NEWLYWEDS
CAN BE
KNOCKED OFF

Books by Amanda Flower

The Katharine Wright Mysteries
To Slip the Bonds of Earth
Not They Who Soar

The Amish Candy Shop Mysteries
Assaulted Caramel
Lethal Licorice
Premeditated Peppermint
Criminally Cocoa (ebook novella)
Toxic Toffee
Botched Butterscotch (ebook novella)
Marshmallow Malice
Candy Cane Crime (ebook novella)
Lemon Drop Dead
Peanut Butter Panic
Blueberry Blunder
Gingerbread Danger

The Amish Matchmaker Mystery series
Matchmaking Can Be Murder
Courting Can Be Killer
Marriage Can Be Mischief
Honeymoons Can Be Hazardous
Dating Can Be Deadly
Newlyweds Can Be Knocked Off

Amanda Flower

NEWLYWEDS CAN BE KNOCKED OFF

Kensington Publishing Corp.
kensingtonbooks.com

For our Geoffrey
Always loved. Never forgotten.

Acknowledgments

First and foremost, I have to thank my readers who have loved all the characters of Harvest, Ohio, for over a decade. You cannot know what it means to me to have such a long-running series. It's a dream of any writer, I can assure you. Bailey, Millie, Lois, and of course, Jethro, thank you too. There will be more Harvest adventures to come.

Special thanks to my amazing agent, Nicole Resciniti. I could not have a better champion of my work who puts me in the position to write what I want to write. That is a gift. I thank too my longtime publisher Kensington. You have kept in me print for over a decade. I am so thankful for and especially grateful to my editor Elizabeth Trout and publicist Larissa Ackerman.

Thanks to my reader Kimra Bell for her eagle eye.

Love and gratitude to my husband, David Seymour. I could not imagine life without you.

Finally, to God in Heaven. Thank you. I don't take any of this for granted.

To return good for good is human, to return good for evil is divine.
—*Amish Proverb*

Chapter One

"How much luggage do you have?" I asked my dearest friend Lois Henry as suitcase after suitcase appeared out of the bed of her granddaughter's pickup truck. I counted three in addition to two duffel bags and her colossal patchwork purse that could double as a knapsack.

Despite the chill in the air, Lois's granddaughter Darcy Woodin was sweating as she lifted her grandmother's luggage from the truck bed and set it on the salt-encrusted blacktop.

That February night, it was a balmy thirty degrees. Gray snow piles topped the four corners of the parking lot like mountains of dirty ice. It would be the end of March before they completely melted away.

It was not the pretty time of winter when children made snowmen and sang carols. Patchy, snow-covered rooftops and grassy fields were blanketed all over Holmes County. We had reached the tired part of winter when the trees lifted their graying branches to the heavens begging for a reprieve. Everything was tinged in a dusty coating of salt.

The bus should have been on the road by now, but Lois had been running late. She left packing until last night and had stayed up all night coordinating her outfits for our five-day stay in Florida. Outfit coordination was very important for Lois: From the top of her red/purple spikey hair to the soles of her bedazzled orthopedic shoes, she cared about every inch of her appearance.

It was pitch black out, but we were able to see with the aid of the electric lampposts around the large parking lot that Harvest Market shared with Swissmen Candyworks, the new Amish candy factory in the village run by my friend Bailey King.

It was eleven at night, and I knew Bailey would be asleep in her bed. That's where I wished I was at that moment.

"I just brought the essentials," Lois said. "It's February in Florida. The weather could be anything from rainy to cold, from hot to dry. I have to be prepared for all of it." Lois adjusted the largest sunhat I had ever seen on the top of her head. It might need its own seat on the bus.

"Millie, I tried to get her down to two suitcases, I promise." Darcy flipped her curly blond ponytail over her shoulder and fanned herself with a glove. "She wasn't having any of it. She accused me of stifling her."

I suppressed a snicker at that comment. No one restricted Lois. Ever.

"I can assure you that I'm not blaming you," I said.

"Lois doesn't need any help when it comes to over-packing."

"Hey, I'm right here," Lois said. "I can hear you. Many things have gone south on my body with advanced age, but I can hear perfectly fine," Lois said. "Besides, how much luggage do you have?"

I held up my single duffel bag.

Lois grinned. "That's perfect. We will say that half of this luggage is yours. See, no problem at all."

I sighed.

My husband Uriah had been across the parking lot speaking to the bus driver for a long while. I could only guess what he had to say to him, but I thought it might be along the lines that Lois and I were prone to get in a little bit of trouble when we were together, so he wanted the driver to keep an eye on us.

Uriah crossed the parking lot to meet us. He was a handsome man even after seventy. His back was straight and his long white beard was freshly combed. His Amish felt hat sat perfectly on the center of his head, but his ears were bright red from the cold. I told him to wear his black stocking cap to protect his ears, but he loved his felt hat and was quite proud of it. It had been my wedding gift to him. Men could be quite stubborn creatures.

He led two large goats behind him. One goat, Phillip, was black and white, and Peter was brown and white. When they saw me, the goats ran ahead of Uriah, and my husband had to jog in order not to be pulled over onto the icy asphalt.

"We're leaving in three minutes," the surly bus driver

shouted into the air. However, I knew he directed his shouts to Lois and me because we were the only passengers not already on the bus.

Seeing Uriah with the goats caused a wave of worry to wash over me. Was I leaving the goats and my new husband too soon after we married? I'd known Uriah my whole life, but it wasn't until we both were widowed that we reconnected decades later. It took me a long time to allow myself to fall in love again even though my first husband Kip had been gone over twenty years.

Lois called our excursion a "bachelorette getaway." Bachelorette wasn't a term that I used as an Amish woman, and even if I did, I no longer qualified as one since Uriah and I had been married for several months and he was my second husband. None of this mattered to Lois, of course; she insisted this was the name she was going to use.

If Lois, who loves to gamble, had her way, we would be on an airplane to Las Vegas for the week. In the end, my friend had the wisdom to recognize that a Vegas trip was not something I would agree to. Instead, she suggested a getaway to sunny Pinecraft, Florida, a small Amish community within the city limits of Sarasota.

Truth be told, I had always wanted to visit Pinecraft. So many of my friends who were in their twilight years spent their winters in the small Amish community there. I believed that *Englischers* would be very surprised to learn that the Amish have "snowbirds" who summer in the north and winter in the south just like the *Englisch* do. We have the capacity to tire of winter just as much as the *Englisch* do.

Even though I was excited for the chance to see a new place and experience the ocean for the very first time in my seventy years of life, I remained unsure, and it wasn't until Uriah urged me to go that I agreed.

"Are you ready to set off?" Uriah asked while Phillip and Peter hopped from hoof to hoof. They thought they were on some kind of adventure because they were coming to town so late at night. They would not find it nearly as fun when I left. I had never been away from them for this long. Part of me was afraid they would forget me and forge a closer bond with Uriah while I was away. I wanted them to be close to Uriah, but because of our history together, I wasn't too proud to admit, I wished to be the favorite of my hoofed friends.

When I had been on my own before the marriage, the goats had been my saving grace. They kept me company on the little farm that I had purchased after my first husband Kip passed away. It was hard for me to imagine getting through the day without seeing them.

Phillip was the wilder one. That wasn't saying much because his brother Peter got into his fair share of trouble too. Phillip jumped in the air and would have pulled Uriah to the ground if my husband had not been ready for it.

"Phillip, control yourself. You don't want all these people to think that we can't tame a goat," Uriah said.

Phillip stopped jumping up and down, but then he looked over his shoulder at Uriah as if to say, "You don't control me." In all honesty, that was true. No one really controlled the goats.

"Millie, can you hold their leads? I'm going to help the bus driver load all this luggage. He's going to need the help."

Lois shook her finger at him. "Not you too, Uriah. I brought what I need. A fashion icon like myself needs options."

I took the leads from Uriah, who laughingly rolled two of Lois's suitcases to the tour bus that was idling in the middle of the parking lot.

"We really should board the bus," I said to Lois. "We are the last people to get on."

However, as I spoke, an old sedan that looked like it had been in a number of fender benders rolled into the parking lot. A young Amish woman got out of the back seat of the car and thanked her driver. She had her bonnet pulled down over her face. She wasn't dressed for the weather. She wore only a hooded sweatshirt over her plain dress, and a long green and blue scarf was wrapped around her neck all the way to the bottom of her nose. She was slight and could have been a teenager judging from her size, maybe even younger.

She turned, and I got a view of her delicate face. Her eyes were wide set, and there was a sprinkling of freckles across the bridge of her upturned nose. Her mouth was pursed together into the shape of a heart. She looked like one of the porcelain dolls that Lois had been known to buy at the flea market. The dolls with their unseeing eyes always made me a tad uneasy. Amish dolls never had faces, and I was much more comfortable with that.

This young woman's face was tense with unease as she looked around the parking lot. She had a small backpack on her shoulder. That was the extent of her luggage, which I supposed made more room for Lois's overpacking.

Phillip pulled on his lead and walked over to the girl. He shoved his nose in her empty hand.

"Oh!" the young woman cried as Phillip nuzzled her hand with his nose.

"I'm so sorry," I said. "Phillip is always excited to make new friends."

I wasn't surprised by Phillip's behavior. The young woman looked sad. My goats sense others' emotions, but I would never say that to Bishop Yoder, my district's longtime bishop, or worse, to his wife, persnickety Ruth Yoder. It wasn't the Amish way to give animals human characteristics. I saw nothing in the writings of the church that would forbid such a thing.

She patted Phillip on the head. "It's all right. He just caught me off guard."

"Phillip is an expert at catching people off guard," I said as I pulled on his lead.

Reluctantly, the goat stepped back.

"Are goats traveling on the bus?" She sounded concerned at the possibility.

I could understand that. I wouldn't want to travel on a bus for over twenty-four hours with Phillip and Peter, and they were *my* goats.

I shook my head. "*Nee*, you don't have to worry about that. My husband brought them so they could say good-bye to me. I'm going to Pinecraft with my friend Lois." I nodded to Lois, who was hugging Darcy good-bye.

Peter baaed at me as if he wanted to make it very

clear that my statement was unfair and he too should be going to the Sunshine State.

She shook her head. "I have never seen goats that are so attached to a person."

I chuckled. "I like to think of them as more like horned dogs than goats."

She smiled. It was a tiny smile, just the slightest curve to the corner of her mouth, but it was the first that I had seen from her since she arrived.

"When is the bus leaving?" she asked.

I looked at the watch brooch that Uriah had given me for our wedding. It was pinned to the lapel of my cloak. It was plain, round, and made of sterling silver. It was much different than the typical wedding gift that an *Englisch* woman would have received upon her wedding, which would have had diamonds, gold, and gemstones of every possible color.

I liked my plain little watch because of the gesture it represented from my husband. I was widowed at the age of forty, and I never dreamed I would marry again. The time in between my first husband's death and my second marriage I realized now was all part of *Gotte*'s plan for my life. I needed to be available to care for my family when they needed me most, which consisted of nieces and nephews and all of my siblings. I also needed to prove to myself that I was self-reliant. I could take care of myself, others, and even solve a murder or two. The murder solving was with the help of Lois, of course. Someone had to be able to drive the getaway car when we got into a sticky situation.

I read the time on my watch. "The bus was set to leave fifteen minutes ago."

She paled. "I can't believe I almost missed it."

"You can thank Lois's overpacking for that," I said.

Across the lot, the bus driver and Uriah struggled to get all of Lois's suitcases and garment bags into the bus's luggage bay.

"Do you have a suitcase with you?" I asked.

She shook her head. "I just have this." She held up her small backpack.

"That's just perfect," Lois said, coming over to join us. "We can say one of the suitcases I brought is yours." She put her hands on her hips. "Can you believe that the driver said that there is a rule of one suitcase per person? Can you even imagine that? I need one suitcase just for my makeup."

The girl's eyes went wide, as if she had never seen a person like Lois before. It was a reaction that I came to expect when Lois met new people. It didn't matter if they were *Englisch* or Amish either. They all had the same awed look on their faces when they encountered my colorful friend for the first time.

"What's your name, sweetie, so I can tell the mean old bus driver that my makeup suitcase is yours?" Lois asked.

"The mean old bus driver," as Lois called him, was half our age.

"Caroline," she stumbled over her own name. "Caroline Ha—Zook." She blushed. "I just got married, and I'm not used to my new name yet."

"It does take some time," I agreed.

"Great!" Lois said. "Caroline Zook." She hurried over the salt-gray asphalt back to the bus. "Mr. Bus

Driver. Mr. Bus Driver. You must put that suitcase back on the bus. It belongs to passenger Caroline Zook."

He looked at the luggage tag. "It has your name on it."

"Yes, that's because it's my suitcase, but I'm letting her borrow it for the trip."

He glared at Lois. "Fine. As long as there is one suitcase per passenger, I don't care how you configure it."

"As soon as I saw you, I knew you were a practical man." Lois smacked him on the shoulder.

He shoved the last suitcase into the bay. "Just get on the bus." He walked away shaking his head.

Caroline bit her lower lip. "I hope I don't get in any kind of trouble for having my name attached to a suitcase that doesn't belong to me. I can't afford another ticket if I get kicked off this bus." She looked over her shoulder as if she was afraid that someone was listening to our conversation. "And I can't go back."

I raised my brow. "Go back where?" I asked.

She looked away. It was clear to me that she didn't want to answer that question. I could understand that. She'd just met me. She didn't even know what order or district I was from. How could she know I was trustworthy? Even so, I couldn't help but be curious about her story. I was also curious as to why she was traveling alone. That was not common for young Amish women. If they had to go somewhere far away, they were at least accompanied by another woman but more often than not by a male family member like a brother or even a cousin. As far as I could tell, Caroline was completely on her own.

She looked around as if she expected someone to jump out from behind one of the lampposts. "I want to get on the bus. I'm ready to go home." Under her breath, she added, "This was a terrible idea."

"What was a terrible idea?" I asked.

She shook her head. "Nothing. I was just talking to myself."

I didn't believe her for a second, but I allowed it to drop for now. Instead, I said, "I don't think that you have to worry about the suitcase. Usually in these cases people agree with Lois just to get her to stop badgering them. I don't think the bus driver will be much different on that accord. If there is any issue, I will be sure to vouch for you."

"*Danki*. I cannot miss this bus." She said that last part barely above a whisper.

"Everyone get on the bus!" the bus driver said. "We're leaving with or without you." It seemed the bus driver's encounter with Lois had sent him into a bad mood. I would have to slip him some of my homemade apple muffins that I brought on the trip to return us to his good graces, or it was going to be a very long trip indeed.

"I'll see you on the bus," Caroline said and hurried toward the rumbling vehicle.

I wasn't able to do that yet as I was still holding Phillip and Peter's leads.

I had thought that it was difficult to leave my diva cat Peaches at home that morning, but as it turned out, it was much harder to leave the goats. They had been my constant companions for the last several years. I had spent more time with them than with any person since moving back to Ohio from Michigan, where I had taken care of an ill sister until she passed.

I scratched them both behind their ears. "Now, you be *gut* for Uriah. I don't want to hear any tales about how the two of you have been misbehaving."

Uriah joined me and eyed the goats. "I'll keep them in line." Then he laughed because we both knew there really wasn't any way to do that.

Uriah gave me a hug, and I felt myself melt into his warmth. After decades of being alone, it was so nice to have a person to lean on again. It wasn't until we married that I had even realized that I missed that. I had learned that I could be happy alone or married. I found that contentment was not in a person but in peace with *Gott.*

He broke off the embrace that was a bit longer than it would normally have been. In our culture, public displays of affection were frowned upon. Rarely did you see an Amish couple hugging or holding hands in public, and kissing wasn't even considered. Just the idea of kissing Uriah in front of all these people turned my cheeks red. If anyone asked why I was flushed, I would blame it on the cold.

Uriah smiled down at me. "Do me a favor. Don't find any dead bodies while you're down there, okay?"

"I won't. I promise. Lois and I don't know anyone in Pinecraft. How would we even be involved in a murder?"

He shook his head. "In my experience, you seem to always find a way."

What I would learn soon enough was it was a promise that I could not keep.

Lois and I were the last to climb on the bus, and we waved to Uriah, Darcy, and the goats as it pulled away from the parking lot. Just as the bus turned onto the road, an Amish courting buggy came careening into the parking lot. The driver pulled back hard on the reins and came to a stop just a few yards from the bus.

The bus driver swore.

There was a murmur through the passengers asking who the young man was, but he was out of the light of the lampposts and no one could see his face.

After so many delays, our bus driver wasn't going to stop to find out. He kept going as if he couldn't leave Harvest fast enough.

Across the aisle from Lois and me, I saw Caroline Zook had sunk low in her seat as if she didn't want to be seen.

Chapter Two

We had just crossed over into West Virginia and wound our way through the Appalachian Mountains. All around us the trees were bare, and what could be seen of the mountains in the dark looked like brown stumps against a gray-black sky. It wasn't the most picturesque time to be traveling across the country.

Lois was bent at the waist holding a plastic bag between her legs as I rubbed her back. In my mind, I willed her not to be sick. We had a long way to go, and I didn't want to make this trip any more unpleasant. Not to mention, she was already on the bus driver's naughty list.

Slowly, she sat up. "I think the nausea has passed, but until we get out of these winding roads, I think I should sleep. Thank heavens I brought my sleeping pills." She set the plastic bag aside and rooted through her massive purse until she came up with a bottle of pills and a bottle of water. She opened the pill bottle, threw two chalk-white tablets down her throat, then chased them with a big gulp of water. She leaned her head back against the headrest and closed her eyes. "I took a little extra. I should be out cold in no time. Wake me up when we're on flatter ground or if we stop to use the facilities. At our age, we cannot miss a rest stop opportunity."

I promised her that I would, and I was very glad that I had given Lois the window seat. Otherwise, I would have been trapped in my spot for hours on end.

I was flipping through a quilting fabric catalog that I had brought with me when I heard the faint rumbling of a snore. I glanced to my right, and Lois was out cold with her forehead propped on the cold glass pane of the window.

As carefully and as quietly as I could, I balled up my cardigan and tucked it in between her head and the glass. She didn't look that much more comfortable, to be honest, but at least if the bus jerked, she wouldn't knock her temple against the glass.

I sat back in my seat and sighed. The sleeping pills would give me a few hours of silence to rest my own eyes or to work on my quilting. I loved Lois dearly, but my friend could talk and talk and talk. And talk some more.

While Lois snored in my ear, I removed my quilting from my bag. It wasn't practical to bring an entire quilt to work on during the trip, but I could not stand the idea of being still for the duration of the long drive. I had compromised in making quilt coasters with candy-patterned fabric. Bailey said that she would sell them on consignment in her candy factory store. If they did well, she said, I could make even more to sell in her family's candy shop, Swissmen Sweets, as well.

I set the small quilting pieces on my lap. As much as I loved making full-sized quilts, it was enjoyable to make something a bit more portable and less time-consuming. A full-sized quilt would take months and months with the help of my quilting circle, Double Stitch. I could make four coasters in an hour. I brought enough material on the trip to make forty. I thought that would be plenty to test at Swissmen Candyworks and see if they appealed to Bailey's customers.

I threaded my needle.

A quiet voice asked, "What are you making?"

I looked up to see Caroline watching me. She was seated across the aisle from me in a seat by herself. The bus wasn't completely full, as most of the snowbirds had flown south right after New Year's Day, and now it was the end of February.

"Coasters. I'm planning to sell them at Swissmen Candyworks."

"Oh, that was the candy factory that was by the parking lot where we met the bus," she said. "I so much wanted to spend a whole day there while I was in Ohio, but I didn't have the time. The trip was very brief."

"You're not from Ohio?" I asked.

She shook her head. "I'm from Florida."

"Pinecraft?" I asked.

"Yes." She paused. "Yes, that's right."

I wrinkled my brow. She didn't sound completely convinced that she was from Pinecraft, but she struck me as a nervous young woman. Because of that, she might've just sounded unsure of everything that she said.

"I have always wanted to learn to sew, but I never did." Her voice was forlorn.

I held my needle suspended in the air. That was very unusual to hear from an Amish girl. Most young girls were taught to sew as soon as they were old enough to hold a needle.

"Your *maam* didn't teach you?"

Her face turned red. "I didn't grow up with a mother. It was just my father and me."

"I'm so sorry to hear that."

Even knowing that she didn't have a mother, it was very curious she couldn't sew. I believed at least one woman in the district would have stepped up and taught her to sew and keep a home. We Amish live in communities, and if it is clear that another member needs support in any way, someone steps up or the bishop asks someone to fill the role for that person.

As one of our proverbs says, "A community is like a quilt, each piece is important to make a whole."

Again, I was curious about Caroline Zook, but I held my prying tongue. Yet even though I didn't speak them aloud, I had questions. Had her mother died? Run away? Had Lois been awake, she would have pulled the entire story out of Caroline.

The young woman shifted in her seat and looked as if she thought she had said too much, but to me, she hadn't said nearly enough.

"I could teach you if you like. We have a long trip,

and we certainly have the time. By the time we cross the Florida border, you will know four kinds of stitches. I have taught many young women to sew, and I have no doubt I can teach you."

She turned back to face me, and her eyes cleared. "I would like that very much. My new husband doesn't know I can't sew, so if I could learn before seeing him again, that would be perfect. I very much want to be a good Amish wife to him. He's the kindest man. He's sacrificed a lot to marry me, and I promised him I would do my very best to fit in."

I raised my brow. "To fit in? Did you marry a man from a different district from yours?"

"You could say that, yes," she said.

When she didn't say anything more, I said, "You scoot by the window in your seat, and I will come over there for our first lesson."

She tucked her small body up close to the window.

As carefully as I could, I shifted away from Lois. She muttered in her sleep, but she didn't wake up. Those sleeping pills must have been very strong indeed.

"Put fifty on the red eight," Lois murmured into my sweater.

I shook my head. Clearly Lois was dreaming about one of her many trips to the Rocksino in Cleveland.

I gathered up my quilting the best I could and slipped into the seat next to Caroline. In the rearview mirror, I saw the bus driver make a face. He had strict rules about staying in our seats when the bus was in motion. It was very possible that Lois and I were the worst passengers that he ever had, from his perspective at least.

I ducked my head. Usually, I was very good at following the rules, but it was clear to me that this young woman needed a friend. Sometimes you have to err on the side of compassion was my thought.

Caroline had her hands folded in her lap. "Are you sure you can spare the material to teach me? I don't want to ruin the piece that you are working on."

"Don't be silly," I said. "I'm making coasters, and they are the perfect pieces for you to learn how to sew on."

I smoothed two triangle-shaped pieces of cloth onto my lap. "The first thing I will teach you is a straight stitch that's to hold two pieces of cloth together. If you can do that, you can do just about anything. Do you know how to thread a needle?"

She shook her head.

We had to go all the way back to the basics, but it was no trouble. I had taught many women to quilt over the years. Every one of them became an expert in the end. I didn't see it being any different with Caroline.

I cut a generous length of white thread and showed her how to put the end of the thread through the eye of the needle. "Now, you try."

She put the thread in or tried to. Every attempt she missed. Her shoulders sagged. "I'm just not any good at this."

I covered her hand with mine. "Do not fret. All it takes is a little patience."

"Patience is something that I don't have. It's why I'm in this mess."

"What mess is that?" I asked.

She looked at me as if she realized that she had let something slip. She cleared her throat. "Let me try again. I will be more patient this time."

I very much wanted to ask her what the mess was that she was in, but I had learned that people would tell me more if I was the one who remained patient. They told their story in their own time. Maybe I would have pressed her more if I had known that her time was so limited.

Within the hour, Caroline had mastered the straight stitch. She held up the two pieces of cloth that she had sewn together like it was a trophy to be admired. "I can't believe I did it. It was so fun too. I can see myself doing this every day. Perhaps I will sell my quilted items in my husband's shop someday. I need more practice, but it's a goal."

"And it is a wonderful goal to have. What kind of shop does your husband own?"

Her face fell as if yet again she believed she said too much. She set the piece back on her lap. "He has a scooter shop in Pinecraft. I suppose quilting will not fit with that."

"You never know. Tourists come into his shop, I would think, and they are always on the lookout for little gifts to take home. You would be surprised what *Englischers* will buy."

"Oh, I know that very well," she said with just the slightest hint of bitterness.

The more I spoke with Caroline, the more I wondered about her.

I smiled at her. "You have been a very good student.

If you wanted to keep at it, I bet you could be one of
the best quilters in all of Florida. Selling in your husband's shop is a very *gut* idea. Do you work at the
scooter shop as well?"

She shook her head. "No, his sister works for him,
and she, well, she can be difficult. I will be looking for
work when I get home. I don't plan to go back to where
I worked before."

"Where was that?" I asked.

"Just for my father." She left it at that.

She set the piece back on her lap. Her eyes shone
with pride. "I didn't know it was possible to be happy
with such a little piece."

It made me wonder how many times Caroline had
been given a chance to make something to be proud of.
It seemed to me that this was a new experience for her.

"You keep going and make a set of coasters for your
new home," I said.

She looked at me. "But this is your business. Aren't
you making these to sell?"

"Yes, but I have plenty for that. You need something
to make your home more like your own."

She looked down at the coaster she was making.
"It's going to take a lot more than a set of coasters to do
that."

"Why's that?"

"I don't believe my husband's family is happy with
our match. His sister, in particular, was upset."

"Did they speak against it?"

"No, but they really didn't have a chance to. Cainan
and I married in secret. We married in such a way be-

cause we already knew how they would feel, and we were right."

"Oh," I said. That was very unusual for an Amish couple. Typically, the district's bishop presided over the weddings in his district. It was hard for me to imagine a bishop marrying two people without consulting with their families first.

As if she knew the questions going through my head, she said, "We married at the courthouse."

That was very unusual indeed.

"What did his parents say about that?" I asked.

"They passed many years ago."

"Oh, I'm so sorry."

She nodded accepting my condolences. "Cainan moved to Pinecraft when he was fourteen with his sister. She married a man from that community."

"Tell me about your husband and your courtship. I just married last summer, and I do enjoy hearing people's love stories," I said.

"I just married two weeks ago," she said just above a whisper. I had to lean close in order to hear her. "Cainan and I wanted to do it for a long time, but since we didn't have our families' support, we just had to make the decision on our own."

"Why were they against it?" I asked.

"It's complicated."

It certainly sounded as if it was.

"I'm sure Cainan is happy that you will be rejoining him. Why did you have to leave so soon after the wedding? What took you to Harvest?"

She bit her lip as if she was searching her mind for

an answer that would not be an outright lie. "I had some unfinished business I needed to take care of to help my father. I should have done it before Cainan and I married, but there wasn't time. Everything happened so fast."

"Oh, and how does your father feel about your marriage?"

A trickle of blood fell from her lip. "He doesn't know yet."

I removed a packet of tissues from my sewing bag and handed them to her. "For your lip."

She dabbed at her lip and examined the tissue. "Oh!" She pressed the tissue back on her mouth.

When she stopped bleeding, I asked, "Tell me about your husband's scooter business."

Caroline visibly relaxed at my change of subject. "They rent and sell scooters as well as bicycles. They even have skateboards. Business is brisk, according to my husband, because bicycles and scooters are the best way to travel around Pinecraft, especially for the Amish."

"Oh, people do not use their buggies as much?"

"Pinecraft is not Holmes County. You will learn pretty fast. They don't have buggies, for one. It's very likely the whole time that you're there, you won't see a single horse."

"No buggies? Then how do they get around?"

"Bicycles and scooters. E-bikes and e-scooters are very popular. Cainan was the first one to introduce them to the community close to four years ago." She continued with her stitching.

I nodded; e-bikes had become increasingly popular in Holmes County as well. They were a great help to ride up and down the rolling hills in the area. We were allowed to use them in our district, but I had never tried one. I prefer my trusty pedal bike.

Not everyone in the district was happy with the e-bikes. The bishop's wife, Ruth Yoder, was the main objector. She had said, "If you ask me, e-bikes are not following the edicts of the faith. It's slipping through a loophole. What's next, Amish folks in electric cars because they can charge their vehicles off the *Englisch* electrical grid? It is a dangerous choice that will lead to more division for our people."

Ruth wasn't completely wrong on that point, but at the same time even our culture had to adapt to keep up with the *Englisch* world. It was the only way for the Amish lifestyle to remain feasible.

Caroline cleared her throat and changed the subject. "Have you been to Pinecraft before?"

I shook my head. "This is my very first time." I blushed. "This is the farthest I have ever been away from home. Just between you and me, I'm very nervous but excited too."

"You will be surprised by how different it is. Very surprised," she said.

I did not know if she meant that as a promise or a warning.

Chapter Three

The bus's overhead lights turned on, and there was an audible groan from the passengers as our eyes adjusted to the bright lights. Outside, it was dark.

"We're here," the bus driver said.

Lois blinked as she woke up from her self-inflicted coma. I had to say I was impressed that she had slept most of the twenty-four-hour trip from Harvest to Pinecraft. She only woke when I shook her shoulder to tell her we were at a rest stop. I, on the other hand, had rested my eyes from time to time, but I didn't believe that I'd fallen asleep at all. Caroline and I sewed through the night, but then she dropped in and out of sleep through the day's drive through the South.

I enjoyed talking with the young lady. She had a sweet soul, and something in me wanted to protect her . . . from what exactly I didn't know. I just had a deep-seated feeling that she needed to be protected.

Lois's colorful hair jutted out from her head in all directions, and one of her false eyelashes hung to the corner of her eyelid. "Are we here? Did we make it? Have you seen an alligator yet?"

"*Ya, ya,* and *nee.*" I reached across the aisle and patted her hand. "Gather up your things. We're here, and it's time for you to lie down in a proper bed."

Lois groaned but quickly pulled herself together, and we filed out of the bus with the other passengers. Caroline was three people ahead of us leaving the bus. I wanted to catch her before she left. I cared for the girl, and she needed a mentor. I wanted to invite her to lunch and perhaps a few more quilting lessons while we were in Florida. I didn't exactly know what Lois had planned for our five-day visit, but I was sure I could squeeze in some time with Caroline as well. I also knew when Lois had the chance to get to know her, she would like her just as much as I did.

Lois's massive purse hit me in the back, and had it not been for the tight quarters of the bus aisle, I would have gone flying. I did bump into the man in front of me.

"I'm so sorry," I said.

He looked over his shoulder and frowned. He was on the younger side for a snowbird, maybe not even sixty yet. His beard was long and curly and he wore thin-rimmed glasses on his nose. "It is all right."

"It was my fault, I accidently whacked her with my purse," Lois said, peeking over my shoulder. "I carry my whole life in here, so it's mighty heavy."

He nodded and turned back to the front of the bus.

"He's a real pill," Lois whispered into my ear.

"Everyone is tired from travel," I said, making excuses for the man. "Just try to be more careful with your purse. Neither of us want to go home with a broken hip."

"Isn't that the truth," Lois said.

Finally, we made our way off the bus. The moment I stepped into the Florida air, my skin felt dewy, and I could smell the salt water. I had never seen the ocean before, so it wasn't a scent that I recognized. I took it in and for the first time thought that this trip south had been worth the long ride after all. Many times on the bus, I had questioned the wisdom of letting Lois talk me into this, but she had been right—it would be *gut* for me.

I felt a small pang in my chest that Uriah wasn't here. He would enjoy it too. I promised myself that we would return together one winter. He deserved to see the ocean; everyone did.

I looked around and we were in the middle of a grocery store parking lot. There was a faint dusting of sand over the blacktop. Also a new sight to me. There wasn't much sand in Holmes County other than what could be found on a children's playground.

Different Amish tourists were met by family and friends that were picking them up.

I looked at Lois. "How far is the place we are staying? Are we walking?" I didn't like that idea in the least. Most of the time I loved walking, and it was my favorite way to travel other than my bicycle, but Lois had a lot of luggage. I didn't know how we would be able to manage it.

"I called an Uber," Lois said. "He will be here any second. There are so many of them in Pinecraft because they drive the Amish around."

"An Uber?" I asked.

"Like an Amish driver, but it's for everyone. There aren't that many of them in Holmes County since the Amish drivers have clinched the market. Also, you have to request an app on the phone. Not too many of you Amish have cell phones that can do that."

I did not understand half of what she said. I had to take Lois's word for it. She was the authority when it came to the *Englisch* world.

Lois waved at a car that just pulled into the lot. "I think that is our driver. I'll check."

While Lois went to ask about the car, I looked around for Caroline. I had lost sight of her when we exited the bus and in the mayhem while everyone tried to grab their luggage and leave as quickly as possible. Everyone on the bus from the driver on down was tired and cranky and wishing for a soft bed. I knew that I was.

"Will you help me load the suitcases?" Lois asked the Uber driver.

He was a young man with a long ponytail and the thinnest mustache that I had ever seen. When he saw Lois's luggage, he sighed.

I knew that it was going to take a bit of time for Lois and the driver to fit all her luggage into his small car, so I went in search of Caroline.

I spotted her standing near the front of the closed grocery store with a young man. The young man was turned away from me, so I couldn't see his face.

"Cainan, I'm sorry. I have told you a hundred times that I'm sorry. How many more times do I have to say it?" Caroline asked.

"You don't even know what you've done by just taking off right after we married."

"I wasn't trying to hurt you or anyone else. Getting married so quickly was your idea, remember? I was against it at first. I didn't want to cause more trouble for your family."

"It's one that I wish that I could take back."

"You can," Caroline said in a soft voice. "It's called divorce."

"We are Amish, Caroline. We don't get divorced. That's something that you will have to remember if you want to live in the Amish Way."

I felt guilty for listening, but the conversation was making me more uncomfortable by the second. I wasn't completely sure that it was a *gut* idea for Caroline to go home with Cainan. He was her husband, but he sounded so angry.

A van pulled up in front of the grocery store, and Cainan grabbed Caroline by the hand. "Come on, that is our ride. We can talk more about this at home."

He pulled her toward the van, and for the briefest of seconds, Caroline's gaze met mine. She had tears in her eyes, but she managed to smile and wave at me before her husband nudged her into the van.

That would be the last time I saw her alive.

Chapter Four

Nearly an hour later we checked into our accommodations, and all I noted about the bungalow was that it was a short distance from the beach. I could hear and smell the ocean before hurrying inside.

As excited as I was to see the ocean, that would have to wait until the next morning, because in my current exhausted state, I would not fully appreciate it.

Lois stumbled into her bedroom across from mine without taking off her makeup or removing the one lone eyelash that was still on her face. Even though I was just as tired, I went through my nightly routine as always. I washed my face, brushed my teeth, put on my nightdress, and let my hair down. I brushed my white hair that when it was down went all the way to the back of my thighs. As quickly as I could, I braided my hair for the night.

When I finally laid my head down on the pillow, I had trouble falling asleep because all I could think about was Caroline waving good-bye to me. I said a silent prayer that I could find her the next day and offer any assistance that she might need, because from the argument that I'd witnessed between her and her husband . . . she had a lot larger problems than just not knowing how to sew.

At some point, I fell asleep, but as usual, I was awake at four the next morning.

Still before sunrise, I held a cup of coffee under my nose. The smell of the coffee and the sound of the sea outside was a healing combination. I was still drowsy from the journey, but I was dying to see the water.

At most, I got three hours of sleep. A nap was certainly on the agenda for later that day, but at present, I could not sleep between my worries over Caroline and my excitement of seeing the ocean.

When the clock struck six, I thought that Lois had slept long enough. I didn't want to miss the sunrise over the water.

I went into her room, which held two double beds, and placed a hand on her shoulder. "Lois. Lois, it's time to wake up."

She waved her hand in the air and almost slapped me in the face. "Five more minutes, Mom. The principal said that I could be late to school."

I snorted. "Lois." I shook her again. This time I took care to keep my head out of smacking range. "Lois, wake up. You said that you want to see the sunrise this morning."

"I've seen the sun before," she muttered into her pillow. "I'm over it."

I stepped back. "You told me that you would say that last night, and I was not supposed to take no for an answer."

"I was lying," she muttered into her pillow.

I snorted. "I made coffee."

She opened one eye. "Did you say coffee?"

I set a mug on the nightstand next to her. I made it just like she liked it with a lot of cream and sugar. Maybe it wasn't exactly how she liked it since I had to use powdered cream. That was all that was in the bungalow, but it was as close as I could get it. I hoped Lois didn't notice the difference.

She rolled onto her side and after lots of muttering sat up and took her first sip of coffee.

She closed her eyes for a moment, savoring. When she opened her eyes again she gasped. "Millie, it's not even light outside. Why are you waking me up at this ungodly hour? I'm supposed to be on vacation."

I tapped my prayer cap on the top of my head to make sure it was still in place. I was fully dressed and ready to see the beach. "You promised me that we would go and see the sunrise our first morning here."

She grimaced and took another sip of her coffee. "I did promise that, didn't I? Can't it wait? We will be here five whole days. There will be many sunrises to see."

I felt my shoulders sag. It wasn't often I'd built things up in my head to be such an event, but I didn't want to wait another whole day to see the ocean when I was close enough to smell it.

"I can just go by myself. When we checked in, the

receptionist said that the path to the beach was clearly marked."

"No, no, no," she said, shaking her head. "What if you get too close to the water and are sucked out into the Gulf, never to be seen again? What will I say to Uriah then?"

"I'm not going to get that close to the water."

"I'm still coming. I want to be there when you see the ocean for the first time. It's a magical experience." She groaned as she stood up and placed a hand at the small of her back. "I am never riding in a bus like that again. My joints are all knotted up, and I have a crick in my neck. I wonder if there is a masseuse in Pinecraft. Do the Amish get massages?"

I eyed her. "Is that something that sounds like the Amish would do?"

She sighed. "Thankfully, we're in the middle of Sarasota. I'm sure I could get a massage here. With so many older folks in Florida, there has to be a big market for treating aches and pains."

I knew Lois was tired because she put on one of her colorful sweatsuits, but instead of spending the time it would take to do her hair, she put the huge sunhat on her head. As for makeup, she powdered her nose, put on red lipstick, and covered her eyes with oversized sunglasses, paying no mind to the fact the sun wasn't up yet.

She grabbed her massive purse from the chair by the door. "This is as good as it is going to get at this ungodly hour. As soon as the sun makes its appearance, I'm going back to bed. I'm on vacation, after all.

Maybe back home I have to get up at the crack of dawn to help my granddaughter Darcy with the breakfast shift at the Sunbeam Café, but I don't have to do it here."

"I appreciate you making an exception for me," I said as we went out the bungalow's front door.

The moment that we stepped outside, I felt a jolt of excitement. I could smell and hear the water even though I couldn't see it yet. To be honest, I was surprised how excited I felt. I'd never thought much about going to the ocean because it never seemed to be a possibility to me. As Amish we were taught to be content with where we were because *Gott* put us there. We were encouraged never to wish for something that we did not have. As the Amish proverb says, "Contentment is discovering the value of what *Gott* has already given to me."

I knew many Amish from Holmes County came to Pinecraft every winter, but that wasn't a luxury I had. I was needed back in Ohio to support my niece Edith and her children, and my quilting circle, Double Stitch, relied on me too. The only way any one of us made a profit was by working together, and the winter was the time when our quilts were in the greatest demand.

Lois pinched her cheeks as we walked down the path. I knew that she was trying to put a little color into her complexion. She did add color but in two small welts on either side of her face.

"I sure hope that I don't meet my next husband on the beach this morning," she said. "I look a mess. This is not how I catch a husband. He could be a real dud if he picks me up while I look like this."

Lois would know, as she had been married four times. She was very good at husband catching. It was keeping the husband that was the real challenge for her.

"You look just fine. And you can't meet your husband here. He would probably be a Floridian. Would you really want to move to Florida?" I asked.

She wrinkled her nose. "Obviously, he would move to Holmes County for me. I can't leave you or Darcy."

I arched my brow at that proclamation. I couldn't think of too many people who would give up the semi-tropical climate for the much colder Ohio weather. It made me wonder how many people who lived in Florida had never seen snow before. Was it as magical to them as seeing the ocean was to me?

"I didn't know that you were looking for a new husband." I stepped over a tiny lizard in the path. If I wasn't so eager to see the sunrise, I would have stopped and examined it. We didn't have lizards of any kind in Ohio. We had salamanders, but I didn't think that was the same thing.

She shrugged her shoulders. "I never know when the next ex will cross my path. It would be good for you to remember that, Millie." She shifted her massive patchwork purse on her shoulder. I was constantly amazed how she could carry the bag everywhere she went. It had to weigh as much as a small child, especially considering all of the oddities that it held. A brick, "just in case," being the most notable.

It was too warm out to wear a bonnet, but I knew the wind would blow my hair in all directions. Instead, I covered my hair with a navy-blue silk scarf. It was the finest thing that I owned and had been another gift from Uriah. I tied it as tightly as I dared under my chin so that it would not blow away.

We came up over the dune onto the sandy path that led to the water. The sky had lightened enough so that I could see the sand, the surf, and the waves. Tears came to my eyes. It was more beautiful than I could imagine. Tiny birds I didn't recognize ran back and forth from the surf, and larger birds bobbed up and down in the water.

"Those little birds are sandpipers," Lois said. "Spritely little things, aren't they? And the giant ones in the water are brown pelicans."

I nodded but was unable to speak.

A young man ran barefoot along the water's edge. He had headphones in and wasn't paying attention to all the beauty around him. I didn't know how anyone would get used to seeing this even if they lived here their whole life long.

Lois looked at me in concern. "Millie, are you all right?"

I blinked at her. "All right? I'm fine. I'm wonderful. Why do you ask?"

"Because you are holding your chest like you might keel over and die. I'm not up on my CPR, so I can't have that."

I looked down, and sure enough, I was holding my chest. I dropped my hand. "I'm just in awe of what I see."

Lois smiled and hooked her arm through mine. "Then let's grab a good seat and watch the show."

I followed her onto the beach, and she stopped about ten feet from the waves. I started to sit down on the sand, and she shook her finger at me. "Not yet." She set her purse on the sand and pulled out two full-sized beach towels. She handed one to me and spread the other on the sand.

I put my towel on the sand next to hers. "I don't even want to know how you fit both of those towels in there."

She grinned. "I have all kind of tricks in my bag."

That was the truth.

Just as Lois and I sat down the sun inched over the horizon, and the sky and sea were awash in pinks, purples, oranges, and reds. In all my seventy years on earth, I had only seen pictures of the ocean. The real thing was so much more breathtaking. It would be etched into my memory for the remainder of my days.

Lois glanced at me and smiled. All the grumpiness in her face was gone. She knew what an important moment this was for me.

"It's amazing, isn't it?" she asked in a hushed voice. Even Lois could appreciate the reverence for the rising sun.

I nodded. I was at a complete loss for words.

She patted my arm.

Finally, the whole sun popped up over the horizon like a ping-pong ball tossed into the air. Tears came to my eyes. I wondered how anyone could sit here and see such an amazing sight and not believe that *Gott* must have had a hand in it. With my eyes open, I took in the sunrise and whispered a prayer of thanksgiving in my heart for the beauty around me. *Gott* could have done so many things when he created the earth, and one of things he chose was beauty. It was a gift to us and a reminder of his goodness to his people.

Lois knocked her shoulder into mine. "Are you all right?"

I smiled at her through my tears. "I am. It is so beautiful."

"It really is," she agreed. "I'm glad that you woke me up. I needed to see this too."

I bumped her shoulder back. "I'm happy to hear you say that, but if you want to sleep in tomorrow, that's fine with me. It's so quiet out here and seems to be very safe. I can make the short walk on my own. We don't have a worry in the world while we are in this heavenly place."

Before Lois could answer me, there was a great shout: "Stop! Stop that pig!"

We might have been a thousand miles away from Harvest, but we knew just who that pig was.

Chapter Five

"Jethro! Jethro! Stop!" Juliet Brook called as she tripped through the sand in her high heels.

Lois and I watched as the little black and white polka-dotted pig ran by us. We both tried to grab him, but that Jethro could run. Not to mention, we were sitting on towels on the sand, and we weren't as spry as we used to be. All we accomplished was flopping on top of each other.

Lois said a few choice words about the little pig as we untangled ourselves.

Jethro had proved his speed time and again—by wreaking havoc and racing through the streets of Harvest—and that he was a troublemaker even if there were no bad intentions. Juliet had never been able to catch him and relied on her soon-to-be daughter-in-law Bailey King to snatch up the pig. Bailey had a gift for pig catching. I didn't know where she got it, since she moved to Harvest from New York City. Were there a lot of pigs running loose in Manhattan? I didn't know, as it was another place I had never been.

Jethro ran up to the waves. They were calm at the moment, but I thought it was safe to assume that the little pig didn't know how to swim.

Lois bent at the waist as if she was setting up to strike. "Let's sneak up on him."

"You couldn't sneak up on anyone," I said. "Leave it to me."

Lois sniffed, but in the end, I believed that she knew this truth about herself because she straightened up.

"Oh, Jethro," Juliet cried. "Don't go in the water!"

Juliet was standing about a hundred yards from us trying to pull one of her heels out of the sand.

Lois shook her head. "I'll take care of her; you get the pig."

I nodded and headed down the beach at a slow pace. Unlike Juliet, I was wearing practical orthopedic sneakers.

Jethro had his snout in the wet sand. I didn't make a noise as I approached. The last thing I wanted to do was spook him.

I was within two feet, and he had his nose buried so deeply into the sand that he didn't notice me. Before he was any the wiser, I scooped him up.

He squealed like he was being murdered and kicked his little hooves.

He was just the size of a toaster but surprisingly strong. I held him out in front of me and did my best to stay out of range of his flying hooves.

"Jethro, calm yourself. Jethro! Stop!" I said.

Jethro froze in midair and stared at me like he had just seen a spirit.

While he was still mid-freeze, I curled his little body into my chest and held him fast. The waves rolled in then and my tennis shoes were soaked through, but it was worth it if the little pig, who had become the mascot of Harvest over the years, was safe.

Juliet and Lois appeared at my side. I was happy to see now that Juliet was no longer wearing her impractical heels but carrying them.

"Oh, Millie." Juliet clasped her hands in prayer with her strappy heels hanging from her fingers. "You saved him. I don't even know what I would do if he was washed out to sea. I thought that he would be a good boy and walk beside me on the beach like he would walk with me at home. He just took off. I think he was enamored with the ocean. He's never seen it before." Juliet was a pretty woman in her late fifties who had a penchant for polka dots on, well, everything from her pig to her clothing. That morning, she wore a yellow and white polka-dotted sundress, and her blond hair was tied up in a ponytail on the back of her head with a matching yellow and white polka-dotted ribbon.

Lois and I shared a look. No one on earth would look at Jethro and say that he was a good boy. At least no one but Juliet.

"I can see why he would be enamored with the ocean. It is my first time seeing it too, and I am mesmerized," I said.

Juliet put a hand to her chest. "I can't thank you enough. I don't know what I would do if I had to run back to the conference and tell Reverend Brook that Jethro was lost somewhere on the beach. The reverend would have been crushed. He loves Jethro so much. I don't know what he would do if something happened to the little guy."

Lois and I shared another look. I had a few guesses what Reverend Brook would do. He'd throw a party at the first opportunity. He loved Jethro because he adored his wife and Juliet loved Jethro, but make no mistake, he would be relieved if Jethro disappeared from their lives.

Juliet held her hands out to me, waiting for me to hand over her pig.

I was a little reluctant to hand Jethro over. It was well known by everyone living in Harvest that Juliet wasn't able to handle her pig. She relied on Bailey to keep him in check, and Bailey was hundreds of miles away. I imagined that Bailey was happy for the respite from pig patrol, but by the looks of it, we could have used her here in Florida.

Then again, Jethro was Juliet's pig, and I couldn't keep him hostage just because I knew that she would lose him later. I handed the little pig over.

She held Jethro to her face. "You are a naughty little boy. How can you go and scare Mama like that? You have taken at least two years off my life."

Jethro responded by licking the tip of her petite nose, Juliet laughed. All was forgiven. Jethro never stayed in trouble for long.

"Juliet, what are you doing in Pinecraft?" Lois asked.

Juliet tucked Jethro under her arm. "My sweet husband is attending a pastors' conference here in the village for pastors and their spouses. It's the first time that we have been able to get away since our honeymoon."

"And you brought Jethro?" Lois eyed the pig, who still had a *gut* amount of sand on the tip of his snout.

She shook her head. "I didn't have a choice. Bailey is in New York recording her candy-making show for Gourmet TV, and my son doesn't have time to watch Jethro as he is now the sheriff of Holmes County. That is why I'm so grateful that you caught him, Millie. Reverend Brook was not happy that we had to bring Jethro with us to Florida, so it is paramount that Jethro does not cause any schedule changes or hiccups to the week's plans. With luck, this will be the only time he gets loose."

Lois shook her head. I knew what she was thinking. There was no way that this was the only time Jethro was going to run from his mistress. There was no chance.

Juliet snuggled the little pig close to her chest. "I knew that the two of you were planning a trip to Pinecraft. What luck it is that we are here at the same time as you!"

"So much luck," Lois muttered.

I knew that Lois liked Juliet well enough. To know Juliet Brook was to like her. She had a childlike innocence about her, but we also knew that if Juliet knew she was near someone she trusted who she could hand the pig off to, she would. Jethro was a cute little oinker, but we hadn't come all this way on a bus to watch a pig that we saw every day back home.

Juliet sighed. "This trip has been an adventure already! Reverend Brook has been in a number of heated church meetings, and now I'm chasing Jethro through the sand. We agreed to come here to relax, but it is nothing like that."

"What are the arguments about?" Lois asked.

"It's the same things that churches have been fighting over for decades. What kind of music should be allowed in the sanctuary, what is the role of women in the church, and the list goes on and on. If you ask me, when the church has a conference like this and fights over these things, they aren't being very Christian. Sometimes I admire the Amish for the fact there are rules and they stick to them no matter what."

"Even Amish rules change," I said. "It might be at a slower pace, but things are different from the time I was growing up. It has certainly been a challenge for most Amish districts to balance their traditional beliefs and allow a few changes so that its church members can be successful in the wider world."

Juliet nodded. "Well said, Millie. Honestly, I wish you could come to one of the conference meetings and talk some sense into all these stubborn pastors. I exclude my Reverend Brook, of course. He just wants to do what's best for his church and parishioners. Sometimes I believe that pastors lose sight of that when their own egos get in the way."

This was true for Amish bishops too. We had a *gut* bishop at the moment, but the bishop before him, who just so happened to be Bishop Yoder's father, was a very strict man, who put his authority first and the people of the district in a faraway second.

"I should get back—"

Jethro began to wiggle in Juliet's arms as he wanted to be freed.

"Jethro!" Juliet chided. "Jethro, control yourself."

"Is the conference very far from here?" I asked.

Juliet shook her head. She turned and pointed down the beach. "It's at the Dutchman Resort right here on the beach. It's about a half mile from here. I thought I was just out for a leisurely stroll this morning on the boardwalk, and Jethro took off like his tail was on fire." She kissed the top of the pig's head.

The little pig sneezed, and wet sand went flying into Lois's face.

"Ahh!" she cried.

"Jethro, you need to cover your mouth when you sneeze. I'm so sorry, Lois," Juliet said as she let go of the pig with one arm so she could reach into her sundress pocket. "Jethro has had a cold ever since we landed in Fort Myers. I believe it is just the change in climate."

Lois pulled a handkerchief out of her bag and dabbed at her face. "Am I going to get sick too? I'm not usually a hypochondriac about these things, but don't pig illnesses transfer to humans?" she whispered to me.

I shrugged. "I have never heard that."

"Swine flu? What about swine flu?" Lois applied hand sanitizer to her face.

Juliet tried to clean Jethro's nose with a tissue, but the little pig was having none of it. He wriggled away and landed on his back on the sand.

"Oh, Jethro, are you hurt?" Juliet cried.

Before she could even touch him, he was up on his hooves and running across the beach again.

"That crazy pig," Lois shouted.

Those were my thoughts exactly.

A large flock of terns landed a few yards from Jethro. Half of them bobbed in the way and the other half settled on the beach and pecked at the sand looking for a bit of breakfast.

When Jethro saw those seabirds, his eyes just about bugged out of his head. He had seen many birds throughout his life and chased a good many of them too. However, he had never seen birds like these.

The birds all turned to face him as one, and Jethro stumbled in the sand. He had not expected the terns to stand their ground. He fell snout first into the sand.

The three of us hurried over to him, but before we could reach him, Jethro pulled his nose out of the ground with a mighty squeal.

He shook his head.

"There's something on his nose," Juliet cried.

Jethro squealed again and jerked his head in all directions, but the crab had clamped both of his claws on the tip of Jethro's nose.

Juliet started to scream. That seemed to scare Jethro just as much as the crab that had a vise-like grip on him.

"Help him! Help him! That crab is hurting him. He could die," Juliet cried.

Now, thinking Jethro could die from a small crab attack was a bit far-fetched, but he could be so scared that he would run into the ocean.

The little pig's eyes rolled back into his head. It was clear that he was on the brink of losing his mind.

"I'll get him," Lois said. She dropped her massive purse on the sand, where it made a craterlike dent, and then lunged for the pig.

Jethro leapt away from her, and Lois landed face first in the sand. I could have told her leaping at the pig wasn't the right tactic to catch him. I supposed it was up to me to catch the troublesome oinker. Again.

While Lois spat sand out of her mouth, Jethro took off toward the ocean.

"Stop him!" Juliet screamed. "He can't swim. He will drown with a crab on his nose." She said this as if it was the worst possible end to the pig's life.

I lifted my skirts and ran after the little pig. My sneakers were squishy from the waves. It was a *gut* thing that I was in shape to run. I had Phillip and Peter, my goats, to thank for that. They were always getting into trouble, and it seemed that I was always chasing them here or there.

I would not say that I was a fast runner by any means, and I was sure that a sturdy speed walker could have gone right past me, but I was fast enough to catch up to Jethro, who had stopped just shy of the pier.

He pulled up short when he got there. He stopped so fast that I almost tripped over him. With three mighty shakes of his head, he sent the crab flying back in the ocean. Before he could take off again, I picked him up and held him close to my chest.

"That is the last time you are running off while on the beach," I told the little pig. "You can't keep putting Juliet through this, not to mention Lois and me."

He looked up at me with the sincerest expression on his face, as if he was promising that he would never do something like that again. I didn't believe him, but I did appreciate that he appeared to understand the gravity of the situation.

His snout was beginning to swell. I could not help but feel a little bit of sympathy for him.

Lois, who still had sand covering the front of her tracksuit, stumbled over to us and waggled her finger at the little pig. "You're lucky I landed on soft sand. I could break a rib falling like that at my age. Or a hip! Do you want to send me in for a hip replacement?"

He licked his snout, where there were two distinct red marks where the crab had got him. Juliet wouldn't be happy when she saw the injury to her pig. I would not put it past her to put makeup on the pig to cover up the imperfections. Juliet had her mind set on the fact that Jethro was destined for greatness and to be a Hollywood star. Any imperfection would be disastrous in her mind.

"Where's Juliet?" I asked.

Lois shook her head. "She's still standing where we left her. She doesn't run. How could she in that dress? I'm all for fashion, but one has to be a little more practical when it comes to walking on the beach."

I agreed with her.

I looked under the pier. It was a new part of the beach to Lois and me. We had not had much time to explore because Juliet and Jethro had showed up.

The pier's pylons were as thick as a man's chest. The wood that made up the pier was battered and weathered to a dusty gray color by the sea.

I noticed something behind one of the pylons; it looked like a shoe. I supposed it would be common for people, especially children, to lose their shoes in the surf. The undercurrent could pull off their sandals and water shoes, but the shoe that I saw was neither of these.

I tucked Jethro under my arm but still held him firmly in place. There was no way that I was going to chase him for the third time that day.

Lois dusted sand off her cheeks.

"It could be nothing," I said. "But I have to check."

"You have to check what?" She shook sand from her hat. "There is a shoe behind the pylon? So what. Someone probably lost it on the beach and it washed ashore with the tide."

"You're most likely right, but still, I will always wonder if I don't check," I said.

Lois groaned. "There better not be a dead body back there. I would really like to have a normal vacation for once."

"Just as soon as I check this out, we can go." In my squishy sneakers, I stepped around the pylon and saw the body of a woman lying in the sand. She was face down and unmoving. "Lois!"

My friend did not hesitate and immediately appeared at my side.

Together we rolled the woman over. There were bruises around her neck. Her hands were tied behind her back with fishing line. My stomach lurched at the sight of her bloody wrists. The woman was in Amish dress, and I knew in my heart who it was before I even saw her face.

Lois felt the woman's neck for a pulse, but I knew it was no use. Sweet Caroline Zook was dead.

Chapter Six

I sat back on my heels in the wet sand holding Jethro in my arms. The little pig seemed to sense my turmoil because he did not fuss or try to get away from me. That was something to be grateful for.

I couldn't look at Caroline's unseeing eyes, so my gaze fell to her feet. One was bare and one wore the simple black sneaker that I had first seen. The bare foot was encrusted with wet sand. Considering the power of the waves, the fact her foot was bare wasn't the surprising part—the tattoo on her left ankle was.

I stared at her bare ankle. There was a small heart tattoo just above her ankle bone. I blinked. I knew that tattoos were common in the *Englisch* culture, but they were forbidden in the Amish world. In our faith, the body was seen as a temple, and we were not to do anything unnatural to it, not even dye our hair. Tattoos were unheard of. How could Caroline have a tattoo and be Amish?

I supposed that it was possible she got it during

rumspringa, or the Amish running-around time when young Amish were given the space and time to decide if they wanted to join the church or leave for the *Englisch* world. Even so, not many Amish revolted in such a way and then came back to the faith. It was such a permanent statement.

"Is that a tattoo?" Lois asked.

I nodded. "It looks like it."

"Then she can't be Amish, can she? A person can't be Amish with a tattoo."

"We met her yesterday on the bus. She was clearly Amish. She was dressed in the Amish way and she told me all about her life as an Amish woman while you were asleep. She just got married and was traveling to Pinecraft to be with her new husband."

"I saw her in line for the bus, but as soon as I took those sleeping pills, I was out," Lois said. "I have to remember to take only one next time. I think that is why I had such a hard time waking up this morning. They were still in my system. The bottle said you could take up to three, so I took four. I'm old; sleeping is hard."

I shook my head and struggled to my feet in the wet sand. I still had Jethro in my arms. "We have to call the police."

Lois nodded. "I'll go back and fetch my purse. My phone is in it."

Her phone and heavens knew what else. The less I was aware of what was in Lois's purse, the better. I didn't want to answer any uncomfortable questions if asked.

Before Lois could even stand up, Juliet was there.

She was bent at the waist as she was carrying Lois's purse. "Lois, you must be in the peak of health if you are able to carry this everywhere you go. Is Jethro all right?" She pulled up short, dropped Lois's purse in the sand, and covered her mouth. "Is that woman . . . *dead*?"

I carried Jethro over to her. "I'm afraid so, and Lois is going to call the police."

Lois fished through her purse and came up with her phone. It really was a wonder that she could find things so easily in there. She just had a talent for it.

I guided Juliet a few feet away from Caroline's body as she cried. In truth, I wanted very much to cry too. I liked Caroline and was hopeful that we could be friends. However, I didn't let myself shed any tears at the moment. There was too much discipline etched in my being to allow me to do that. It is not the Amish way to have strong emotions, either *gut* or bad, in public. We have those behind closed doors, and if we can manage it, during prayer alone with *Gott.*

Juliet wept into Jethro's shoulder. The little pig looked at me in a pleading away as if he wanted to escape his mistress's tears. I didn't take him away from her. I had enough to contend with. I was glad Jethro seemed to have the *gut* sense not to try to escape Juliet's arms. Maybe he finally learned his lesson, as the last time he escaped he was snapped onto by a crab and found a dead girl. That would be enough to shake anyone to their core.

Lois slung her purse over her shoulder. "The police are on the way."

As if she beckoned them on, we could hear the sirens of the approaching police cars. The noise startled the flock of terns, and they took off in a flurry of feathers and complaints.

To my surprise, the two police cars drove right onto the sand with sirens sounding and lights flashing. This was all it took to drive the sandpipers and pelicans from the beach as well. I couldn't say that I blamed them. If I had been able to fly away, I would have taken off too.

An ambulance parked on the side of the dune, as it couldn't come on the sand. I could see just the top of it peeking up over the dune and its flashing lights reflecting on the sand.

Bystanders who were combing the beach for shells or just out for a morning stroll avoided the area too. I noted how different the general reaction to police in Pinecraft was to Holmes County. Back home, half the village would have come out to see what all the commotion was about. Here, everyone seemed to want to be as far away from it as possible.

A police officer got out of the car. He wore a gray T-shirt under a bulletproof vest and navy-blue shorts. His vest said "Sarasota Police" in bold yellow letters across his chest. There was a gun and badge on his belt. I didn't think that I had ever seen a police officer in shorts before. However, I could understand why he was wearing them. It was already beginning to feel warm, and it was only eight in the morning. I couldn't imagine what it felt like standing on the beach at noon.

Another man got out of the second car. He was a bit older and wore a button-down shirt and dark pants. His hair was combed back from his face. He wore giant sunglasses that covered half of his face.

"Did one of you call in an accident?" the second man asked.

Lois raised her hand. "It was me." She held out her hand to the older man.

He looked down at it with a scowl on his face. "I don't shake hands. There are too many germs in this world, and people aren't as careful with their hygiene as they should be."

Lois dropped her hand. "Well, I never. That is not the thing to say to make a favorable first impression."

He scowled at her. "I'm Detective Marcs, and I am not here to make a good or bad impression."

Lois opened and closed her mouth.

I was afraid of what my friend might say, so I jumped in. "We understand, Detective, and we are so grateful that you came so quickly. As you can imagine, we are distraught at our discovery this morning."

He nodded. "You found a body on the beach? I wish I could say this was the first time that I have gotten a call like this in the early morning, but I cannot. I have been a police officer in Sarasota for over thirty years. You would not believe the things that I have seen wash up from the Gulf."

If there was something worse than a dead body, I most definitely didn't want to hear about it.

"People can be drunk and reckless," Detective Marcs said. "It leads to many of the accidental deaths this close to water."

"I don't believe her death was accidental," I said.

Detective Marcs gave a sharp turn of the head to look at me. "What are you saying? Suicide?"

"No. Murder."

Chapter Seven

Detective Marcs glared at me, and I realized my error in judgment. I wasn't dealing with Chief Brody or even Deputy Little back home in Holmes County. Detective Marcs didn't know me, and he wasn't going to take my opinions into consideration during his investigation like the officers I knew back home did.

"Why would you say that?" the detective asked.

I couldn't take back what I said, so there was nothing I could do but continue on. "Because there was fishing line tied around her wrists." I took a breath. "And I could be mistaken, but it looks like she was strangled. She could not have done that to herself."

He glared at me. "How would you know this?"

I frowned. "We had to make sure that she wasn't still alive. I saw it when Lois was taking her pulse."

He pursed his lips together. It was clear to me that the detective had a lot more he wanted to say to me but was trying to control his emotions.

"Detective, you are going to want to see this. It appears the woman was tied up," one of the officers said. Several more police officers had arrived while I had been speaking with the detective.

"I will be there in a moment," the detective called back. "Secure the scene. Check the area to the high tide line for evidence."

The officer nodded and went back under the pier.

Detective Marcs turned back to me. "You seemed to have studied the body quite closely. I believe most women, especially Amish women, would have shrunken away from a dead body, not gotten close to it to look for signs of foul play."

Before I could speak, Lois chimed in, "You will learn really fast that Millie is not like most Amish women. She's a crime solver. She has solved several murders back in Holmes County, Ohio. In fact, we *both* have. She would have never solved all of those murders if it hadn't been for me too."

The detective studied me. "What is she rambling about? You solved a murder—"

"More than one," Lois chimed in. "It wasn't like it was a one-time deal. We are bona fide sleuths."

I wished Lois was one foot closer to me so I could poke her and tell her to stop talking. The detective didn't need to know any of this. It would only make him concerned that we were the ones who found the body. And more suspicious.

Even so, I could not lie. "We have helped the sheriff's department back home with a case from time to time. You have to remember the majority of Holmes County is Amish or Mennonite. The police aren't able to receive the same truthful answers from my community that I can as an Amish woman. The Amish don't trust the police, and that is for good reason, as they were persecuted when they lived in Europe."

"You're telling me that because some European police officers were unkind to the Amish over two hundred years ago, the county sheriff in Ohio consults *you* when he is trying to solve a murder."

"It sounds outlandish when you put it that way," Lois said.

"That's because it is outlandish," Detective Marcs growled. "The two of you are trying to make a fool out of me. A young woman is dead. This is not a spectacle for a couple of senior citizens to make a mockery of." He stomped away to the crime scene.

"Who are you calling a senior citizen?" Lois asked.

I stepped on Lois's foot.

"Ouch, Millie, I just have sandals on and you have on sneakers. How is that a fair fight?"

"I had to do something to stop you from telling Detective Marcs about the murders we solved back home. You might think you're helping, but you're not. You're making us look like we are suspects."

"Suspects? Why would he suspect us, a couple of old ladies? I never heard anything so ridiculous. We didn't even know the girl."

I bit the inside of my lip. Lois may not have felt that way because she slept for most of the bus ride between Ohio and Florida. However, after talking to Caroline for hours on end, I felt like I knew her very well. I knew her well enough to know that she was anxious about returning to Florida and starting her new life with her husband. At the time, I had thought those were normal newlywed jitters. No one really knew what they were getting into when they got married. I believe this is especially true for young Amish women, who are sheltered much of their lives. While traveling on the bus, I had wondered if Caroline regretted her decision to marry. However, once she agreed to marry her betrothed, it would have been very difficult to change her mind. The Amish don't have long engagements. When a couple agrees to marry and the marriage is approved by their family and their bishop, everything moves very fast.

I thought about my own marriage to Uriah. We married a few days after agreeing to. Now, part of that had to do with our age and because we had known each other since childhood. There wasn't much we *didn't* know about each other already. From what Caroline said, I don't think she had the same circumstances with her husband.

Juliet walked over to us and hugged Jethro to her chest. "This has just been an awful trip. Reverend Brook has been so on edge over the all the politics in the conference, and Jethro is misbehaving because he doesn't have his routine."

"Or Bailey," Lois piped in. "He really needs Bailey."

Juliet, who I have never seen mad in my life, narrowed her eyes at Lois. "I can take care of my pig."

"No one is questioning that," I said and gave Lois a look.

Lois shrugged. I can't say that I disagreed with her, but clearly it wasn't something that Juliet wanted to hear.

"And now there is a dead body," Juliet wailed. She burst into tears.

Lois and I shared a look. Most of the time, Juliet was happily oblivious to what was going on around her. A person could steal her wallet right out of her polka-dotted handbag and she would thank them for stopping to talk to her. Clearly, there was something going on with her that was much more than her pig finding a dead person, because honestly it wasn't the first time it had happened, and she'd never taken it this hard.

Before Lois and I could get to the root of Juliet's emotional outburst, Detective Marcs returned. He stared with wide eyes at Juliet burying her tearful face into her pig's side. "What is wrong with her? Did she know the victim?"

I shook my head. "*Nee,* I don't believe that she did. She is just shaken up over everything that has happened. It has been quite a difficult morning, as you can imagine."

He eyed me. "You don't seem to be upset."

"I'm heartbroken for the girl, but I will save my tears for the time when I can shed them in quiet."

He looked from Lois to me to Juliet and back again. "You can cry at the police station, because that's where you're going right now."

"What?" Lois asked. "Are we under arrest?"

"No," Detective Marcs said. "But you are witnesses . . . maybe even persons of interest. We can talk about it more when we get to the police station."

Juliet's wailing grew worse.

Chapter Eight

Lois and I didn't have much choice but to go to the police station. Thankfully, I was able to convince the detective that Juliet should be allowed to return to her resort with Jethro in tow. She had been down the beach when we found the body. What's more, there was a real risk of Jethro getting loose in the police station and causing all kinds of chaos.

To be honest, I think Detective Marcs agreed that Juliet could leave because of the crying. It didn't seem to me that the detective was all that comfortable with Juliet's emotions.

One of the young police officers escorted Lois and me back to our bungalow so that we could change our shoes, which were soaked, before going to the police station. When we reached the bungalow, Lois changed not only her shoes but her entire outfit. She put on floral leggings and a bright pink caftan top.

"There's no time to do my hair properly." She rooted through her suitcase and came up with a bright green bucket hat. "This will have to do." She turned around and showed me. "What do you think?"

"It's a statement."

"Good. That's just what I want it to be. I'll do my makeup in the back of the cruiser," she said.

I shook my head and followed her out of the bungalow.

The young female officer looked to be about the age of Lois's granddaughter. She was petite with a wide mouth and black hair that was tethered to the top of her head in an intricate braid.

"I'm Officer Billings and I will be taking you to the station. The detective should be there shortly after we arrive." She pointed to a police cruiser.

Lois and I got in the back seat. I noted that we were behind a metal grate that kept us from reaching the driver. I could not help but wonder who else had sat there.

Lois leaned forward and held on to the bars as Officer Billings pulled away from the bungalow. "Tell me, Officer Billings," Lois said, "is Detective Marcs always in a foul mood like that? He must be a complete bear to work with."

She glanced over her shoulder and seemed to be shocked that Lois's face was so close to the grate. "He's been at the Sarasota Police Department longer than I have been alive. There's nothing that comes to Sarasota that he hasn't seen, from alligators to sharks to hurricanes to tourists."

Lois sat back. "Tourists are on the same list as alligator, sharks, and hurricanes?"

"Tourists cause more trouble for the city than the other three combined," Officer Billings said.

Lois and I shared a look. ——

"This isn't his first body on the beach either," Officer Billings added. "Sadly, there are a few drownings every year."

"Amish drownings?"

The back of Officer Billings's neck turned red. "I don't think I am at liberty to say that."

Lois leaned forward again. "Was there another Amish murder on the beach?"

The officer changed the subject. "There is the station up ahead. We have a full docket today. Mostly snowbird complaints. We are in the height of snowbird season and they honestly cause more trouble than the alligators."

"So how often is there an alligator sighting?" Lois asked.

"I'm sure someone sees one in the area at least once a day. You don't have to worry about them in the salt water, though, unless there is a hurricane. Then they really could be anywhere. I've even seen one on a roof after a hurricane."

Lois's eyes were huge.

I patted her leg. "It's not hurricane season. All should be well."

"Thank goodness for that. I don't want to see any flying alligators *Sharknado* style."

I wrinkled my brow. "Sharkwhat?"

I had no idea what she was talking about. Apparently Officer Billings did, because she chuckled. The *Englisch* could be really odd at times. I had learned to live with it after all these years, especially when it came to Lois.

Lois sat back in her seat and pulled her makeup bag from her purse. I watched in awe as she applied foundation, blush, eye shadow, and false eyelashes to her face.

She was just touching up her lipstick when Officer Billings said that we had arrived at the station.

"I'm impressed," I said. "I have never seen you do your makeup that fast."

"I typically like to linger over my makeup, but there's no time for that. I've learned how to do this on the run. I've been known to put on eyelashes while driving too."

My jaw dropped. "Please don't ever do that when I'm in the car with you."

"Millie, it is only in the most desperate of situations, like being late for a date."

I shook my head. Lois and I were locked in the back seat of the police cruiser, so we had to wait for Officer Billings to let us out.

"If you ladies will follow me, I will put you in the interrogation rooms so that the detective can speak to you," the officer said.

"Rooms. Does that mean that we will be separated?" I asked as I climbed out of the car.

"Yes," the officer said. "It's standard procedure with witnesses."

"We are just witnesses, right?" Lois asked. "Not persons of interest."

Officer Billings didn't say anything to that.

"Why can't we be together?" I asked. "Lois was with me the whole time. We have the same story."

"Then there will be nothing to worry about, as your stories will match." She opened the door to the police station, and we went inside.

I would have to say that the police station in Sarasota was much different than the sheriff's department in Holmes County, which was a 1960s octagonal building that was built for utility, not for looks. The inside of the Sarasota station looked like it was from a magazine. Potted palm trees sat in three corners of the room, and the wall and floor colors were very fitting with the ocean of teals, blues, and greens.

"This is the prettiest police station that I have ever been in," Lois said.

Officer Billings looked over her shoulder. "Have you been in many?"

"My fair share. A number of my husbands were compulsive gamblers. You tend to get into a bit of trouble with your bookies if that's what you're into and need to be bailed out."

"Husbands?"

"Just four," Lois said. "I'm not any good at marriage."

Officer Billings raised her brow at this but made no more comment. I thought that was for the best. It was never *gut* to have Lois start speaking about her ex-husbands. She had a lot to say about them, and then we might be here all day.

Officer Billings led Lois and me to a doorway at the end of the hall. "Ms. Henry, I would ask you to step inside here."

I peeked around Lois. The room was bare and gray,

and the only furniture was a metal table and set of folding chairs.

"I feel like I'm on *CSI* or something." Lois stepped into the room and then looked over her shoulder at me. "See you on the other side."

Officer Billings closed the door.

The officer then led me up a flight of stairs into what looked like an everyday office with cubicles and ringing phones. At the end of the floor, she unlocked the door and gestured for me to go inside.

I found myself in an office. I looked at the walls and saw photographs all over the room of Detective Marcs shaking hands with official-looking folks. I didn't see any personal photos that might have been him with his family. I wondered if he had any family or if he chose these photographs because they suggested importance and power.

"Why aren't I in a room like Lois's?" I asked.

"Would you prefer to be in an interrogation room?"

"*Nee*, but I'm just wondering if there is a reason to bring me here."

She shrugged. "It is where Detective Marcs asked me to put you. I have learned after all these years it's best not to question him."

I swallowed. That sounded ominous.

Just as I sat in one of the hard plastic chairs across from the detective's desk, Detective Marcs stepped into the office. When the detective walked behind his desk, Officer Billings stepped into the doorway.

"Billings, thank you for bringing Mrs. Schrock to my office. You can leave now," the detective said. His voice was stern.

"Do you want me to speak to her friend?" Officer Billings asked. "Or would you like to question her too?"

"You question the friend," he said. "But give her some time to cool her heels."

I knew how much Lois was going to hate that and suspected that the detective did too, which was exactly why he did it. He could have left me in a quiet room for quite a while, and I would be all right. But then again, I was Amish. Amish women were taught to be patient and take advantage of quiet. Lois hated waiting, and she hated quiet. She would run from the police station when this was all over. I couldn't say that I blamed her. I was looking forward to getting out of there too.

Officer Billings nodded and stepped out of the room. She was about to close the door when I spoke up. "Can you please leave the door open? It is not proper in my culture for a woman to be alone in a room with a man she does not know."

She looked to the detective, and he nodded. Leaving the door open, she walked away.

"*Danki*, for being so understanding," I said. "I am not fearful of anything improper, but appearances are important too."

"I can respect that, Mrs. Schrock," he said.

"Please call me Millie. I was Mrs. Fisher for most of my life, and there are times that I forget that my new last name is Schrock. In the Amish world, we just address each other by our first name unless the person we are speaking to is a leader in the church."

He nodded. "All right, Millie. You can call me Detective Marcs."

I suppressed a smile. I had expected nothing less from him.

"Let's go back to the start of this morning," Detective Marcs said. "Why were you there?"

"Lois and I were on the beach to see the sunrise, and we ran into Juliet Brook, a friend from back home in Ohio. Her pig was loose and we caught him for her. Her pig escapes a lot, so we know how to catch him. I would say that everyone from Harvest does. It's just something about living there. Going to the café, eating candy, and catching the town's pet pig."

The detective looked at me like my goats Phillip and Peter were tap-dancing on my shoulders. I guessed I couldn't blame him for that. A person really had to go to Harvest to truly understand what I was talking about.

"You caught the pig and found the body." He made a note on a tablet of paper on his desk.

I shook my head. "We gave Jethro back to Juliet."

"You said the pig was the one that led you to the body." He narrowed his eyes like I had fibbed about part of my story.

"He was," I said. "But he found her the second time he got loose."

He pinched the bridge of his nose. "The second time."

I nodded. "Juliet was anxious and had trouble keeping him under control. He's a very adventurous pig. Have you ever watched *Bailey's Amish Sweets*?"

"What?"

"It's a television show on Gourmet TV. Bailey is Juliet's soon-to-be daughter-in-law and she's usually much better at keeping track of Juliet's pig than Juliet, but she's in New York shooting her show. Sometimes Jethro is on the show, but I assume they didn't need him for these tapings. Tapings are what Bailey calls them. I can't say that I exactly know what that means. I have only seen snippets of the program that Lois has shown me on her phone. I don't have a television."

"Yes, I understand that Amish don't have televisions." He scowled.

I took a deep breath. I was rambling, and I knew that was because I was nervous. I never spoke like this when I was being questioned by Deputy Little or Sheriff Brody back home. However, I knew both of them well and they trusted me. Detective Marcs didn't know me at all and doubted the majority of what I was saying.

He pinched his nose again like he was starting to get a headache. I could only guess how much worse his headache would be if he spoke with Lois. It was a very *gut* thing that he assigned that job to Officer Billings.

"Go back to the part the about escaping the second time." He released his nose and folded his hands on the notepad in front of him.

I told him about how Jethro escaped from Juliet's arm and ran under the pier. "That's where we found her. As soon as I saw Caroline, my heart was broken. She was so young and had so much life to live. It's so tragic."

"Wait! What? You said Caroline."

I nodded. "That's her name."

He flattened his hands on the desktop. "You knew the dead woman?"

I nodded. "We rode on the bus from Ohio with her.

Her name was Caroline. She's from Florida originally. She never told me what she was doing up in Ohio. I suppose I just assumed that she was visiting relatives since there is so much crossover between Holmes County and Pinecraft. She was returning to Florida to be reunited with her new husband."

He stared at me. "And you didn't think that this was worth mentioning to me before?"

"I would have, but you didn't give Lois or me a chance to say it. You sent us off with Officer Billings just as soon as you could."

"As soon as you said that you were crime solvers what was I supposed to do?"

Crime solvers had been Lois's term, not mine.

"Tell me everything that you know about her. Don't you understand that since you can identify her, we will be able to find and notify her family that much sooner? This is a breakthrough. The Amish aren't the easiest to find when they don't have public records. Some of them don't even go to the dentist. The faster we can tell her family, the less likely they will hear it through gossip in the community."

My heart ached. I hadn't thought about that all. Maybe it was because Holmes County in a lot of ways was such a small place. Everyone knew everyone else or knew someone who knew someone else. There were only really two degrees of separation in Holmes County, even less in Harvest. But Pinecraft was a small community in a much larger city, a place with city crime and city problems. I wasn't in rural Ohio any longer.

"I do apologize." I folded my hands in my lap. "You're right. I should have said it to you right away or told

Officer Billings if I did not have the chance to tell you on the beach."

He gave a gruff nod and seemed to be pacified with my apology. Maybe he thought that I was going to fight back. "Do you know Caroline's last name?"

"Her married name was Zook," I said. "She said that her husband owns a scooter shop in Pinecraft."

The detective nodded. "It must be Zook's Scooters. It's popular with Amish and English alike. You will have to excuse me for a moment. I need to send one of my officers out there to tell the family." He stood up from his desk and walked out of the room.

As the door gently closed behind him, I folded my hands in my lap as the enormity of my mistake hit me. I prayed that no one reached Caroline's husband with the news before the police did. I knew better than most how quickly news traveled in the Amish community. Even though Lois and I found Caroline very early in the morning, the police presence would bring people to the beach to see what was happening. The news that an Amish girl was found dead under the pier would travel quickly.

A few minutes later the detective came back. "You are free to go for now," he said. "It's likely that I will want to talk to you again. Please stop at the desk to sign your statement."

I stood up. "What about Lois?"

"Officer Billings is recording her statement, and she should be able to leave soon as well."

I nodded and walked to the door.

"Millie?"

I turned to face him. He was leaning against the bookshelf behind his desk. "Don't leave Florida without clearing it with me first."

I nodded, knowing exactly what that meant. I was a suspect.

Chapter Nine

I walked back into the under-the-sea waiting room, signed my statement, and found Lois sitting in a chair by the exit rooting through her giant bag. After a moment, she came out with a tube of lipstick. She reapplied her bright pink lipstick and smiled at me.

I pointed at my teeth. "You have a bit on your front tooth."

She rubbed her teeth and it went away. "I'm glad all of that went a bit faster than I thought it would," she said. "I was afraid that we would be here all day and lose vacation time. We have so much that we want to do and see."

I nodded absently.

"Are you ready to leave?" She studied my face.

"*Ya*. It's my hope that we don't have to come back here again." I looked over my shoulder, half expecting that Detective Marcs was just behind me to drag me back inside the police station.

"Mine too, but I do like the lobby. It might be the

prettiest one that I have ever seen. Too bad it's wasted on a prison."

"It's not a prison," I said. "It's the police station." I opened the door for her, and we walked out.

The first thing I noticed when I stepped outside the police station was the humidity. I could feel the small hairs that had escaped their bobby pins start to curl.

Lois removed the hat from her head, and I had to stop myself from gasping. The state of her hair was startling. She was typically all put together when it came to outfits, but I could see now why she was so upset with her appearance. Even though it was nothing like my Amish garb, I knew that she took great pride in her clothes, makeup, and hair.

She touched the top of her head. "It feels like a mop."

"It sort of looks like a mop too, like a mop that was recently used to clean up punch."

Lois gave me a look. "Millie, you don't have to be so accurate with your description." She slipped the hat back onto her head. "I'll have to wait until we return to the bungalow to fix it. If I see any eligible men between then and now, I'll be very upset."

"You can't really see your hair with the hat on."

"Really? So, you can see some of it?" She removed her hat again and tucked all of her hair under it. "That was very rude of the police to not offer us a ride back to our bungalow. It must be at least a mile from here. That's too far for a couple of old women to walk in an unfamiliar place and unaccustomed to the heat."

I pointed to a large building down the block. The sign read THE DUTCHMAN RESORT. "Isn't that where

Juliet said that Reverend Brook was having his meetings?"

"It is, and since there are so many out-of-town folks there, I'm sure we'll find a taxi."

I wasn't sure that we needed a taxi. To me it looked like a half mile to the resort, and Juliet said it was a half mile between the resort and the bungalow I shared with Lois.

Lois and I walked toward the conference center. A large posterboard sign out front said WELCOME PASTORS AND DELEGATES.

"Delegates for what?" Lois wanted to know. "Are they nominating the next president?"

"They must be delegates from the churches to vote on things and such."

"Who knew churches were so political?" Lois asked.

I refrained from comment on that.

There was a line of taxis with drivers outside the center waiting to take people anywhere they wanted to go. I wanted to hop right into one and start this day over again. It had been a very long morning.

As if it came down in a heavy cloak, the weight of the day fell on my shoulders. Tears pricked my eyes. I could not believe that Caroline was dead. I had not known her long, but I had liked her. She was so excited to return to Florida and start her life with her new husband, and she wanted to impress him by learning to sew. There had been a vulnerability about her, and I instantly wanted to take her under my wing and protect her. In my mind, I had already made plans about future sewing lessons while I was in Florida with Caroline.

She was to be my friend. All of that was ripped away. I blinked away my tears. I made a promise to myself then and there. I would find out what happened to her.

Lois was looking around the resort while I struggled with my emotions and was completely unaware of how I was feeling. That was for the best. I didn't believe I could speak about it without crying, and crying out in the open was not the Amish way.

"They have a coffee shop inside," Lois said. "I have to have a latte if I want any chance of salvaging this day."

Before I could stop her, she ran into the conference center through the revolving door. I went up to the door, unsure how to enter.

A man behind me said, "You just walk through the gap when it appears and then you come out the other side."

I looked over my shoulder at him. "I believe it's the timing that has me nervous."

"I can help you." He offered me his arm. He was a tall man with dark hair brushed back from his forehead, and he wore glasses and a button-down shirt and slacks that were so crisp, they appeared to have been ironed just minutes ago.

After a brief moment of hesitation, I took it, and he led me through the door.

When I was on the other side I thanked him and dropped his arm. It would not be becoming for anyone to see me touching a stranger.

He smiled with bright, straight white teeth. "It was no trouble at all. Are you here for the conference?"

I shook my head. "*Nee,* but I do have friends who are attending."

"Oh? Who is that?" he asked.

"Reverend Brook and his wife, Juliet."

He flashed his teeth again. "I know them very well. I must say that Reverend Brook has been steady leadership on two of our committees. Had he not been there, I'm convinced the committee members would have come to blows."

"Blows? I thought this was a conference for pastors."

"It is, and in my experience, pastors are the quickest to anger when they disagree. I am happy Reverend Brook has been able to keep everyone on an even keel."

"Reverend Brook has always been a steadfast man, and his calmness is well known in our community. I have always appreciated that about him as well."

"Any friend of Reverend Brook's is a friend of mine." He held out his hand to me to shake.

I looked at it. In Amish culture, it was believed to be a rude for a man to offer a handshake to a woman he didn't know. The norm was if the woman wanted to shake your hand, she would extend her hand first. In most cases, the woman would not offer a handshake. Touching strangers, even in the most innocent experiences, wasn't the norm in the Amish world. Touching anyone in public was unusual. Even knowing all this, I briefly shook his hand because I didn't want to appear rude to a friend of the Brooks.

"I'm Ross Hanniford. I'm a local pastor in Sarasota. My family has been here for over twenty years. I'm running the conference this week, and, as I said, I am so glad that I have Reverend Brook here as a voice of reason. It's something that the conference desperately needs."

I removed my hand as gently as I could from his grasp. "Millie Fisher Schrock," I said. "Did you live somewhere else before coming to Sarasota?"

He nodded. "I grew up in Wisconsin and could not wait to get away from the cold weather. Florida has been great. Except for the occasional hurricane, I don't have any complaints."

"That's *gut*," I said. "And I'm glad that you invited Reverend Brook to your conference. You made a wise choice. No one in Harvest—Amish or *Englisch*—has a bad word to say about him."

"The only problem with Reverend Brook is the pig." Ross wrinkled his nose as if Jethro was close enough to smell. Not that the pig smelled poorly. Juliet made sure that Jethro was always clean and presentable. He might be the most manicured pig on the planet.

"Jethro?" I asked as if I didn't know the answer.

"Yes. He has been all over the conference center, and Reverend Brook's wife Juliet is running this way and that in tears because she can't get the pig to behave. A church conference is not the place for a pig."

I agreed that it was not.

"I have asked the reverend to leave the pig in his hotel room for the time being, but he said the hotel staff will not allow Jethro to be in the room unsupervised."

I couldn't blame the resort on that point. "Juliet is my friend. I will talk to her about taking Jethro off her hands for a few hours here and there, so she can enjoy the conference. I know she does not want to worry Reverend Brook."

"That would be wonderful. We really only have a few days for these meetings before the pastors scatter across the country again, and we don't have time for interruptions like this."

Lois returned with two coffees in hand. One was a giant iced concoction with whipped cream and sprinkles, and the other was a medium paper cup.

"There were so many flavors to choose from, like a key lime matcha latte. Whoever thought of that?" Lois asked. "I played it safe and got a double sugar cookie latte, but we will have to come back for us to taste them all." She sighed. "Or for *me* to taste them all. I got you a boring black coffee with nothing added, just how you like it." She held the paper cup out to me and I took it from her hand. "Back by the coffee shop, there is a full Amish restaurant just like the ones at home. I can't say that I'm dying to go there. We could go to a restaurant like that for breakfast, lunch, and dinner every day in Harvest. However, if you are craving home cooking, it is an option. I'm excited for all the fresh seafood I can eat."

Pastor Ross watched Lois with an amused smile on his face. "I take it that you two know each other."

"I guess you could say that," Lois quipped. "We have been the best of friends since birth."

"Lois." I jumped in before my friend could tell Pastor Ross our life story. As the head of the conference he surely had many other things that he could or should be doing. "This is Pastor Ross Hanniford. He is running the conference that Reverend Brook and Juliet are attending."

"Very nice to meet you," Lois said. "You will have to excuse my appearance. It's been a wild morning and I haven't had the time to do my hair."

He grinned. "What could be a wild morning for a couple of kind women like you?"

"We went to the beach and—"

"Pastor Ross?" A younger man came down the hallway. He was tall and lanky and took loping strides like he was in a hurry. He wore black trousers, loafers with no socks, and a polo shirt with the name of the conference embroidered on the pocket. "Pastor Ross, I'm so sorry to interrupt, but Simon Blind would like to talk to you about his afternoon session. He's not pleased with the room placement."

Pastor Ross shook his head. "The only way Simon Blind would be happy was if I let him speak from my pulpit. That's never going to happen."

"He's threatening not to present."

Pastor Ross pursed his lips together. "He's made this threat before."

Lois cleared her throat.

"Oh, I apologize," Pastor Ross said. "Ladies, this is Scott Lawrence. He works for my church and for the conference. I would not be able to do all of this without his help. He's truly a godsend."

Scott's face turned bright red.

"Scott, this is Millie Schrock and . . ." He trailed off.

"Lois Henry," Lois said.

"Yes," Pastor Ross said as if he needed to give her approval of her own name.

"They are friends of Reverend Brook and Juliet," Pastor Ross said.

"Oh." Scott pushed his floppy blond hair out of his face. His hair was long enough to touch his shoulder, and he nervously played with it every few seconds. I watched with fascination as it always went back into place.

"The people with the pig," Scott said.

Pastor Ross chuckled. "As my right-hand man in my ministry and in this conference, Scott has been dealing with the antics of the pig the most. You've done a fine job too."

Scott shook his hair. "I don't know about that. Every time that I think I have the problem solved, the pig pops up again, causing even more trouble. I don't know why Reverend Brook and Juliet brought him with them."

"He's a comfort pig," Lois piped up. "Juliet needs him for her nerves."

Scott narrowed his eyes for just a moment as if he was seriously doubtful of that statement.

"I have good news for you, Scott," Pastor Ross said. "These two ladies have agreed to take Jethro away from the conference from time to time. Isn't that kind of them to offer?"

"I could track him down right now and hand him over," Scott said. "It would only take a moment. It's pretty easy to track him down. You just follow the general outcry and sound of disturbance."

Pastor Ross laughed. "We will talk with Juliet and Reverend Brook about it first before handing the pig over."

Scott scowled. If I was Jethro, I would stay as far

away from the pastor's assistant as I could get. There was no love lost there.

"I'll speak to Simon." Pastor Ross turned to Lois and me. "Ladies, it was so nice to meet you. I hope we will meet again during the conference. A friend of the Brooks is a friend of mine."

"It was lovely to meet the two of you," Scott said with a bright smile.

Lois cocked her head and smiled at the pastor as if she were taking him under consideration for husband number five. I could see why, and I knew the signs when Lois was scoping out a new husband. Her cheeks flushed, and her eyes trained in on her target. Pastor Ross was a very handsome man in a groomed sort of way. His nose was slightly too large for his face, but he made up for it by having perfect skin and a thick mane of gray hair. I guessed he was in his late fifties, which was a bit on the young side for Lois if she asked me.

Lois and I said our good-byes and turned to walk out of the resort. She whispered in my ear, "No wedding band. He's fifth husband material."

"Lois, he's too young for you," I whispered back. "You could be his mother."

"Mother? That's a stretch. I'm keeping him under consideration. He has nice teeth. It's hard to find a man with good teeth at our age. I don't take a set of pearly whites for granted any longer."

I shook my head. "There are plenty of taxis outside. Let go back to the bungalow and regroup."

Lois smiled. "Regroup for what? Because we have a murder to solve?"

I nodded. "It's exactly for that."

Just as we were leaving, the revolving door spun, and Detective Marcs and two police officers walked into the resort's grand foyer. They had a determined set to their jaws, and recognition flickered in the detective's eyes when he saw me.

Lois grabbed my arm. "I don't think they are here for the key lime matcha."

Pastor Ross frowned. "Can I help you, Officer?"

Detective Marcs shot a look in my direction and then addressed Ross. "Yes, I'm looking for Ross Hanniford."

Pastor Ross stepped back as if he had been slapped. "I'm Pastor Ross Hanniford. How can I help you? I hope that nothing has happened to any of my parishioners."

"No, sir, not that we know of," Detective Marcs said. "It's about your daughter."

Pastor Ross blinked. "Did you find Caroline?"

Scott gasped, and my heart fell to my stomach.

Chapter Ten

"**I**s there somewhere we can talk in private?" the detective asked, giving me a very pointed look.

"Yes, of course." Beads of sweat gathered on Pastor Ross's forehead. "There is a small meeting room right by the elevators. We're using it for committee meetings, but it should be empty right now."

With one more glance in my and Lois's direction, Detective Marcs followed Pastor Ross to the room. The other officers followed close behind. Scott Lawrence shifted back and forth and then finally seemed to come to some sort of decision. He followed Pastor Ross and the police down the corridor. He played with his hair the entire time.

I felt shaky. I knew that Pastor Ross must be Caroline's father, but he wasn't Amish. Then of course, I remembered the tattoo on Caroline's ankle. Did she convert to the faith to marry her husband? That did happen, but it was extremely rare. It had become even rarer with the passage of time. It's far more common for a young

Amish person to leave the faith than for a young *Englischer* to join the faith.

"Whoa," Lois said. "That English pastor is Caroline's dad? How? She's Amish."

"She didn't grow up that way, I take it." I held the coffee just under my nose.

Lois shook her head. "Detective Marcs looked like the vein on his forehead was about to burst when he saw us. It had to look suspicious to him that we were standing with the dead girl's father just a short while after leaving the police station."

"It's not a *gut* impression of us, *nee*."

"Detective Marcs is going to come looking for us after his talk with Pastor Ross."

"I would assume so." I sighed. "I wish that I knew more about Caroline. I thought on the bus ride that we shared so much with each other, but I realize now, you can't know someone really well in that short a time. It takes years."

"That's the truth. You still surprise me, Millie, after seventy years on this earth together." She sipped her questionable coffee drink and got whipped cream on the tip of her nose. She wiped it away. "Did you know that Pastor Ross was Caroline's dad before the police arrived? Was that what the two of you were talking about?"

I shook my head. I held the coffee in my cold hands, and they warmed quickly. The steam from the cup soothed me. Even though it was warm and in the eighties outside, the thermostat inside the conference center must have been set to Arctic Circle. I had been shivering since the moment I stepped inside the building. I quickly told Lois about meeting Pastor Ross Hanniford and his complaints about Jethro.

"You offered to take Jethro off Juliet's hands while we were here?" Lois held her latte out in front of her as if it were a shield to ward off troublesome pigs. "Why would we do that? Don't we have enough problems with the murder? I mean, by what you said, that handsome detective might think you and I are suspects, since we rode the bus with Caroline."

"I know I should have consulted with you before saying anything about Jethro, but Pastor Ross sounded desperate to get Jethro away from the conference."

"I'm not surprised he did. Anyone with any sense wouldn't want that pig close to an important event."

Lois and I turned around and saw Detective Marcs walking to the entryway. The officers who had come into the resort with him were nowhere to be seen.

"I hope the two of you have a very good reason for being here. It was my understanding that you were going back to the place where you were staying after leaving the police station," the detective said. "And yet here you are."

"Are you trying to keep tabs on our movements, Detective Marcs? One would think that a detective from the Sarasota Police Department has much more important things to do than monitor a couple of ladies on vacation."

"I'm a police officer in Florida. During the winter all I do is monitor old ladies on vacation," he said with a slight smile on his face.

"Was that an actual joke, Detective?" Lois asked.

The barest of smiles disappeared from his face.

"We just stopped in on the way back to our bungalow for a bit of coffee," Lois said. "As you know, it has been a very challenging morning, and believing that we could face one more minute of it without coffee is just unrealistic."

He stared at Lois as if he was trying to decide if she was always like this or was rambling to put him off. I would happily tell him that she was always like this if he asked.

He turned to me. "What were you doing with Reverend Hanniford, then?"

"How is Pastor Ross?" I asked.

"How is it that you know Reverend Hanniford?"

"I don't know him," I said. "I just met him. Lois and I stopped by here for coffee, as she said, and to check on Juliet. Her husband is a pastor and attending the conference here at the Dutchman Resort. She was the one with the pig on the beach."

"Ah, yes, the pig lady." He pursed his lips. "I find it quite strange that the two of you seem to be everywhere that I turn when it comes to Caroline Zook."

"It's merely a coincidence; I can assure you. I didn't know that Pastor Ross was connected to Caroline in any way until you and your officers arrived," I said. "I simply was chatting with him about our mutual friends."

"Reverend and Mrs. Brook," Detective Marcs said.

"*Ya*." I sipped my coffee. It was finally cool enough to drink, and I thought it was safe to say that Lois was right. I needed coffee before I could face much more of this day, and it wasn't even lunchtime yet.

The detective squinted at me as if he was trying to judge my level of honesty. He relaxed slightly as if he had accepted my answer. I gave a sigh of relief, but I knew I wasn't out of trouble yet as far as the detective was concerned.

"How is Pastor Ross?" I asked again. "He seemed like a very nice man. And why did he say that you found Caroline? Was she missing? Is he really her father? She was in Amish dress. Did he know that she joined the Amish?"

The relaxed expression on his face dissolved into irritation. "Mrs. Schrock, I have spoken to your sheriff Aiden Brody, back in Ohio, and he spoke very highly of you. He said that I should trust what you have to say. However, you're not in Ohio any longer, and I am not nearly as trusting as your rural county sheriff. I would ask you to leave the resort and stop talking about Caroline or anything to do with her death unless I ask you a specific question about it. I imagine talking about murder wasn't your intent when you came to Florida."

"It wasn't," Lois chimed in. "But it sort of follows us wherever we go."

"Please leave the resort. You are not welcome here." He scowled.

I didn't like to be dismissed, but Lois downright hated it. So when I noticed her shift her stance beside me, I was on my guard.

"You don't know if we are welcome here or not. This

resort doesn't belong to you, and our friends are staying here. You don't have to be so rude." Lois adjusted her purse strap on her shoulder. "We're just trying to help."

He glared at Lois. "The best way you can help is to stop trying." With that, he stomped out of the resort, leaving Lois and me standing at the entrance with our mouths hanging open.

Chapter Eleven

"Stop? Stop?" Lois grumbled we walked out of the resort. "It's clear to me that he doesn't know us at all. We never stop."

This was true. "It was kind of Sheriff Brody to put in a nice word for us," I said.

"What else could he say? We have been a big help to the sheriff and his department the last few years. He has come to rely on us."

I thought "tolerate" was a better word than "rely," but I didn't correct Lois.

"Do you still want to get a cab to go back to the bungalow?" I asked.

"No, I'd rather walk. I need to work off some steam; that detective really riled me up."

"I can see that. It's a short walk. Let's go back to the bungalow, rest for a bit, and get on with our day."

"And eat," Lois said. "I'm starving. I should have gotten a muffin at the coffee stand."

"We have snacks back at the bungalow, but I think we are both due for a nice meal out."

She looped her arm through mine as we proceeded down the sidewalk. "We are, and despite everything, I'm determined to enjoy this beautiful day. Look at this weather. You can't beat it."

I had to agree. The sun was now high in the sky and the leaves on the palmettos along the sidewalk shone. After a long Ohio winter, it felt like paradise, and it would have been were it not for the death of Caroline Zook.

"Millie Fisher Schrock, what are you doing here?" a very familiar voice asked from behind us.

I turned around and saw Ruth Yoder walking through the conference center lobby. Her silver hair was tethered perfectly back into an Amish bun, and her prayer cap sat squarely on the top of her head. Not a single stray hair fell out of place. It wouldn't dare. Ruth wore a short-sleeved, dark purple dress, black tights, and sensible black sneakers.

My outfit was identical to hers in many ways, although my dress was olive green. However, I could not say that my white hair was as pristinely in place. It had been quite a morning.

I knew that I would have a lot of surprises in Pinecraft, but running into Ruth Yoder had not been on my possibility list. Finding a dead body had been more expected than seeing Ruth.

"Ruth? What are you doing here?" I asked.

"I should be asking you the same thing. You never said that you were going to Florida at our last Double

Stitch meeting. You just said that you and Lois were going on a trip."

"I didn't know where we were going at the last meeting. She told me where we were headed two days before."

"That's truth," Lois said. "Our destination was a surprise for Millie."

Ruth glowered at Lois. To say the two of them had a long history of dislike for each other was a fair statement. Ruth, Lois, and I grew up together. Even at a young age, Ruth didn't approve of my close friendship with an *Englischer*, and she thought Lois was *gut* hearted but could also have her wild moments. Ruth always said that Lois was a bad influence on me. She would have much rathered that I only have Amish friends like she did.

But she was very wrong. Lois had not been a bad influence on me. She never pressured me into doing anything against my faith or upbringing. Our friendship was built on mutual respect. I didn't agree with all her choices, but to be frank, she didn't agree with all of mine either. That didn't mean we loved each other any less. As the proverb says, "Be slow to anger and quick to forgive, and you will have friends for as long as you live."

I applied this proverb to my friendship with Ruth as well, but she would be insulted if she knew. Ruth was easily insulted.

"I don't remember you saying anything about going to Florida," I said.

Ruth sniffed. "I wasn't certain that we were going to

make the trip, and it didn't seem worth causing any up-roar within the district that the bishop and I would be gone if it wasn't to be. If I had my way, we wouldn't have left. There is too much work to be done in the district, but Bishop Yoder insisted. He claims this con-ference was a *gut* chance to connect with *Englisch* churches." She shook her head. "He could have con-nected with *Englisch* churches in our own county, if you ask me."

"You're here for the conference?" I asked.

She stared at me as if I had just asked her the most ridiculous question that she had ever heard in her life.

"Why else would I be here?" she asked. "An Amish bishop doesn't take vacations from community, unlike some."

Lois opened her mouth as if she was about to speak, but the last thing I wanted was for them to get into an argument in the middle of the sidewalk right in front of the resort.

"My husband is on an important panel," Ruth said.

"What's the panel?" I asked.

"Interchurch relations about how the churches in a community can work together for the betterment of all. As you know, Bishop Yoder has always had a close re-lationship with Reverend Brook. Together they have done a lot of good for Harvest, and our district and his congregation collaborate well together. Even so, it's difficult for me to be here."

"Why is that?" Lois asked. "This is the perfect time to be away from Ohio. February is the pit of the year up north."

Ruth scowled at Lois, but I didn't know if it was because she disagreed with what Lois had to say or it was the mere fact that Ruth always scowled at Lois. If Ruth ever smiled at Lois, there was a very good chance Lois might faint straight away.

"The bishop and I are needed at home. We are always needed at home. It is our position set forth by *Gott* himself."

"That sounds a little holier than—"

Even though I agreed with Lois about Ruth's opinion of herself, I cut her off. "Everyone in the district knows how hard you and Bishop Yoder work for the community," I said.

She pursed her lips together and nodded as if that was the only correct response to her statement.

Lois stood right next to me, and I saw her roll her eyes out of the corner of mine.

Ruth shook her head. "I told Reverend Brook it was not *gut* that both of us would be away from the quilting circle at the same time. Who will be there to keep the ladies on task? We are coming to the tail end of winter. This is the time when most of the quilting must be done."

"Aww, Ruth, I don't think you need worry about that at all. Winter goes on in Ohio until April," Lois said. "You will have plenty of time to quilt."

Ruth glared at her because she believed no one could run the circle as well as her—or the district as well as her husband, for that matter.

"Leah, Raellen, and the others have been quilting for a long time, Ruth," I said. "They will have everything well taken care of. You don't have anything to worry about."

She folded her arms across her chest. "That shows how little you know. I will have to fix so many things when I return home. I have a headache just thinking of it."

I had complete faith in the ladies in Double Stitch. They would do a fantastic job with the quilting circle with both Ruth and me gone. I envied them a little. They would be able to have meetings without Ruth interjecting orders for an entire week. I would have loved to quilt under those conditions. The ladies would be having a fine time, of that I was certain.

I decided to change the subject. "Did you come down on an earlier bus?" I asked.

Ruth wrinkled her nose. "We came down by train."

"I would have thought that you would be on the Amish bus."

Ruth frowned at her. "I have no interest riding in a bus. I believe that a train is much more appropriate for a beloved Amish bishop. We were able to have the privacy of our own compartment."

"Maybe we should go back by train," Lois said.

I shook my head. I knew the expense would be much higher than the bus. Lois was paying for the trip as a gift for me, and that alone made me uncomfortable. I was not used to accepting such lavish gifts.

"What have the two of you been doing since you arrived?" Ruth glanced at Lois's bucket hat. "Have you been to the beach? Is that an *Englisch* beach hat?"

Lois pulled down on the hat to make sure all of her haphazard hair was well covered. I was certain she didn't want Ruth, of all people, to see the purple-red mop on the top of her head any more than she would want a prospective fifth spouse to see it. Ruth would comment about it for the rest of our days on earth.

"Millie and I were just at the police station because we found a dead body this morning," Lois said as if she was describing a leisurely walk on the sand.

I groaned.

Ruth stared at her. "Please tell me you're lying."

"I'm not," Lois said and looked to me. "Why doesn't she ever believe me?"

"She's not," I agreed.

Ruth threw her hands into the air. "Millie, it is bad enough that you find dead people back in Holmes County where everyone knows you, but now you're doing the same thing in Florida?"

Lois put a protective hand on my shoulder. "Millie can't help it if dead people show up wherever she goes."

"I do hope finding the body is the end of it," Ruth said. "You couldn't possibly know the person who died."

"That's where you're wrong." Lois reveled in that fact for a moment. "She came down on the bus with us. She's not from Harvest, though. She was just visiting."

"What was her name?" Ruth asked. "I have a very good memory, and maybe I know her or her family."

"Caroline Zook," I said. "She's from Pinecraft. Zook is her new married name." I paused. "Her maiden name was Hanniford. She was Pastor Ross Hanniford's daughter."

"I know her." Ruth gasped. "I know her quite well, in fact."

Chapter Twelve

"How do you know her?" Lois asked.

Ruth shot her a look. "Through Pastor Ross, of course. Pastor Ross is a longtime friend of Reverend Brook and has even traveled to Harvest to see the reverend. When he came, Bishop Yoder and I were invited to the Brooks' home for dinner. It was only right that we were invited. If Pastor Ross was really interested in how interchurch relations worked between *Englisch* congregations and Amish districts, my husband, who leads the most prominent district in Harvest, was the one to ask."

"And Caroline was with him at the time?"

"*Ya,*" Ruth said. "This was a few years ago. She couldn't have been more than thirteen or fourteen."

"How was she?" Lois asked.

"Quiet," Ruth said. "But in my mind that's how a child should be in a room of adults. Pastor Ross spoke about how talented Caroline was with facts and fig-ures. He said that she was going to be a successful engineer someday or maybe even work for NASA." She sniffed. "That is not the future I believe is best for a woman, but I held my tongue. The *Englisch* ways are different."

"I think that's amazing," Lois said. "But—"

"Did she agree with that?" I asked. "That she wanted to be an engineer?"

"She was a child. She said nothing at all. Even though they were *Englisch*, the pastor raised his daughter right not to speak in a room of adults unless she was spoken to. We did not speak to her."

I bit the inside of my lip and wondered how many times in her life Caroline had been silenced. I wondered if in the end she did what she wanted to do. By marrying an Amish man, she would not be continuing in her school or having anything to do with spaceships or whatever it was the *Englisch* called them.

Ruth looked over her shoulder. "I have to get back. Bishop Yoder and I have just arrived, and he has meetings this afternoon. We need to check into our rental."

"You're not staying at the resort?" Lois asked.

Ruth glared at her. "An extravagant *Englisch* resort is not the place for a bishop to stay. It would be very unbecoming." She walked away without saying good-bye, but I wasn't startled by that. It was Ruth's typical method of departure. What did surprise me was everything that we had learned about Caroline and her tentative connection to Harvest. She had visited Harvest at least once when she was younger, but what would have motivated her to go back a second time?

As we walked back to the bungalow, I was mesmerized by the bright green parakeets in the tree that were hanging by their feet pecking at the fruit. We certainly didn't have birds like that in Ohio.

I was so distracted that I didn't even realize that Lois had stopped walking until I was jerked backward by our linked arm. "Lois, what is wrong?"

She stopped in front of an entrance to a parking lot. In the middle of the parking lot was a small, freestanding stucco building with large bright blue shutters. The stucco was painted beige. Dozens of scooters and bicycles were parked in front of the store, and there were three cars in the lot. Above the door, the sign read ZOOK'S SCOOTERS.

Was it any coincidence that these four places—the resort, the bungalow, the police station, and the scooter shop—were all within a mile of each other along the road parallel to the Gulf? What it did tell me was Dutchman Resort and Zook's Scooters were close enough to where Caroline's body was found for the killer to be from either one of those places. They could strike and go back to the resort or the scooter shop with no one being the wiser. I shivered at the dark thoughts swirling around in my head.

"Our rest and snacks will have to wait," Lois said.

They would indeed.

Lois and I walked up to the scooter shop.

"We should rent scooters to get around Pinecraft. It seems like it's the best way to travel around here," Lois said.

"I think you might be right."

Lois grinned. "I always wanted to be a tough biker girl."

"You'll be on a scooter," I said.

"A small technicality that I am willing to overlook."

I opened the door to the scooter shop, and we stepped inside. The shop had bicycle wheels and tires hanging from the walls. An antique-looking scooter was suspended from the ceiling. All of the shelves were bare pine wood, and the floor was dusty concrete. I wouldn't have expected much more from a working Amish shop.

A thin Amish woman stood behind a high counter to the left side of the room. "May I help you?"

"*Ya,*" I said. "We would like to rent two e-scooters for the week."

"Do you have a reservation?" the young woman asked.

"No," Lois said. "We just happened to be walking by your shop, and it looked like a much better way to get around."

The woman sniffed. "We really recommend that people have reservations. We are at the height of tourist season. We're fully booked out for the next two months until the snowbirds fly home around Eastertime."

"Do you have anything at all?" I asked.

"I'll check." She stepped away from the counter and went into the back room.

"They have scooters," Lois grumbled. "There were a least a dozen e-scooters sitting outside the front door."

"They could already be promised to other customers."

Lois shook her head. "Millie, you are always willing to give every person the benefit of the doubt. It's one of your most endearing and annoying qualities."

"*Danki*, I think."

Lois lowered her voice. "That young woman had quite a chip on her shoulder for being Amish."

"Amish can be rude too," I said. "It's not just the *Englisch*."

"Isn't that the truth."

We heard footsteps coming from the back room, and they were a lot heavier than those of the young woman.

She appeared, but she was followed by a tall young man who was most likely nineteen or twenty. His eyes were red and his skin was blotchy. He had just the beginning of an Amish beard growing on the tip of his chin, but it was little more than a few fine hairs.

He swallowed. "Tabitha tells me that you want to rent two e-scooters, but you don't have a reservation."

This no reservation issue was really becoming a problem for Zook's Scooters.

Lois and I nodded.

"We do apologize for not having a reservation," I said. "We just arrived by bus from Ohio last night, and we didn't know scooters were the best way to move around Pinecraft. We certainly understand if you don't have any available."

His face relaxed just a bit, but he still looked like he could burst into tears at any moment. "We do have a couple older model e-scooters in the back. Everything else is reserved. If you are all right with those, we can rent them to you."

"All we care about is if they go or not," Lois said. "We're low maintenance gals."

Lois said this ironically in her case.

He nodded. "Tabitha, go ahead and start the paperwork, and I will get the scooters."

She nodded but didn't look happy at the fact that the

young man, who I was almost certain was Cainan Zook, Caroline's husband, agreed to rent us anything at all.

Lois and I filled out the paperwork and put down our deposits as well for renting the scooters.

"You can wait outside," she said. "Cainan will bring your scooters around the front of the shop."

Lois and I shared a look. So, it was confirmed now the young man was Cainan Zook. I did not like Tabitha's tone when she asked us to leave, but I was grateful that Lois and I might have a chance to speak to Cainan alone.

We stepped outside the shop, and Cainan Zook was pulling two e-scooters around the corner of the building. The scooters had seen better days. They were scratched up and the paint was all but chipped off. The tip of one handlebar was bent at a weird angle.

"What in all that's jinky are those?" Lois asked.

Cainan's face turned bright red. "They look a lot worse than they actually are. At the height of the season, we just haven't had time to repaint them."

"They are going to need more than a couple swipes of a paintbrush."

"Are they safe?" I asked.

"I think so," Cainan said.

"You think so?" Lois yelped.

This was one of those times when I was in full agreement with Lois. Maybe we should give up on the idea of the scooters.

"Let me test them out for you," Cainan said. He leaned one of the scooters against the building and took the second scooter into the parking lot.

It took a couple of tries, but he was able start the scooter and ride it around the parking lot.

"He makes it look easy," Lois said.

I knew it couldn't possibly be that easy.

He took the second scooter out, the one with the bent handlebar, and did the same thing.

After he parked the second scooter, he let out a breath. "I wasn't sure they would even start."

"You are not giving us confidence in your product, young man, when you say things like that." Lois adjusted her purse strap a little higher on her shoulder.

"They should be fine for you," he said without an ounce of confidence. "But if you don't want to take them and would like a refund, I understand."

"We will take them," I said. "Their appearance doesn't matter."

"That's what I said about a couple of my husbands," Lois muttered.

I rolled my eyes at her. It was a trait that I had picked up from Lois and not one of which I was proud. However, it was useful from time to time.

"*Gut*," Cainan said. "I'm glad that we were able to accommodate you. Is there anything else I can help you with?"

I nodded. "We are both so sorry to hear about your wife's passing. Lois and I met her, and we were very fond of her."

His upper lip quivered. "You knew Caroline?"

I nodded.

He sat on the edge of the curb. "I'm just trying to forget all of it. It will be easier that way."

Chapter Thirteen

"**Y**ou need chocolate," Lois said. "It won't cure anything, but it might help."

"Lois," I whispered. "He just lost his wife. Candy isn't going to help."

"I know, but at least you're eating something delicious while being miserable." She rooted in her bag and came up with a full-size candy bar. She held it out to Cainan.

He shook his head. "That is kind of you, but I'm really not that hungry. I don't know when I will ever be able to eat. Today has been a nightmare."

The curb looked extremely low to me, and if I sat on it, it was unlikely that I would be able to get up again without assistance. Even so, looming over Cainan didn't seem like the kindest way to speak to him when he was in such a terrible place.

Slowly, I sat on the curb two feet from Cainan, and I faced him. He wasn't looking at me. Instead, he stared blankly out into the parking lot.

"I'm Millie Fisher Schrock, and this is my friend Lois Henry from Holmes County, Ohio. Lois and I met Caroline on the bus to Pinecraft from Harvest, Ohio," I said. "I chatted with her most of the trip down. She was a very kind young woman and spoke very highly of you. She told me all about your scooter shop and how you started it on your own. She was so proud of you."

He looked at me. His eyes glistened with tears, but none fell. "She always encouraged me. It's something that I loved most about her. Everyone needs someone in their corner. Caroline was that for me. I can only hope that I was the same to her. I don't know if that is true, though."

"Why do you say that?" I asked.

"I told her going on that trip to Ohio was a mistake. We had just married. She should have stayed home with me." He gripped his hands so tightly that his knuckles turned white.

"Does she have family in Ohio?" I asked.

He turned back to the parking lot. "*Nee.*"

"Then why did she go there?"

"She felt like she had to. I told her she didn't. There was still a defiant independence about her that she could not shake. She did not fully understand the Amish world. I was her husband; she should have done as I said. That is our way."

Lois made a gagging gesture that I was grateful that Cainan could not see.

Spousal relationships were just as complicated in the Amish world as they were in the *Englisch* world, and perhaps more so because faith was the third party in an Amish marriage, and that could be interpreted a myriad of ways by both husband and wife.

I was of the belief that a husband and wife should come to decisions together through prayer and conversation. One should not order the other what to do. That would only lead to resentment. I believed if Caroline had survived, and she and Cainan continued down this strict understanding of marriage, resentment, not faith, would be the third party in their union.

"Why did she have to go to Ohio?" Lois asked.

I could tell from my friend's tone that she wanted to get to the root of Caroline's reason for traveling to Ohio sooner rather than later.

He shook his head. "It's not my place to tell."

"Did you tell the police?" I asked.

He looked up in surprise. "Why would I tell them? It had nothing to do with what happened to her."

I wasn't so sure about that. I knew if I told Detective Marcs that Cainan was withholding this information from him, he would press Cainan and perhaps even take him to the station like he had Lois and me. On that curb, Cainan Zook looked like a lost boy, and I had an urge to protect him. I knew that Caroline had loved him very much. Any time that she mentioned him, her face would light up. For that reason, I wanted to protect him for her too.

At the same time, I wanted to know why Caroline had gone to Ohio. Whatever the reason was, it was an emotional one. Caroline had seemed to be very shaken up when she first climbed onto the bus, and she had been late getting to the bus too. Had Lois not been loading her seemingly endless pieces of luggage, Caroline would have missed the bus entirely. If she had, would she still be alive today?

"I'm going to go test out the e-scooters," Lois said.

I believe she sensed this conversation would go better if I spoke to Cainan alone. She was right too. I had found that there were things that Amish were comfortable telling me but not telling an *Englisch* person. There was a constant fear of judgment from the *Englisch*.

Lois rolled the e-scooter with the straight handlebars out onto the gravel and sand parking lot.

While she tried to start the scooter, I said to Cainan, "When the bus arrived last night, I saw you."

His head whipped around to face me.

"You were there to pick up Caroline." I paused. "It appeared that the two of you were in the middle of some kind of argument."

"Were you spying on us?" He wrinkled his forehead.

"Not at all. I was looking for Caroline because I wanted to invite her to lunch during the time Lois and I were in Pinecraft. As I told you before, I liked her very much."

He scowled at me. "If you liked Caroline so much, you wouldn't be asking these types of questions. Why are you torturing me by reminding me that one of our last conversations was an argument? Do you really think I don't beat myself up about that already?"

"It is not my intention to upset you," I said. "I want to understand what happened to Caroline."

In the parking lot, Lois rode back and forth on the e-scooter. She seemed to know what she was doing, and she almost ran into a parked car only once.

She waved her hand in the air. "The brakes work great!"

That was a relief.

"Why? Because you spent one day with her? That hardly seems to be enough to make you ask these questions."

"It was long enough to care about someone," I said. "And I can offer you some help in this case. Lois and I have been involved in this sort of thing before."

He narrowed his eyes. "What sort of help?"

"Do you want to know what happened to her?" I asked.

"Of course I want to know that. If I never find out it, will keep me up at night for the rest of my life." He put his head in his hands and said something that I could not hear.

"What was that?"

His head was still down, but he turned his neck to look at me. "I'm afraid it was my fault."

I folded my hands in my lap. "Why would you believe that?"

"As you said, we were arguing. I drove her away from our home. She went to the beach, I am sure. She always went to the water's edge when she was upset. When I heard that she died on the beach, it made the most sense to me."

"Where do you live? Close to the beach? Could she walk there?"

"She could be there in a matter of minutes. We lived here," he said. "We live in an apartment over the shop. I promised her that one day we would move, since it would be too small a place to raise a family. For just the two of us, it was just right. There is even a worn path behind the scooter shop that leads to the beach."

I pressed my lips together. What he was telling me was it was not only easy for Caroline to walk to the pier in the middle of the night, but also easy for him. As much as I knew that he was heartbroken over his wife's death, it did not dismiss him as a suspect. I had learned over my years of life that the most seemingly loving and caring people were capable of doing the most terrible things.

"What did you argue about?"

"I was frustrated and resentful. I am not too proud to be able to admit that now. I was still angry at her for leaving so soon after we were married. She doesn't understand what it means to be an Amish wife."

"Because she grew up *Englisch*?" I asked.

He stared at me. "How did you know?"

"By chance, I met her father today." I didn't go on to say that I had made the connection because the police had stopped at the Dutchman Resort to tell Ross Hanniford that his daughter was dead.

"You have only been in Pinecraft for one day and you know all this." He narrowed his eyes. "Who are you?"

"I have already told you. I am a person who cared about Caroline and wants to help. Lois and I have a unique experience when it come to this sort of thing."

"You don't know what you're getting yourself into. Sarasota, Florida, is very different from Ohio."

"I imagine that it is, but human nature remains the same. Do you want our help? Because if you do not, I will leave you be. I don't want to cause you any more pain."

He kicked a pebble in front of him with the tip of his sneaker. "*Ya.*" He swallowed. "Because the police think I killed my wife."

Lois squeezed hard on the scooter's brakes, sending gravel flying in all direction. "Did you say the police think you killed your wife?"

Cainan nodded.

"Then we have to help you," Lois said.

I agreed with Lois that we should help Cainan Zook, but I didn't want her telling him outright like this without hearing his whole story. I also couldn't get his argument with Caroline the night before out of my head.

"Why do the police suspect you?"

"Because someone told them that we were fighting a lot."

I blinked. "Who told them that?"

"I don't know, but the detective said something like 'I know you and Caroline had a rocky marriage.' He was right. It was rocky. Not because we didn't love each other, because we very much did. I have loved her since before I was baptized." His voice cracked. "And I will love her the rest of my life."

"And how old are you now?" Lois asked.

"I'm twenty-one."

"Oh!" Lois exclaimed.

I guessed that Lois thought he was just a teenager, like I did.

"How long have you been married?" I asked.

"One month, but for half of that time, Caroline was in Ohio on her fool's errand."

"What was the fool's errand?" I asked.

He shook his head. He wasn't ready to answer that question just yet, but I was certain that he would when he began to trust us. He wanted our help, after all.

"Do you think the errand is why she was killed?" I asked.

"I don't know, but I would guess that it had to do with her father. She moved out of his house three months ago. He was furious. He even sent the police out to find her."

"Did they?"

"*Ya.* She was staying with a friend of hers who has an apartment in Sarasota. She lived there until we married."

"Did the police make her go back to her father's home?" Lois asked.

"*Nee.* How could they? She was over eighteen, an adult."

"Did the police tell her father where she was?"

"I don't think so. She never heard from him again," Cainan said. "If they told him anything, I suppose it was that she was safe and didn't want to go back home."

I folded my hands into my lap. Pastor Ross Hanniford was sounding more and more like a suspect in his own daughter's murder.

Something else struck me. This meant that the Sarasota Police Department would have a missing person report on Caroline from three months ago. However, Detective Marcs didn't know her identity until I told him who she was. To be fair, he might not have worked on that other case. I was certain that by this time he had connected the dots between the two cases.

"Why did she leave her father's home?" Lois asked.

"She no longer felt safe there."

My eyes went wide. "Was he hurting her?"

He shook his head. "*Nee*, it was nothing like that."

"Then why didn't she feel safe?"

"I cannot answer that question. My wife made me promise not to tell."

"Cainan, the reason she left could be the very reason she was killed. If you want us to help you, we need to know," I said.

"*Nee*." He folded his arms across his chest. "I won't betray her. I will take it to the very grave."

If he wasn't careful, the grave would come sooner rather than later. It had for Caroline.

Chapter Fourteen

The door to the scooter shop opened, and there was a stout Amish man standing in the doorway with a short black beard. His hair was covered with a straw hat. "Cainan, how long are you going to be? We have a group coming in soon to pick up their e-bikes."

"I was just finishing up with these ladies who are renting two of our older scooters." Cainan made a face. "I am sorry that this is all we have."

"Don't be," Lois said. "They work. We aren't going on joyrides or anything like that. We just need them to get from point A to point B. They will work just fine for that."

The other man folded his arms over his broad chest. "I am surprised that you are renting *that* scooter."

Cainan met his eyes as if in a challenge. "A scooter is a scooter. As Amish we don't dwell on material things."

His eyes went wide and he almost looked impressed

with Cainan's answer. I could not help but wonder what it was about the scooters, other than their general worn-out appearance, that surprised the man that Cainan rented them out.

Lois held out her hand to the newcomer. "Lois Henry, and this is my friend Millie Fisher. We are so excited that you had a couple of scooters to spare for us."

He glared at her hand, did not shake it, and then scowled at Cainan.

"Ladies, this is my brother-in-law Malachi Grabill. You met my sister Tabitha inside. They help me out with the shop as much as they can. I couldn't run it without them."

Malachi nodded as if he was placated by the praise. I had feeling that Malachi was the type of man who required a great deal of praise to be satisfied.

"I can't be here all day," Malachi said. "I have other work that needs to be done." He stomped back into the shop and slammed the screen door behind him.

"I am sorry about that. My brother-in-law knows everything one can about batteries for the scooters and bikes, but his disposition is not always the friendliest."

"Not to worry," Lois said.

Cainan stood up. "I must return to work. We have a large tour group arriving soon. Tabitha and Malachi will need my help. Tour groups tend to be the most demanding, and from what I gathered, not a single one of them has ridden an e-bike before. There will have to be a lot of training."

I started to get to my feet as well, but I wasn't nearly as graceful as Cainan. Lois noticed my wobbling and pulled me to my feet. When I was upright, I dusted sand off the back of my dress. "*Danki*. That curb is a lot lower than it looks."

"Especially at our age," Lois said. "You'd need a crane to get me off that curb."

"Are you sure you shouldn't take some time from work?" I asked Cainan. "You received the most terrible news."

"It's better for me to stay busy. *Gott* has meant us for work, so I will do my best to keep up with it. It is not wise to dwell on what might have been."

"*Gott* grieves," I said softly. "Even Christ himself grieved when his friend Lazarus died. I don't believe *Gott* would judge you for mourning your wife."

"Others will judge me." He glanced over his shoulder, and his sister Tabitha's face was visible in the window.

When she caught us looking at her, she disappeared from view.

He sighed. "It is winter and the height of the season. There are so many reservations for scooters and bicycles. My sister Tabitha and my brother-in-law work here at the shop with me, but with so many reservations, they would not be able to keep up without my help. I can't afford to grieve. Not right now." He took a step toward the door.

"Cainan," I said. "I have one more question."

He looked over his shoulder and gritted his teeth in preparation for whatever it was that I was going to ask. He waited.

"What is the name of the friend that Caroline lived with before she married?"

His shoulder relaxed. I must not have asked the question that he most feared. I wished I knew what that question was, because I certainly would have asked it or made Lois do it.

He looked at me. "Her name is Kimber. She works at Double Dutch Ice Cream." With that, he went back inside the shop.

Lois walked over and stood beside me in front of the door. "That was a detour worth making. We got some answers."

"And a lot more questions," I said.

"You said that you would help him. Is that what you're going to do?"

I nodded. "It is. At this point, I don't know him well enough to know what his role really was in Caroline's murder, but he does appear to be devastated at her death. I want to give him the benefit of the doubt but also keep my eyes open to what he might have done or what he might know. He's not telling me everything."

"Always give people the benefit of the doubt," Lois said. "But don't remove them from your suspect list until you have their alibi."

I nodded. That was exactly what I planned to do.

"Let's take these e-scooters for a spin. We need a little practice before we take them on the road. No one wants to end up in traction."

I grimaced.

Lois held the second scooter for me.

"I'm not so sure about this," I said. "I've never ridden one of these before."

"You will pick it up in no time. You are a pro at riding your bike even when those two crazy goats of yours are running behind you. This will be easy for you."

I wasn't as certain about that.

"Hop on, and I will show you," Lois said.

Lois gave me the scooter without the bent handlebars, which was very kind of her. She showed me where the start button was and how to work the brakes. "Push this if you want to go faster or pull back to slow down." She pointed at a lever on the handlebars. "Got it?"

"I think so."

"Great! It's high time that we get back to the bungalow and rest for a spell." She hurried over to her scooter, hopped on, and rode out of the parking lot without even a backward glance at me.

I pressed the start button and pushed the lever. The scooter jerked forward and I nearly fell off. When I was on the smoother pavement on the side of the road, the ride was a bit easier. Even so, I was still wound as tight as a bobbin in a sewing machine. Thankfully, the road had a bicycle lane, but even with the extra space, I tensed up every time a vehicle sped by me.

Up ahead, Lois was having the time of her life. She rode at top speed and disappeared around the corner that led to the bungalow. I wasn't nearly as confident with my driving.

As I came around the corner, I saw Lois swerve around a jogger who made a rude gesture at her as she passed. "Yahoo!" she called back at the jogger.

I didn't blame the jogger. Lois was just inches from running him over and would have if he hadn't jumped out of the way.

Lois skidded to a stop in front of the private road that led to our bungalow.

Pumping my brakes as gently as I could, I stopped beside her. "Lois, you must be more careful when you are on the scooter. You're going to kill somebody. You terrified that poor jogger."

"Don't be such a downer, Millie. I knew exactly what I was doing, and I was in control the whole time."

I had my doubts about that.

"These scooters are great," she said. "We will have no problem getting around Pinecraft with these. Also, they will be easy to stash somewhere if we have to do a sting for the investigation."

"Let's hope it doesn't come to that," I said.

Lois started her scooter back up and laughed. She rode away, and as usual, I followed her. I had been following her for decades. I saw no reason to stop now.

I turned onto the private road that led to the bungalow. Ours wasn't the only one on the street. There were six in total, plus the main house where the owner lived. From what the owner said, she made enough on rentals of the bungalows that she traveled overseas most of the summer. She was always here in the winter, as it was the high season.

"I have my reservation right here," a furious voice said. "Right here!"

I slowed my e-scooter and then brought it to a complete stop. I knew that voice; I would recognize it anywhere. I dismounted from the scooter and wondered what I should do next.

"Psst! Psst!" came from behind a large palmetto along the lane.

I turned and looked. Lois waved me over.

I rolled my scooter over to her.

"What is she doing here?" Lois hissed.

"I don't know," I whispered back.

"Did you tell Ruth Yoder where we were staying?"

"*Nee,* you were there for the whole conversation," I said.

"She found us somehow. The woman is a bloodhound, I tell you. She leaves no stone unturned. She found us and now we are doomed." She covered her eyes with her hand.

"We don't know that she was looking for us."

Lois dropped her hands and rolled her eyes. "Why else would she be here? This is really killing my vacation vibe. First a dead person and now this. I'm going to need a vacation after this vacation to recover."

I would need the same.

"She looks like she is having a disagreement with Bernice, the owner. We should go over and help her," I said.

"Help who? Ruth or Bernice? Are you crazy? I'm not going over there. Ruth is going to chop my head off the moment she sees me."

"Chop your head off?" I asked. "She would never."

"It's just an expression."

"The *Englisch* have the worst expressions."

"What I mean is she is going to blame me for whatever she is yelling at that poor woman about." Lois stuck her hand in her purse and came up with a bottle of water. She took a long drag from the bottle. "Talking about Ruth dehydrates me. That's how bad it is." She thrust the bottle at me. "Drink."

I waved away her offering. "I'm fine. We can't just go to our bungalow and pretend we didn't see her."

"Why not? I think that is an excellent plan."

"First of all, we have to walk by her to get to our place."

"Not when we go to the beach first, then come in from the ocean side of the bungalow."

"I have a feeling that Cainan would not want his e-scooters in the sand."

"Oh, for Pete's sake, you win. Let's go see what she's here for."

I patted Lois on the shoulder. "You're a kind woman, Lois Henry."

"No. I'm begging for trouble. It's what my mother used to say about me, and I'm starting to think she might have been right." She took another sip from her water bottle before dropping it to the bottom of her bag.

Lois and I inched over to Ruth and Bernice, the owner of the Bungalow Garden.

"What are my husband and I supposed to do?" Ruth asked. "This is very unprofessional on your part. You should be ashamed that we have no place to stay."

Bernice was a tall woman in a wrap skirt over a one-piece swimming suit. Her long silver hair fell down her back in a braid, and she wore a floral headband on the top of her head. Despite Ruth's harsh tone, she was unfazed. "I don't know what to tell you. There are plenty of hotels in Sarasota. You should have no trouble finding a room even in the high season."

"We are Amish!" Ruth said as if her plain dress and prayer cap didn't already give that away. "We can't in *gut* conscience stay in an *Englisch* hotel with all the noise and carrying on and a bar! My husband is the bishop of our district back in Ohio. It would be shameful."

"Go online and rent a house, then," Bernice said. "I can't discuss this with you any longer. I'm late for my yoga class." She went back into her house and shut the door.

Ruth threw up her hands in disgust.

"I say we make a run for it," Lois whispered. "I think we can get past her without being seen."

"We have to help," I whispered back. "They don't have a place to stay. Our bungalow has two bedrooms."

"Mildred Fisher Schrock, don't you dare!" Lois's eyes narrowed. She was serious if she used my full first name that she knew very well I disliked.

"What choice do we have?"

"So many. There are so many choices. This is not one of them."

"What are the two of you doing here?" Ruth cried.

It seemed my argument with Lois had grabbed Ruth's attention.

I plastered a smile on my face. "Ruth, I was just about to ask you the same thing. Lois and I are staying here this week. We're in bungalow number four." I cleared my throat. "As we were walking up, we noticed that you seemed to be having a misunderstanding with Bernice, the owner."

"It wasn't a misunderstanding on my part. She is a devious woman and claims that I didn't reserve a bungalow for the bishop and me even though I mailed in the request months ago."

"You made the reservation by *mail*?" Lois asked as

if it was the most ridiculous thing that she'd ever heard. "Did she send confirmation back?"

"*Nee*. But this is how we have always done reservations to stay in Pinecraft, and this is the first time that the host claims she never got the letter. I'm furious, and now the bishop and I don't have anywhere to stay."

"You Amish folks really need to use hotels.com or something or ask an English friend to do it for you," Lois said under her breath.

"Did you take the bungalow I requested for my husband and me?" Ruth narrowed her eyes at Lois. It was no surprise to anyone that she blamed Lois. She always blamed Lois.

"Nope, I made the reservation online and got an email confirmation like everyone else," Lois said and started to roll her scooter away. "Well, you're nothing if not a resourceful woman and will figure something out." She looked over her shoulder at me. "Come on, Millie, we have much to do this week. We are burning sunlight."

I cocked my head at Lois. "Please," I mouthed.

She glared at me.

"Just one night," I mouthed.

She let out a great sigh, and I knew that was all the confirmation that I needed.

I turned back to Ruth. "Why don't you stay with us for tonight until you can find a place?" I asked. I made a conscious effort not to look at Lois because she would have murder in her eyes. One murder that week was enough for me.

Chapter Fifteen

Lois unlocked the door to the bungalow, and Ruth went in first. She sniffed, "It seems that Bernice is very fond of the beach theme."

It wasn't a compliment, and I didn't correct Ruth because what she said was true. The bungalow was decked out in seashells, rope, sailboats, and fish, from the ceramics to the wallpaper.

"You owe me," Lois whispered.

I knew I did. Ruth Yoder and Lois had been nemeses in childhood. Ruth was always a very strict Amish girl and she didn't approve of the fact that my closest friend was a "wild" *Englischer*. She didn't understand why my parents let me spend time with Lois, but I knew why. Lois grew up next door to my family farm in a troubled home, and she spent most of her time on my farm to escape the chaos at her house. My parents were two of the kindest people anyone ever knew, and they let Lois come over whenever she needed to because they knew that was the best way to show *Gotte*'s love to her.

What's more, my parents trusted me. They knew that Lois's "wild ways," as Ruth would call them, would not rub off on me. I had a set path ahead of me in the Amish way of life, but that didn't mean I could not be friends with a person who chose to live differently. *Gotte*'s love is boundless and without such rigid human boundaries.

When Lois graduated from high school and moved away and I married Kip, we lost touch for many years. However, we reunited in our golden years, and it was like we had never been apart. As expected, Ruth did not approve, nor was she thrilled to have her old nemesis back in her life.

"Lois and I can share her bedroom. It has two beds," I said, eager to change the subject. "So, you and the bishop are welcome to the second bedroom."

"For one night," Lois said.

I gave her a look and turned back to Ruth. "Where is your luggage?"

"It is still at the Dutchman Resort with my husband. We arrived here later than expected, and the bishop had to go straight into his first meeting. I decided to leave our luggage at the conference and walk here to check in. He planned to bring the luggage later when he was done for the day."

"How is the conference going?" I asked. "Have you seen Jethro at all?"

"Juliet brought the pig?" Ruth shook her head. "I never thought she would be that irresponsible."

"Bailey was in New York," Lois said.

"Still, there had to be someone from her church that would take the pig for a few days." She patted her prayer cap. "I'm going to go freshen up. It's been a very trying day."

"Let me gather my things first," I said.

I hurried into the bedroom and tucked my few belongings back into my duffle bag and shuffled back out of the room.

Without another word, Ruth walked into my bedroom and shut the door.

We could hear the lock click after her.

Lois dropped her purse on the small sofa that was in the combined eat-in kitchen and living room. "I hope you're happy."

"I wouldn't say happy." I glanced at the door, hoping that Ruth wasn't listening, but I was sure she was. Ruth loved gossip just as much as Lois did. I believed that was one of the reasons the two of them were at odds so often, because they were always trying to out-gossip each other. I glanced at the door.

Lois shoulders sagged. "I'm trying to appreciate the kindness of your heart, Millie. You are a better person than I will ever be."

"Rubbish," I said. "I know you would have done the same thing . . . eventually."

Lois snorted. "I'm going to freshen up myself and lie down for a bit. Then we can make plans for our next steps."

I nodded. "It sounds like a *gut* strategy. I think I will walk on the beach. I need to clear my head."

Lois frowned. "Do you want me to come with you?"

Her face sagged with exhaustion. I knew she needed a nap. I could probably use one too, but I would never be able to fall asleep. My head was spinning too much.

Between Caroline, Cainan, Jethro, and now Ruth, it was a lot to take in, especially on a vacation.

"*Nee,* you stay here and get some rest."

"What if you find another dead body?"

"I won't," I assured her.

"You've said that before." She walked off to our bedroom.

Before I left the bungalow, I changed my shoes. I had brought the one pair of sandals that I owned with me. I rarely wore them, but I was not willing to sacrifice another pair of sneakers to the sand and waves.

I stepped out of the bungalow and made sure the door was locked behind me. I wanted Ruth and Lois to be as safe as possible. I was acutely aware that there was a killer loose in Pinecraft. He or she didn't have any reason to come after my friends, but one could never be too careful. It was a hard lesson I'd learned over the years.

The sandals felt odd on my feet and I wasn't wearing stockings, which was also odd to me. Ruth would have been horrified if she could see me. However, I had to admit the breeze on my feet and legs was welcome. The only place that I ever went barefoot was at home on my own farm, and only in the summer.

At the end of the boardwalk that led out onto the beach, I removed my sandals and carried them in my hand.

The sand was warm, but not too hot. I suppressed a girlish giggle. The tiny grains tickled my toes. It was a moment to embrace, to bask in the pure joy of having my toes in the sand. I felt free. It wasn't an emotion that came over me often as an Amish woman.

When Lois and I had walked out onto the beach at dawn, there had been scarcely anyone on the sand except for a few joggers and shell seekers. Now the beach was close to full. Everyone appeared to be relaxed and happy. One would never know that a woman had died here just hours ago.

The sand was full of beachgoers, but there weren't that many people in the water. Paddleboarders in wet suits, and young children with parents who would have preferred to be curled up on a beach towel with a new book. That sounded lovely to me as well. Perhaps when things settled, Lois and I could go to the bookstore in town and find something to read. It would be nice to have a true vacation, not one with murder and unexpected guests.

I had not intended to walk all the way to the pier, but I could not help myself from going in that direction. I didn't think that police missed anything. Detective Marcs, from what I saw, was a very thorough officer when it came to his investigations.

Even so, I wanted to take a peek at the crime scene again. Lois would be furious at me if she knew I'd walked this far and this close to where we found Caroline's body without her. She hated missing one second of sleuthing. "Sleuthing" was her word for it, not mine.

There was crime scene tape around the pylons where Caroline was found, but now the tide was a bit higher and that place where she had lain was just a few inches underwater. As the tide rose, it would be several feet under the water soon enough.

A piece of crime scene tape had broken away from the pylon and floated listlessly in the water. Something about seeing that piece of bright yellow plastic in the waves broke my heart all over again at Caroline's demise. I wished that we had had that second sewing lesson. I wished she had confided in me on the bus as to what she was doing in Ohio. Had she, I might have been able to help and she would still be alive.

"What are you doing here?" a ragged voice asked.

I turned to see Pastor Ross Hanniford standing a few feet away. He was still dressed for the conference in dress shoes, slacks, and a button-down shirt, but he stood in water up to his ankles. He appeared to be completely unaware of it.

"Pastor Ross," I said. "I'm sorry if I came up on you in surprise. I just wanted to come and pay my respects."

"The police told me that you were the one who found my daughter this morning."

Actually, Jethro was the one who'd found Caroline, but I didn't think this was the time to mention it. He already had his negative opinion of the little pig. I didn't want to add to it.

The friendly face that greeted me at Dutchman Resort was gone. Now he looked at me with suspicion. In truth, I was suspicious of him as well.

I nodded. "When I ran into you at the Dutchman Resort, I had no idea that Caroline was your daughter. Lois and I really were there to see how Reverend Brook and Juliet were faring."

He frowned as if he didn't quite believe me. Then he turned and stared at the crime scene tape that marked the spot where his daughter's body was found. He didn't cry, just stared. I could not imagine the turmoil that he was feeling. I had faced much tragedy in my life but had never lost anyone so dear to me in such a violent way, much less a child.

"The police said that her hands were tied behind her back," he said. "Did you see that?"

I nodded, but then I realized that he wasn't looking at me. He was just staring at the same spot under the pier. He didn't see my nod. "*Ya*, I did see that."

He nodded. "I told my daughter that marrying into the Amish world was a mistake. She thought she knew them, but as you can see, she was very wrong."

I wasn't sure if he'd forgotten that I was also Amish or if he just didn't care. However, I was willing to give him grace. He had just lost his daughter, possibly his only child. I realized I knew very little about the Hanniford family.

As much as I wanted to ask those questions, I held my tongue. I stood in front of a stricken father in the depths of grief. This wasn't the time.

"Can I get you anything?" I asked. "Is there some-one I can call for you?"

He looked at me as if he'd forgotten that I was stand-ing there. Then his face cleared, "No, thank you. I'm sorry if I came off harsh. I always suspected Caroline ran off with that Amish boy. There was nothing that I could do to discourage her infatuation with him. When I reported her missing months ago, the police said they found her and she was safe. They also told me that she was an adult and had a right not to tell me where she was. I knew where she was. I could have gone to her then, but I was too stubborn. I wanted her to come back to me groveling and begging to be let back home." He shook his head. "Time passed and I felt differently. I was sorry for my part in her leaving, but I was too pride-ful to go find her and tell her so. Pinecraft is small. I always thought I would just run into her someday. I wanted to tell her that it was all right. That I wasn't upset that she left me for the Amish. I just wanted her back in my life in any way that she saw fit." He closed his eyes for a long moment. "I won't have that chance now."

I didn't know what to say. The only thing that came to mind was platitudes that I knew would be of little help. I wanted to tell him that I would be praying for him because I would, but it seemed like such a hollow promise in that moment, even though I knew it was far from hollow.

Someone cleared their throat behind us, and I turned to see Scott Lawrence standing just out of reach of the water.

"Scott, what are you doing here?" Pastor Ross asked.

"I came looking for you." He glanced at the crime scene tape floating in the water. "I did try to call and text you several times. We're setting up for the after-noon conference sessions. I know that you usually like to go over the roster and meet with each speaker beforehand. When I couldn't get hold of you, I thought you might be here."

"I had my phone off," Ross said. "I needed a mo-ment alone."

Scott nodded. His face was marked with concern. "I understand that, Pastor Ross. Would you like me to take over the conference from here on out? I have the schedule, and with all your hard work leading up to it, everything is running smoothly."

Pastor Ross shook his head. "No, no, it will be good for me to get back to it. I'm afraid if I go home I will just crumble."

A slight frown appeared on Scott's face, as if he wasn't completely happy with this answer. Just as quickly as I saw it, it was gone. He turned to me. "It's nice to see you again. You will have to excuse me, as I have forgotten your name."

"There is no need to apologize," I said. "It has been a trying day for us all. I'm Millie Fisher Schrock from Ohio, but you can just call me Millie."

He blinked. "I didn't know you were from Ohio. Whereabouts?"

"Harvest in Holmes County," I said. "I would say that most of the Ohio Amish here are from Holmes County."

"Or close to it," he mumbled.

"Do you know it?" I asked.

"No, no." He shook his head. With that, he led Pastor Ross away and left me wondering why he had just lied to me.

Chapter Sixteen

After Pastor Ross and Scott left, I walked back to the bungalow. When I arrived, I found Ruth's bedroom door open. Her shawl was on the bed, but she was gone. Perhaps she had gone back to the Dutchman Resort after bit of a rest. It was a short walk, maybe half a mile, after all.

The door to the bedroom that I now shared with Lois was closed. Slowly, I opened it and found Lois sleeping on her stomach, looking every bit like a starfish that had washed up on the beach. She had her arms and legs splayed out, and she drooled on her pillow.

There was an armchair in one corner of the room with a throw blanket on it. As quietly as I could, I picked up the blanket and covered her with it.

She murmured into her pillow something about dice, but other than that, she did not stir.

While Lois slept, I planned for what we should do about the rest of the investigation because after seeing crime scene tape wrapped around the pylons and Pastor Ross's clearly broken heart, I wasn't giving up. I didn't care what Detective Marcs thought of that either.

Although I hadn't asked him outright because I didn't want to upset him more than he already was, I got the impression that Pastor Ross thought that the Amish were responsible for his daughter's death. I would even go as far as to believe he might blame Cainan Zook.

What was surprising to me was that he apparently knew that Caroline had been in love with Cainan, so as he admitted, he knew where to find her. Instead of going to the Zooks and asking about Caroline, he went to the police and filed a missing person report.

That seemed to be going a bit out of his way to involve the police.

A dark thought clouded my mind. Was it because he knew that Caroline was in danger, and he wanted to build his case against the Amish?

I shivered. That seemed a bit too far, and I promised myself that it was a theory that I wouldn't share with Lois because she would clamp down on it hard.

Just because the thought crossed my mind, I had to put Pastor Ross Hanniford on my mental suspect list. Cainan Zook was there as well. Both of them loved her and were devastated that she was dead. However, there were times that misplaced love led to murder, so I couldn't count them out.

There was a great groan from the bed beside me.

Lois rolled over on her back and stretched her arms in the air like she was shaking her fists in victory. Victory for what, I wondered. The world's greatest nap?

"Oh!" Lois cried and dropped her hands at her side. "I needed that. What time is it?"

I looked at the little pocket watch that Uriah gave me that was pinned inside my pocket. "It is after four."

"After four!" She sat up in her bed. "I was asleep for hours."

"Maybe three," I said, "clearly it was something that you needed."

"Did you sleep?" she asked.

I shook my head. "There were too many thoughts running through my head to let me rest."

She nodded. "What's the plan?" She knew me well.

"I think we go to the Dutchman Resort for dinner tonight."

She smiled. "I thought you were going to say something like that."

While Lois got ready for dinner, which included putting on a new outfit and redoing her hair and make-up after sleeping on them, I filled her in on my walk on the beach.

Lois smoothed her caftan over her hips and tied a braided belt around her waist. "When in Florida, flowy dresses are a must."

"You look very colorful," I said, and I meant it. Lois wore more colors than were in the massive Christmas tree that was set up on Harvest's square every holiday season.

"I will take that as a compliment. I assume that you are ready to go," she said.

I nodded. The only changes that I had made were to put my walking shoes back on and tuck a few stray, windblown hairs back into place after my walk on the beach.

Lois opened the bedroom door and looked left and

right, as if she were afraid that someone was going to mug her right in the middle of the bungalow's tiny living space.

"Ruth is gone. She was gone when I got back from the beach."

Lois let her shoulders relax, but her eyes were still wide as she took in every detail of the bungalow's interior. "Her shawl is there," Lois said with a foreboding tone to her voice. "As long as one of her articles of clothing is inside the bungalow, we aren't safe."

"We aren't in any danger from Ruth Yoder," I said.

"Speak for yourself. This is her chance to snuff me out with a pillow in the middle of my sleep. We are keeping that bedroom door locked all night long. No exceptions."

I rolled my eyes as expertly as Lois would have done herself. "It's just one night."

"You and I know that it's going to be more than one night. Ruth is the tightest wad that I have ever met, even more so than my third husband. If she and her husband can stay here for free, she is going to jump at that chance no matter how uncomfortable it will be for all of us, including her. I think she wants to spend her time in Florida with me as much as I do with her."

I wrinkled my nose because I knew she was most likely right.

We left the bungalow. I hoped that Ruth didn't plan to come back soon. She didn't have a key, and I didn't know how long she would be gone. However, that couldn't be helped. She wouldn't have a cell phone or some *Englisch* way to contact us, but she could have left a note as to how long she would be gone so we could make sure that she was able get back inside.

Lois and I decided to walk along the sidewalk to the Dutchman Resort instead of along the beach. Lois said she couldn't walk on sand in her hot pink sequined tennis shoes. That was fine with me. After my last moments on the beach with Pastor Ross, I wasn't eager to go back right away.

At the resort, there was a side entrance that went right into the restaurant. A line gathered outside the door.

Lois eyed it. "This is going to be a sizable wait for Amish fried chicken."

Lois adored fried chicken.

"Do you want to go somewhere else?" I asked.

She shook her head. "No, we are here to eat, but we are also here to snoop."

A hostess with a clipboard walked up to us. She was jotting down names and the sizes of the parties.

"Can I take your name?" the young woman asked.

"Put it under Lois," Lois said. "And it's just the two of us."

The hostess nodded and made a note on her clipboard. "There is a wait for a table," the hostess said, looking frazzled. "We have a large conference here this week, and it seems every last one of them is eating here. Add that to tourist season, and you have a mess."

I nodded. "We heard. Is it the pastors' conference?"

She nodded and moved to the next party. The poor woman didn't have time to chitchat.

A second hostess gathered up a stack of menus. "Yoder, party of six."

Three groups started to step forward and the young girl's eyes bugged out of her head. Frantically, she looked at her list again. "Sam Yoder, party of six."

There was an audible groan as two of the Yoder parties retreated.

Next to me Lois's shoulders began to shake.

"Don't laugh," I said out of the side of my mouth.

"I'm not." Even as she was saying it, she sounded like she was choking as she swallowed a chuckle. "It's just calling Yoder in a place like this is asking for half of the population to stand up," she managed to say.

I snickered.

"See! It is funny." She grinned from ear to ear.

"Stop it," I hissed, but I was smiling. It was nice to have a light moment for a change. It seemed like the second we had stepped off the bus in Pinecraft, everything became so heavy. Even before Caroline Zook was killed I had worried about her after witnessing the argument between Caroline and her husband Cainan.

"Lois! Millie!" a sweet Southern voice called.

We turned to see Reverend Brook and Juliet walking toward us. Reverend Brook wore what I was beginning to view as the Floridian pastor uniform of dress pants and a polo shirt. Juliet was in her typical polka-dotted sundress. This dress was black and white. She looked like she was ready for a tea party, or at least the photos I had seen of such events in library books.

"Are you waiting for a table?" she asked.

"We are. We have a long wait." I shrugged. "That's not a problem. It must mean the food is *gut*."

"No, you don't. We have a reservation, and you will eat with us."

I shook my head. "We don't want to cause any trouble."

"No trouble at all, and it's the least we can do after you saved Jethro from the Gulf this morning."

I didn't believe that Jethro had been in any danger from drowning in the Gulf. The pig had been leery of the waves and rightfully so. However, I didn't say anything to that point because my stomach rumbled with hunger. Lois and I had not had a real meal since we arrived in Florida. I didn't even mind that we would be eating the same fare as we could have gotten at home. There was comfort in familiarity, especially in a time and place where nothing was familiar.

"This is perfect," Juliet said. "Our reservation is for four, but our friends decided not to come. The husband is the keynote speaker tonight, and he wants the extra time to prepare. I believe they are opting for room service." She glanced around the room. "Looking at this crowd, I believe he made the right choice. It might take some time to be served."

"That's quite all right," Reverend Brook said. "I'm done with speaking for the day, but I do have some evening meetings." He smiled at Lois and me. "We would love for you to join us."

We agreed and stepped out of the line. Reverend Brook gave the hostess his name, and we were whisked away to a table.

The *Englischers* in front of us in brightly colored shirts and shorts narrowed their eyes. It seemed that no one was happy waiting too long for fried chicken.

"Now, that's service," Lois said as we sat down at a

table for four. A waitress set warm rolls and glasses of water on the table for all of us.

I think what struck me the most about the restaurant was it looked just like all the Amish restaurants back in Holmes County with oak tables, paddle back chairs, a long buffet that looked like it was ready for Thanksgiving, and handmade quilts framed on the walls.

Lois must have thought the same thing because she said, "It's like we never left home."

I read the paper menu in front of me. I wanted to be comforted that night, so I opted for the beef stew with dumplings. I doubted that it would be as *gut* as my mother used to make it, but it would be familiar.

Lois shook her head after we ordered. "I don't know how you can eat stew when it's ninety degrees outside."

I set my water glass back on the table. "It's freezing in here."

"Floridians do love their air-conditioning," Juliet agreed with a shiver. "I almost got the stew myself."

"Fried chicken is the only way to go in this scenario," Lois grumbled.

I thought it was best to ignore her comment, and I turned to Juliet. "Where's Jethro this evening?"

Juliet wrinkled her petite nose. "They won't let him in the restaurant, so he's back in our room. The resort doesn't want us to leave him alone in the room, but I don't know what else to do. Reverend Brook has a full schedule, and as his wife, I need to be at his side. My hands are tied, and I have nowhere to turn."

I could feel Lois staring at me. She was willing me not to offer to take the pig, but I really didn't want Jethro to get in any more trouble. I heard myself say, "Maybe we could take him from time to time when he's not allowed to be with you."

I had told Pastor Ross that I had planned to do as much. I'm sure with the shocking loss of his daughter, he hadn't had the time or the capacity to mention it to Juliet and Reverend Brook.

Lois slathered a roll with apple butter and shoved it in her mouth. I appreciated her discretion.

Juliet clasped her hands at her chest. "That is so kind of you, Millie. You are always willing to pitch in when someone needs a hand. There should be more people like you."

Lois ate another roll. Her cheeks bulged out like those of a chipmunk gathering seeds in the autumn.

"How is the conference going?" I asked, hoping Lois would stop shooting eye daggers when I moved the conversation away from the troublemaking pig.

"It's excellent," Reverend Brook said. "There is a great lineup of speakers, and I think people are really learning from each other. Sometimes conferences like this can be a bit competitive as pastors try to prove that what they are doing works best to get parishioners in the pews. I'm of the belief that there are many ways to reach people for the Lord, and not all of it takes place in a sanctuary on Sunday morning. Pastor Ross Hanniford has done another wonderful job of putting this together."

"How is he?" Lois asked. "We were with Juliet when the body was found. Of course, we didn't know who the victim was at the time."

Juliet looked as if she might cry at the mention of the murder. "I can't even think of it. It was so horrible. I have never been involved in something like that, and to find out it was the daughter of a friend . . . Well, it just could not be worse."

"The poor man is stricken," Reverend Brook said. "Everyone admires him as he continues on with the conference after such a tragedy. I know in some ways he already felt like he lost his daughter to the Amish." He grimaced. "I don't mean for that to sound like an insult of any kind, Millie. I believe we've known each other long enough now that we can speak candidly."

"We have and we can," I said. "But there are Amish at the conference, so Pastor Ross must not have a terrible opinion of us all."

Reverend Brook buttered a roll. "A few bishops were invited, including Bishop Yoder from your district, Millie. We are in Pinecraft, and Pastor Ross felt like it was essential to show how English churches and Amish districts can work together for the betterment of the whole community. Did you know Bishop Yoder and his wife Ruth are here?"

"We know," Lois said in a deadpan voice.

"Pastor Ross is not against the Amish. He lives in Pinecraft. He has many Amish friends like we all do when you live in such close proximity to the culture. He just did not expect his daughter to join them. It's one thing to be friends. It's an entirely different thing to be family."

"It is unusual for an *Englischer* to join the Amish

way," I said. "It's much more common for an Amish person to leave the faith."

Reverend Brook nodded. "Yes, and that is something Pastor Ross knows well. When he learned that his daughter left for the Amish, he was upset. He called me, and we talked about it at length. He knew she was very close to one particular Amish young man she had known since she was a child." He glanced at me. "But I don't believe that he ever thought that she would give up her life and going to college to marry him. He thought that it was just a passing amusement until she went away to college."

"But it was much more serious than that," I said.

"Apparently so." He licked his lips. "It's not unheard of for pastors to lose track of what their children are up to. There are so many people relying on us for emotional and spiritual support that at times the ones at home are ignored." He looked to Juliet. "I try my very best not to let that happen to us."

Juliet reached across the table and squeezed her husband's hand. "You do a fine job. Both Jethro and I appreciate you very much."

He nodded and sipped his water. "Pastor Ross was upset that she didn't want to see him and she left, and her refusal to see him did surprise me. I have known Caroline since she was a little girl. She was always extremely close to her father. Her mother left the family when she was just a baby. Not everyone can handle the pressures of being a pastor's wife, and a pastor's wife in a church the size of Pastor Ross's is even more stressful. She handed him the baby and left."

I frowned. If Caroline was so close to her father, why would she leave him like that with no good-bye, no note? What had happened? What had he done to make her leave? What had she done? I looked down at my hands as I considered all I had learned. At the moment, Pastor Ross, as much as I liked him, was my main suspect.

Chapter Seventeen

After dinner, Reverend Brook went back to his meetings, and Juliet ran up to her room to fetch Jethro. Lois and I waited in the lobby.

Lois sighed. "Did you really have to agree to take the pig? We already have Bishop Yoder and Ruth in our bungalow."

"We don't want Jethro to get ejected from the resort because he's alone in Juliet's hotel room." I arched my brow at her. "Do we?"

She folded her arms. "I guess not."

"Look at it this way—Ruth will hate it."

Lois's face broke into a smile. "You're right! She will hate to be sleeping under the same roof with Jethro. She might hate it so much she will leave! Millie, you are a genius!"

"I have my moments." I chuckled.

"I doubt that Ruth will be able to spend one night in the same place as Jethro. She's going to run screaming from the bungalow." She clapped her hands together.

I eyed her. "She will have to spend one night. She and the bishop don't have a place tonight."

"Okay, one," Lois conceded. "I'll make sure Jethro pays special attention to her." She rubbed her hands together.

Maybe this wasn't the best idea I'd ever had after all.

Juliet came into the lobby walking Jethro on his pink and red polka-dotted leash. I supposed that it had been a gift to Jethro from Juliet for Valentine's Day. Juliet would certainly lavish Jethro with gifts on every holiday, not just the major ones.

"Aren't you the best pig in the whole world," Lois said in a singsong voice. She bent over and picked up Jethro. She snuggled the little pig under her chin.

Juliet's eyes widened in surprise. It was no secret that Lois had a gift for making excuses not to watch Jethro. For the most part, Bailey King was the one who took on the pig and sometimes I would help.

Jethro's eyes bugged out of his head, as he was just as shocked.

"We will be happy to take Jethro for the night," Lois said. "This way you don't have to worry about him getting into any trouble."

Juliet blinked and glanced at me as if she was checking if I noticed Lois's change of heart. I had noticed it all right.

"If you're sure," Juliet said. "The two of you are on vacation. I don't want Jethro to keep you from having a good time."

Lois tickled the pig's snout. "How on earth could he

do that? He's just the sweetest little oinker. We will take good care of him, I promise."

"We will," I said.

Juliet's shoulders sagged in relief. "It's only for a few days. The conference will be over on Thursday morning. Reverend Brook and I will be going to West Palm Beach for the weekend to relax before we go home. Thankfully, we will be staying at a pet-friendly hotel that time."

I frowned. I wanted to ask her if "pet-friendly hotel" was the same as a "*pig*-friendly hotel." I guessed that the staff was expecting dogs, maybe a cat or two, not a pig. However, I stopped myself from saying anything about it. Lois and I were set to leave on the Amish bus back to Harvest early Friday morning. The last thing we needed was Jethro on that bus with us.

Before leaving the resort, we stopped in the Amish bakery and bought items for breakfast. I chose some sourdough bread for toast in the morning. Lois gravitated to the giant donuts and cinnamon rolls.

Jethro was a perfect gentleman on the walk to the bungalow. From what I could tell he was grateful not to be trapped in Juliet's hotel room. He was a pig built to roam, and that was what he did all over Harvest. Coming to Florida and being on such a short leash must have been difficult for him.

Back at the bungalow, Lois and Jethro split a cinnamon roll. I didn't say anything to Lois about not giving sweets to the pig. She seemed content to have Jethro with us, and I didn't want to ruin that even if I did know that she was most happy about Jethro's presence because he might chase Ruth away.

There was a knock at the bungalow door.

Lois had a piece of cinnamon roll halfway to her mouth, and she froze. In an ominous whisper, she said, "They're here. Jethro, brace yourself, young man."

Jethro's eyes bugged out of his head, and I went to the door.

I opened the brightly painted door and found Bishop Yoder, Ruth, and their two small suitcases on the other side.

"It is about time that you opened the door," Ruth said by way of greeting.

I smiled. "It's nice to see you again, Ruth, and I'm happy to see you, Bishop."

The elderly bishop smiled. While Ruth, Lois, and I had recently turned seventy, Bishop Yoder was knocking on the door to ninety. I could tell this from the deep wrinkles on his face that were to the point that it was difficult to see the color of his eyes. However, other than the sun damage to his skin, his back was straight and his hands were strong.

"It was very kind of you to let Ruth and me stay with you, Millie. It is a true illustration of being a good neighbor," Bishop Yoder said.

"I know that the two of you would have done the same for Lois and me if we were in the same spot."

The bishop held up his hand in greeting to Lois. "It's *gut* to see you, Lois. Ruth and I will be so busy with the conference, you will hardly know that we are here."

"We are happy to have you," Lois said with a huge smile, and Jethro had an equally large smile while sitting on her lap. It was clear to me that the two of them had made a pact to drive the Yoders away from the bungalow.

Ruth removed her lace shawl from her shoulders and neatly folded it. As of yet, she had not noticed Jethro on Lois's lap, and I wasn't going to bring him to her attention.

"*Danki* for letting us stay here. It's been a flurry of activity since we set foot in Pinecraft. I don't know—" She stopped mid-thought. "Is that Jethro?"

"It sure is," Lois said as if Jethro was her firstborn and she was proud to unveil him to the world.

"Millie, what is the meaning of this?" Ruth wanted to know.

Bishop Yoder rolled their suitcases inside the bungalow and gently closed the door. He hurried off to the room that he and his wife were going to share. It was clear to me that he had no interest in getting involved in an argument over Jethro yet again. As a resident of Harvest, he had been in many such arguments before.

"Juliet was having difficulty juggling Jethro and supporting her husband at the conference, so she asked Lois and me to take the pig for a few days," I said. "We know how important the conference is to Reverend Brook, so we were happy to help."

Ruth clenched her jaw as if she were trying to compose herself before she spoke. "This is utterly ridiculous. Juliet always has trouble juggling her pig and everything else. She should never have brought him to Florida in the first place. What was she thinking? I have always thought that woman has no common sense, but this just proves me right. Reverend Brook should have put his foot down with his wife for once and told her to keep the pig at home."

"He is her comfort pig," Lois said, coming to Juliet's defense. "She needs him nearby."

"That is just a made-up role for *Englischers*. How can anyone find comfort in a pig?"

Lois put her hands over Jethro's ears. "Don't listen to her. She doesn't know any better."

Ruth's face flushed, and I thought steam might just come out of her ears.

Lois hugged Jethro to her chest like he was her child she was protecting. "He's here, and there is nothing that can be done about it."

"I can think of a few things that can be done," Ruth muttered under her breath.

Lois looked down to hide the grin spreading across her face. As much as she didn't want to take Jethro on during our vacation, she was getting a lot of joy out of the fact that Ruth was so upset.

I perched on the arm of the small sofa and folded my hands in my lap. It was amusing at first to see Ruth so put upon by the presence of the pig, but I didn't want anyone to be uncomfortable, even Ruth. "Jethro will sleep in our bedroom," I said. "You won't have to worry about him. We will make sure that he stays out of your hair."

Ruth sniffed. "I know how that pig is. He is an escape artist. You might want to keep him in your room, but he will find his way out. If I find him in my bed, I make no apologies for what I might do."

As if he could understand her, Jethro's eyes went wide and then he buried his face in Lois's chest. Lois patted the little pig's back. "Don't worry, Porkchop, I got you."

I didn't think calling him "Porkchop" was going to make Jethro feel any better.

Ruth wasn't wrong that Jethro was an escape artist. Perhaps taking Jethro off Juliet's hands was a bad idea after all.

The bishop came out of their bedroom. "It is very kind of you to let us stay here," he said, giving his wife a glance. "We were in a difficult spot finding a place to stay, and, Millie, it does not surprise me at all that you extended an invitation to the little pig too. You have always had a kind heart. Ruth and I both admire you for that." He glanced at his wife again.

"*Ya,* we do," Ruth grumbled.

I had never felt so admired in my life.

"We have an early morning, and I have some studying to do for my meetings tomorrow. I will bid you all good night." Bishop Yoder wheeled his suitcase into the bedroom and closed the door.

After the door was shut, Ruth turned back to us. "Don't the two of you make this trip more difficult for me than it already is. You cannot know how hard it was for me to leave all my responsibilities behind in Harvest. I don't know what I will find when I return home or how many messes I will have to clean up."

"I think Harvest will survive without you for a few days," Lois said.

Ruth glared at her.

I wrinkled my nose. "What do you mean by that? Is something wrong?"

"Can't you see that something is wrong? I'm sleeping under the same roof as a pig. Pigs belong in barns, not homes."

I frowned. I knew that couldn't be what she meant by the comment.

She turned to Lois and Jethro and wagged her finger at the two of them. "I have my eye on you two. Don't you forget it."

With that, she opened the door to the bedroom and then slammed it behind her.

Lois beamed. "She is so annoyed."

"We should not relish someone else being upset," I said.

"Oh, Millie, there are times that you are no fun at all." She kissed Jethro on the top of the head. "Nice work, my friend."

The little pig looked as bewildered as ever.

Chapter Eighteen

I was out on the beach and the gentle waves ran over my bare toes. The sand was cooled by the water and felt refreshing.

Suddenly, just when I felt comfortable standing in the sand and surf, a huge wave came in from the depths of the ocean. I tried to run away from it, but my feet were glued to the sand. I couldn't move, and the wave overcame me. As I was tossed and turned by the ocean, I saw that there was another person in the current with me. It was Caroline Zook, and she was dead. I knew in a matter of moments I would be too.

I sat up in bed gasping for air. Jethro, who was sleeping at the foot of my bed curled up like a cat, jumped to his feet and squealed. Lois in the bed next to us turned on the light. However, she couldn't see because she had a leopard-printed sleeping mask over her eyes.

She turned her head this way and that. "Who's there? Who's there?"

"Lois, it's just me," I said. "I had a bad dream."

She couldn't hear me tell her to take her eye mask off because she had a set of earplugs in.

"Millie, what's wrong? Are we under attack? Is it the Cold War again?" She waved her arms back and forth like she was trying to swat away a wasp.

I got out of bed and removed her eye mask from her face, then pointed at her ears.

She removed her earplugs. "What on earth is happening? You scared me to death."

"I'm sorry," I said. "I had a nightmare."

I sat back down on my bed and gulped air. Jethro walked over and poked at me with his snout. He could be a compassionate little pig when he wanted to be. Jethro and I were forming quite a bond on this trip. I could understand how Bailey King always pitched in when the pig needed to be looked after. He was a lovable little oinker, as Lois would have called him.

Lois patted her hair. Her purple-red spikes were poking out from her head in all directions. If she could see it, she would have been horrified. Lois took great pride in her coif.

Jethro lay across my lap with a heavy sigh. He was much more like a cat than a pig, although my ginger cat Peaches would have been horrified at the comparison.

"He looks sad," Lois said. "He must be missing Juliet."

"And I'm sure she's missing him too. Juliet and Bailey are his people. Everyone else is a poor substitute."

"Maybe he should go back to her today. Ruth is annoyed with his presence, but I didn't get the impression that Bishop Yoder has plans to move to another hotel.

We might be keeping Jethro from Juliet for no reason." Lois sighed. "I'm enjoying how much Ruth hates sharing the bungalow with him, but I don't want the little oinker to be depressed. No one wants a down-and-out pig on their hands."

This was true.

"Maybe. At least we will make sure he spends some time with Juliet today." I glanced at the electric clock on the nightstand. It read five thirty in the morning. I was surprised that I had been able to sleep so late. "It doesn't seem like there is much point in going back to sleep at this hour."

"Speak for yourself," Lois said, lying back down and pulling the blanket back over her legs. "I have another two good hours of sleep calling my name." She put her eye mask back on and rolled over.

I stood and quickly dressed for the day. I knew Bishop Yoder would be up soon, and I would not be caught walking around the bungalow in my nightdress. I shivered at the very idea of him seeing me in such a state. I was very grateful that both bedrooms had their own bathroom attached to them.

After I wrapped my hair in an Amish bun at the nape of my neck and secured my prayer cap on my head with hairpins, I went out into the common room.

I held the door for Jethro, but he opted to climb onto Lois's bed and go back to sleep. The two of them were out before I shut the door.

I wasn't the least bit surprised to find Bishop Yoder sitting at the kitchen table. His Bible was open in front of him at the table, and he held a steaming cup of black coffee in his hand.

"Good morning, Bishop. I'm so sorry to interrupt," I said.

He looked up from the Bible. "You're not an interruption, Millie. My wife and I are staying with you and Lois. We are the ones who are interrupting your trip."

"We are happy to have you," I said. I didn't believe a little fib on Lois's behalf would hurt anything.

"You have always been a loyal friend to Ruth. I have witnessed it myself over the years. I know there are times that Ruth can be . . . prickly, but she really does care about you and all the ladies of the church. In particular, I know how important Double Stitch is to her. She is able to quilt with her dearest friends. For her, that is the greatest gift of all."

This surprised me, taking into the account the number of times Ruth complained over this and that about Double Stitch. However, I knew Ruth well enough that I could imagine her both loving it and criticizing it too.

"And Lois?" I asked with a smile.

"She likes Lois well enough too." He gave me a knowing smile.

That sounded like a huge endorsement to me.

"The two of them take joy at being at odds with each other." He turned back to his Bible.

Ruth was the bishop's second wife, as his first wife died when she was barely thirty. He had a large family, as he had children both with his first wife and with Ruth. I knew him as well as I knew all the men in the district except for Uriah, my husband, of course. I knew the main facts of his life but little else.

In the Amish community, the men and women socialize in very different ways as adults. It wasn't uncommon at the church meals after services that they were separated. The women worked on preparing the meal and running this way and that after the children, while the men tended the fires and visited with each other.

I might have known Bishop Yoder better if we were of the same gender—or the same generation, but he was a grown married man while Ruth and I were in *rumspringa*. He was already well on his way to being a leader in the district. No one in the district was surprised when Bishop Yoder was selected.

I poured coffee into the metal mug by the stove. While my back was to him, Bishop Yoder asked quietly, "Millie . . . is everything all right? Before you came out of your room, I thought I heard a shout."

I felt my face flush. "I'm sorry if we disturbed you. I had a bad dream and startled Lois awake."

He nodded. "I hope that you are feeling well now."

"*Danki.* It was just a dream." Even as I said this, memories of that terrifying dream and Caroline floating in the sea water came back to my mind. I tried my best to push them away.

He nodded, but by this time, he was fully back into his Bible study. I hated to interrupt him, but this might be the only chance I would have to speak to him without Ruth chiming in with her opinions, of which she had many.

"I dreamt of Caroline Zook," I said. "The woman who died. My thoughts have been so preoccupied over her that now I am dreaming about her."

Bishop Yoder looked up from his Bible. "Oh, I am sorry to hear that. It is such a terrible thing that has happened. I cannot imagine what Pastor Ross is going through. What do you think the dream means?"

"Means?" I asked. "I don't know that it means anything at all. It was a nightmare."

"There are times that *Gott* sends us messages through dreams."

I frowned. "Do you really believe that?"

"Was it not the case with Daniel and so many other fathers of the Old Testament?"

I knew that he was right. "I do not know in my case if the Lord is trying to tell me something or if it was dreams of an overactive imagination."

"It could be both," Bishop Yoder said. "*Gott* can use the circumstances of the world to share his messages to us."

I nodded and thought on it. My dream came back to me in bits and pieces.

"Isn't it against the Amish way to interpret dreams?"

"I don't believe it is," the bishop said. "*Gott* will use any means he can to tell us something we need to know or to teach us a lesson."

This made me wonder if *Gott* was just sharing information with me or teaching me a lesson. To be honest, it felt less like a lesson and more like a warning.

Chapter Nineteen

Lois came out of our room at a quarter past eight. I had already been to the beach to see the sunrise. This morning, I had walked in the opposite direction from the pier. I wasn't ready to face that spot again so soon.

Jethro followed her out of the room like he was an obedient pup. He kept looking up at Lois as if asking her permission to go here or there. In all the time that I had known the little pig, I had never seen him so attentive to a person's wishes, not even Bailey's, and she had the very best control over him.

"Looks like you have Jethro eating out of your hand this morning." I set my second coffee mug on the small kitchen table.

"Watch this." Lois held her hand down to the pig. "Shake."

He tucked his small hoof into her hand, and Lois shook it up and down.

"He is quite smart." Lois beamed with pride. "I think we will have a nice time with him today."

I clamped my mouth shut to keep myself from reminding her that she wanted to deliver the little pig back to Juliet and Reverend Brook at first chance.

"Where are the Yoders?" she asked.

"They already left for the conference," I said.

"Can't say that I'm sorry I missed them. Maybe this rooming arrangement won't be as bad as I thought. Ruth and I just need to stay out of each other's way. I worried that they would be a bother with Ruth making constant demands."

"Lois, both Ruth and Bishop Yoder have not been a bother. They are so busy with the conference all day and into the evening, they are barely here."

Lois sniffed as if she wasn't in full agreement with that. She poured herself a mug of coffee. "I do have a fun day planned for us."

"Oh," I tried to keep the disappointment out of my voice.

She eyed me. "Believe me, you will enjoy it."

"I'm sure I will . . ."

"But you want to find out who killed Caroline."

"*Ya*, I believe the dream that I had is encouragement to keep going." I also thought that it was a warning of some sort, but I wasn't going to tell Lois that last bit. "What are we doing?"

"We are going kayaking to see the manatees."

I blinked. When Lois said that we were going to Florida, seeing the wildlife there that was so different than I was used to in Ohio had been on the top of my list. She was right, I would love that excursion, but guilt tightened around my heart. I shouldn't be out in the world enjoying myself when Caroline was dead.

"It's through the church conference. It is one of the activities that they have for attendees, but Juliet scored us some tickets too. While we are communing with nature, we might learn a thing or two about the murder."

"How?" I asked.

She smiled. "I have on good authority that Scott Lawrence, Pastor Ross's right-hand man, will be on our excursion."

"Oh?"

She nodded. "Juliet told me this. Now, who would know Pastor Ross better than him, and the reasons the pastor was so upset with his daughter for marrying an Amish man?"

I wrapped my hands around the coffee mug. "He's an employee. Would he really know so much of Pastor Ross's relationship with his daughter?"

"Many times, assistants know more about their employers than employers know about themselves."

"What about Jethro?" I asked. The thought of taking the little pig on the kayak was terrifying.

"I've been texting with Juliet. She and Reverend Brook will meet us at the launch site and take the pig off our hands for a few hours." She patted Jethro on the head. "You're not meant for water sports, my little oinker."

I did my best to hide my smile. If Lois knew I was amused by the fact she had bonded with the little pig, she might put up her guard against him again.

I wasn't sure how we were going to ride our e-scooters to the park where we were to meet up with the kayaks with Jethro in tow, but Lois had already thought of that to. She rolled Jethro in a towel and tucked him in her purse. His head peeked out of the open bag. He didn't seem bothered with it in the least.

Not knowing how long the kayaking journey would be, I packed a small bag with snacks, water, and sunscreen. The sun was bright, and I knew our Ohio winter skin would burn quickly.

"Ready?" Lois asked.

I nodded.

Outside, Lois jumped on one of the e-scooters and started it. I tentatively turned on the second scooter and was happy to hear it roar to life. Even though the scooters were in working order, I hoped that the launch site wasn't too far away. These contraptions were not meant for long journeys.

As if she could read my mind, Lois looked over her shoulder. "It should be a ten-minute ride. The park isn't too far from here." With that she kicked up the kickstand and rolled down the lane.

Jethro looked back at me from his spot in her purse with terror in his eyes.

I followed closely behind Lois. It took me a full five minutes to begin to feel comfortable on the scooter again. I felt the slightest breeze could tip me over.

Up ahead of us was a sign for a park. Lois made a sharp turn into the driveway leading into the park, leaving me very little time to turn.

Jethro squealed as they careened onto the gravel.

I let out a sigh of relief when Lois parked her scooter at a bike rack under a giant magnolia tree. I stepped off my own scooter with shaky legs.

"That was exhilarating," Lois said.

Jethro and I shared a look.

I parked my scooter next to Lois's. "We don't have bike locks."

"I don't think we have anything to worry about. Do you see our scooters? They look like they are about to break apart at a moment's notice."

If she was trying to make me feel more confident about the scooters, it wasn't working.

"Millie! Lois! Yoo-hoo!" a sweet voice called.

I looked up from the scooter to see Juliet in a white and yellow polka-dot skirt and matching sleeveless blouse, and Reverend Brook in khaki pants and a polo shirt, walking up to us.

"My heavens," Juliet said, walking straight up to Jethro. "You made it." She placed her hands on her cheeks. "Did you bring Jethro here on that?" She pointed at the mangled e-scooters that Lois and I had rented from Zook's Scooters.

"Sure did," Lois said. "Your piggie loved it. Who doesn't like the wind blowing his ears?"

Jethro flattened his ears against his head. He did not look like he loved it.

Lois lifted the pig out of her purse, unwrapped him from the towel, and handed him over to his mistress.

Juliet held him close. "My little angel. I could barely sleep last night without you." She looked up at Lois and me. "He usually sleeps in the bed between Reverend Brook and me."

"How romantic," Lois said.

Reverend Brook cleared his throat. "We should get

going too, my dear. We don't want to hold up Lois and Millie, and we don't want to be late for our tour either."

She nodded. "Reverend Brook and I are going to visit some botanical gardens today." She glanced at the kayaks. "It's the other excursion that the conference organized. I'm not much for water sports."

"You can't kayak in those heels," Lois said. "That's for sure."

Juliet looked down at her feet. "These old things? They are the most comfortable shoes I own. I can walk for miles."

"It's a wonder that her feet still work at all," Lois muttered under her breath.

"I'm so glad to have Jethro back." She smiled at Lois and me. "Thank you for taking such good care of him. Happily, there aren't any more conference meetings until after lunch. Everyone has the option to go on one of the excursions or do something on their own. Reverend Brook and I chose a stroll through the botanical gardens, but Lois said that you would enjoy the wildlife excursion more."

"Thank you for putting us on the kayak trip," I said. "I was hoping to have a chance to see the natural side of Florida while we were here. It's so different from back home. I've never seen anything like it."

"It is our pleasure. I told Reverend Brook that it was the least we could do for you for taking care of Jethro while we were in meetings."

"I would have taken cash too," Lois whispered.

I stepped lightly on her foot in warning. Lois might believe that she was whispering, but her whisper was the same as some people's outside voice.

"We can't thank you enough for taking Jethro," Reverend Brook said.

"Is Pastor Ross here?" I asked. "Or will he be going to the gardens?" I looked around for any sign of the conference leader.

Reverend Brook shook his head. "I believe he is taking the time to take care of things related to his daughter. These excursions were already on the schedule for the conference. Not even pastors and Amish bishops can sit in meetings talking about doctrine and church politics all day long. This break came at the perfect for everyone, but especially for Pastor Ross. He has much that he has to take care of."

"I can imagine there is much to do," I said.

Reverend Brook nodded. "His loss is so great. It's impossible to fully understand without living through it yourself. However, I pray none of us will ever be put in that position."

"Amen," I agreed. "But *Gott* always has a plan even if it's not something that we can understand on this side of life. One day it will all make sense. In the meantime, we must meet Pastor Ross with compassion and kindness. As the proverb says, 'Kindness, when given away, keeps coming back.' I'm glad that he has this time to take care of all he needs to do."

Reverend Brook nodded. "If you ladies will excuse me, I see one of the pastors on my committee across the way there." He patted his wife on the arm. "I just need a word with him before we leave. He's on my panel this evening."

"Of course, my dear," Juliet said and beamed at her husband.

After Reverend Brook left, Lois cleared her throat. "I believe you said Scott Lawrence was going to be on this kayak trip. Is he? I could see why Pastor Ross might ask him to stay back and help him."

A strange look crossed Juliet's face.

"What is it?" I asked.

Juliet lowered her voice. "I—I don't know if I should say this."

"Say it," Lois encouraged. "We are all friends here."

"I believe the two of them are a bit at odds at the moment. I heard them argue outside the auditorium at the resort." She looked around as if to make sure that no one overheard us.

"What were they arguing about?" I asked.

Juliet shook her head. "I heard the angry voices and turned around and went the other way. I didn't want anything to do with it."

Lois sighed. She was thinking what I was thinking. Had we been there, we would have inched closer to the two men so that we could eavesdrop. I supposed not everyone was as nosy as we were. Unfortunately.

Juliet looked around. "I did hear one thing, though."

"Oh?" Lois and I leaned forward.

"Pastor Ross shouted at Scott, 'It's your fault.'"

"What's his fault?" Lois asked.

Juliet shrugged.

Lois and I shared a look. Could it be that Pastor Ross blamed his assistant for his daughter's death? And if that was the case, why didn't he just go to the police?

I looked around the gravel parking lot. People milled around while waiting for instructions about the kayaks.

Most of them were in shorts and church T-shirts. At the same time, guides unloaded kayaks from large trailers. They laughed as they worked.

I finally spotted Scott Lawrence close to the water. His back was to us, but he was staring out into the estuary with such concentration that I didn't know if he was even aware of all the commotion around him.

Reverend Brook came back. "Are you ready to go, my dear?" he asked his wife.

She nodded. "Thank you again, ladies," Juliet said. "I know Jethro will be eager to get back to you soon. He has so much fun with the two of you."

She tucked Jethro under her right arm and looped the other arm through Reverend Brook's.

"Have a nice time at the botanical gardens," I said with a wave.

As we walked away, Lois said, "We're still stuck with the pig?"

"I thought you liked Jethro now."

She sighed. "I do. He serves the purpose of keeping Ruth away from me. But is he happy? I can't tell. I don't speak pig."

"He wasn't happy with the scooter. I know that."

Lois waved away my comment. "He loved it. He just has an odd way of showing it." She lowered her voice. "But I must say knowing that Pastor Ross and Scott are fighting is very interesting. He must have blamed Scott for what happened to Caroline."

"Wouldn't he go to the police, then?" I voiced the thoughts that I had earlier.

"I'm not saying that Scott killed her, but that doesn't

mean he didn't play a part." She glanced over at Ross, who was at least a hundred feet from where we stood. "And it's going to be our job today to find out what part that is." She paused. "And not fall in the water. My hair looks way too good today to get wet."

Chapter Twenty

A young man with bright yellow hair and swim trunks far too short to be considered modest cupped his hands around his mouth. "Everyone from the Pinecraft Clergy Conference come over here! It's time for your safety chat."

Lois hiked her purse onto her shoulder. "Safety chat? How deep is the water in the estuary? Should I be concerned?"

"I'm sure it's just part of their procedures," I said.

"Gather round! Gather round!" the young man cried.

Slowly, the group of roughly thirty men and women formed a semi-circle around him. I noted that there were several Amish men in the group, but no women. I would guess that the strictest districts would have viewed kayaking as inappropriate for women. I was glad that Bishop Yoder was more lenient on such rules.

A young man whistled. "Good morning, everyone. I'm Blane. I'll be your guide today. Are you ready to see some manatees?" He pumped his fist in the air.

Lois bumped my shoulder. "He is way too excited for this early in the morning."

"The gentle giants come to our estuary in the spring every year. We are just at the beginning of migration, so there are not as many manatees here as there will be in a few weeks. However, our drone spotted several snoozing near the mangroves. I have a great feeling that we are going to have a sighting today! At times, the manatee will float very close to your kayak. Do not reach out and touch them. They are highly protected, and just touching a manatee is against the law. Are you ready?"

"He really needs to cut back on the caffeine," Lois said.

Scott Lawrence stood at the very end of the semi-circle. He was looking at each person in turn with an openly curious expression. When his gaze settled on me, our eyes locked. He was the first to look away. I could not help wondering what he knew about Pastor Ross and his daughter Caroline. If he was as indispens-able to the conference leader as Pastor Ross had led us to believe, he might know quite a lot, just like Lois had said.

Instead of staring down Scott, Lois was swiveling her head back and forth as if she was looking for something or someone.

"Scott is right there," I whispered.

"I know. I'm not looking for him. I have a bigger target I'm worried about."

"Who?" I asked.

She shook her head. "Ruth. What if she is part of

this trip? She will finally have her chance to take me out. Death by drowning isn't my first choice."

"You don't honestly think that Ruth would go kayaking, do you?"

"That is a very good point, Millie."

Blane noisily cleared his throat. "No talking during the safety talk." He gave me and Lois a look.

Lois and I both blushed and silently listened to the instruction about how to put on our life jackets, how to hold an oar, and what to do if the kayak were to capsize.

When the talk ended, he said, "Now, we will hand out life jackets and oars. Wear your life jacket the entire excursion and always know where your oar is."

Chatter picked up in the group as kayakers waited for their gear. To my surprise, Scott Lawrence waved at me and then walked over to Lois and me. Lois elbowed me in the ribs as he approached as if I didn't notice.

Scott smiled down at me. "I'm happy we are meeting at a happier time." He cleared his throat. "After Pastor Ross and I left the beach yesterday, he told me of your connection to Caroline."

"I'm sorry to say it wasn't that much of a connection, but in the short time that I knew her I had grown fond of her."

"Did she tell you why she was in Ohio?"

His eyes narrowed just a tad, and it immediately put me ill at ease. Had I known why Caroline Zook traveled to Ohio, I don't know that I would have told him. Not that I would lie. That would be very much against my Amish culture, but one can tactfully withhold information without bearing false witness.

"She did not tell me. I just knew she was eager to get home."

"Not home to her father and home congregation, but to her new Amish life, I take it."

I frowned.

Lois took that opportunity to hold out her hand. "We haven't formally met. Lois Henry. I'm Millie's friend and investigating sidekick."

I groaned inwardly. This was not something to announce to someone who might know something about Caroline's murder.

"Investigating sidekick?" Scott asked, clearly confused.

Lois gave him a beady look. "Yes. Millie is the Amish Marple of Holmes County, Ohio."

"Amish Marple?" Scott asked confused.

"You know. She's Amish, and she investigates murders like Miss Marple."

"Who is Miss Marple?"

"Don't they teach you anything in school anymore? Miss Marple. Hercule Poirot. Agatha Christie." She ticked the names off on her fingers.

His face was blank.

"It's the video games," Lois lamented. "Kids just don't read anymore."

"We have been praying and thinking of Pastor Ross," I said, hoping to change the subject.

His face turned downward. "Thank you. I have been amazed with his strength. The team and I can't believe how much of himself he is pouring into the conference after his loss. I told him that I would be happy to take more of the load off his shoulders, but he refuses. He is welcoming the distraction. What I fear is what will happen when the conference is over and we all go back to our normal lives. Then the loss will hit him."

"Like a ton of bricks," Lois said and patted her purse.

Scott didn't know, of course, that she patted her bag because she had a brick in there. Who would have thought a seventy-year-old woman was carrying a brick around in her handbag?

"Are you going out on the kayaks?" Lois asked as if she didn't already know.

He nodded. "Pastor Ross and I both signed up for this excursion, but I suggested he stay back and rest. He has had very little time to himself since the conference began, and he is in desperate need of it." He shielded his eyes from the bright sun. "I'm glad at least in this one case, he followed my advice. He wants to keep busy, but I know from experience that this will all catch up with him in a few days."

I nodded. This was true. The lead pastor would not be able to outrun his grief forever. However, I could understand wanting to hold it at bay for a few days before succumbing to the worst of it.

Scott cleared his throat. "We're so happy that you have been able to help Reverend Brook with Jethro the pig." He laughed as if he couldn't believe he was saying the words. "Reverend Brook is a big part of our team, and especially now, with Pastor Ross in such a difficult place, we are leaning on him more and more. It would be difficult to do to with a pig running loose in the resort."

"I'm surprised that there are so many Amish at the conference," I said. "How did that come about?"

"We're in Pinecraft, and it only seems right to include the Amish community that might want to participate. Not every district that we extended an invitation to came. Some Amish are more willing to work with the English, and some less so. Pastor Ross has been great friends with Reverend Brook since their seminary days, so he asked him to invite pastors or bishops from his area. I believe Bishop Yoder is from your district."

I raised my brow. I had not expected Scott to know this.

As if he noticed my surprise, he said, "Ruth, his wife, told me that she and the bishop were staying with a friend from her district and mentioned your name."

"Oh, yes, both Ruth and Bishop Yoder are staying with us," I said.

Blane whistled. "Hey, folks. Let's stay organized and make quick work of picking up your gear so we can spend as much time as possible on the water."

The crowd clapped, which seemed to be exactly what Blane had been hoping for because he pumped his fist in the air for a second time.

From then on, the line moved quickly to receive life jackets, oars, and kayaks. Before I knew it, I was wearing a life jacket and carrying my oar to the water. The guide had the kayaks ready for each person.

A young woman in a long-sleeve T-shirt and shorts held her hand out to me to help me into the kayak. "Have you been in a kayak before?" she asked.

I shook my head. "But I have been in many canoes."

"If that is the case, you should be fine. It's the same principle."

I hope she was right as I awkwardly stepped into the kayak, which bobbed dangerously back and forth under my weight.

I gathered the hem of my skirts in my hand and settled on the seat.

When I was in place, she pushed my kayak into the water. At first, I was certain that I would tip over. I closed my eyes for a moment and held my oar at my chest. I let the gentle waves rock me and I found my sea legs, so to speak. When I opened my eyes again, I saw most of the kayaks were gathered in the widest part of the estuary waiting for instruction.

When I trusted the kayak to hold me upright, I relaxed. As instructed, I paddled toward the middle of the inlet. I bit my lip and watched as Lois clumsily climbed into her kayak. If anyone was going to capsize, it was going to be my friend. If she did, I would have to jump into the brackish water after her. She was going to be most upset about her ruined hair.

As I paddled, I was happy to learn that the young woman was right. The kayak was very much like a canoe in how it maneuvered. By the time I reached the group, I was much more comfortable.

Lois wasn't having the same luck. While I had paddled to the middle of the estuary, she was still trying to climb into her kayak.

Every time she lowered herself into the kayak, she wobbled, and she stepped out into the shallow water by the bank.

I was about to paddle over to her to offer some encouragement when there was a cheer. She was in the kayak and floating out in the water. She looked completely out of her element.

I found myself smiling. I knew that Lois said that she set up this excursion so that we could track down the killer, who was very likely attached to the pastor's conference in some way. However, I also knew she picked the outing and not the botanical gardens because it's what I would most want to do. Kayaking would not have been her first choice.

I paddled over to her. "You okay?"

"I think so. I'm not much of an outdoorswoman."

That was an understatement. Lois's idea of an outdoor adventure was an open-air flea market. Hunting down a bargain was her sport of choice.

"Can you believe that the woman who put us in the kayaks wanted me to leave my purse behind?"

I raised my brow. "It might be because of the extra weight."

"I don't care what it is. I don't go anywhere without my purse. What if I need something?"

If she ever needed the brick at the bottom of her purse, I just might faint, but I knew better than to say that aloud.

"Cool. Cool," Blane said. "We're all here. Since we're such a big group, we're going to split you up into three groups of ten. Don't you worry, every last one of you will get to see a manatee! It's going to rock your world."

Since Blane previously said that it wasn't full season yet for manatees to be migrating through this area, I didn't want to get my hopes up.

"I'll take the first group of ten," Blane said. He

waved his hand at the first section of people, which included Lois, Scott, and me. I was happy to see that Scott was in our group because there were a few more questions that I wanted to ask him about Caroline's death.

"Let's go!" Blane cried.

Lois seemed to be a bit unsure about the paddle. I stayed back and showed her how to use it.

"I think I got it now," she said, and she paddled around in the water.

"Go ahead of me, so I can keep an eye on you," I said.

"I can take care of myself, Millie," she huffed, but as she said that, her kayak rocked back and forth. "On second thought, that's a good idea."

Blane wasn't waiting around to make sure that all the guests knew what they were doing. Instead, he shot into the mangrove. The guests paddled furiously to keep up. Lois, being Lois, went at her own pace, so by the time we made it to the mangrove, there was a sizable gap between the last kayak and hers. As much as I wanted to paddle faster to catch up with the group, I didn't want to leave Lois behind.

"We should have done a tandem kayak," Lois shouted from a few yards ahead of me. "Then you could steer this thing."

There wasn't much steering required at the moment. Inside the mangrove, there was a narrow aisle that was just wide enough for one kayak, but it was also very easy to get caught in the tree roots and branches if one wasn't looking.

Lois proved that to be true. The nose of her boat became tangled in a branch.

"I'm stuck," she cried. "This was a terrible idea to come here. This is where I'm going to die and be eaten by alligators and bugs. I don't know what's worse."

A bright white bird landed on a mangrove branch just right of my head. It shook its head at me while it moved it back and forth. He was unlike any bird that I had ever seen. He had a long, curved beak that made a semicircle from the middle of his face.

I paddled forward until my kayak ran up against Lois's. "You're not going to die here," I said. "It's four feet deep. We could walk out if we had to."

"In these snake- and alligator-infested waters? No, thank you."

"I thought alligators were only in fresh water."

"I'm not going to risk it on what you think."

While we were talking, I deftly untangled Lois's kayak from the mangrove, and using all my strength, I moved her kayak so that it was pointed straight ahead. "Just paddle and you will make your way out. When we are in open water, it will be easier to stay out of trouble."

"I don't know about that. I seem to find trouble wherever I go."

I wasn't going to argue with her about that. "The water is shallow enough here that you can just push off the sandy bottom."

After nudging Lois's kayak through the mangrove, we finally peeked out onto open water. Just as we came out, a large white bird flew over our heads, and Lois screamed. "We should have gone to the botanical gardens."

I was pleased to see when we came out and Lois

calmed down from her near bird attack that Blane was waiting for us. The rest of the kayakers were in the middle of the estuary pointing and taking pictures with their phones.

"Whoa, the two of you were really stuck back there. You keeping it together?" Blane asked.

I nodded. "Thank you for waiting for us."

He smiled. "It was no trouble. We will be in this inlet for a while. We have a couple of manatees up ahead. As you can see, everyone is going gaga for them. I can't say I blame them. I have seen manatees hundreds of times in the wild, and it never gets old."

"Oh, I want to see," Lois said and began to paddle in the direction of the other kayaks. It seemed all her distaste for kayaking was forgotten in that one moment.

I followed Lois with Blane just behind me.

We slowed down the closer we came to the group so we wouldn't scare the animals.

"See the smaller one there? It's a calf. He was born here last year and is about a year old now. He will be with his mother for another year at least. Then he will venture out on his own. However, he will never stray too far away from his original pod, as they always come back to the same spot in the winter to rest and stay warm."

The mother dipped down into the depths every so often and came up with a mouthful of seagrass.

The calf seemed happy to float near his mother and lift his nose in the air so that kayaks could get the best look at him. They didn't even look real. They were like legless hippos. I had seen hippos in the Cleveland Zoo. I was in awe of the Lord's creation and his goodness to create such creatures. Surely they had a purpose like everything in creation did, even if that purpose was simply to bring this small group of kayakers joy.

As I watched the mother and calf, I said a silent prayer of thanksgiving to *Gott* for his creation.

When the mother came up again, she munched on seagrass and nudged her little one with her snout like she didn't have a care in the world, but I knew she did. Deep scars crisscrossed her back, and I gasped when I counted as many as seven.

As if he knew what caused my reaction, Blane said, "Those are made by motorboats. The estuary is a no wake area, meaning motors are not allowed to be used on boats until the boat reaches deep water. The reason for that is the scars on the mama manatee's back. Sometimes a boater doesn't even know a manatee is right under his boat, and he cuts into the manatee's back with the propeller, being none the wiser. The rules have helped to lessen this, but not everyone listens, so you still find creatures like that young mother with scars like these."

"How awful," I said.

Blane nodded. "That's why eco-trips like this are so important. I'm a firm believer if people saw the wildlife we were trying to protect, they would be more likely to want to protect them too."

I nodded.

He paddled ahead of me. "Let's all get into a circle so everyone can have a clear view of the manatees."

It took some time and, in Lois's case, having me push her kayak into place, but we finally had a makeshift semicircle around the manatees. The calf put his snout into the air and lifted his head as if he wanted to see what we were up to. The mother was unfazed by all the movement, but I suspected she knew she could leave at any time if she felt that her calf was in any danger.

"Oh, look, there is another one!" someone in the semicircle cried.

She was right. A much larger manatee came into the inlet. Just judging on the fact that it was so much larger than the mother manatee, I had to believe that it was a male.

"I think I see another one too."

In the confusion, I felt a bump under my kayak. I peeked over the side into the water to see if I hit something. Perhaps there was an old tree stump or rock that I had run aground on. As I did this, I felt the bump again, and the next thing I knew I was in the water flailing.

Lois screamed, "Woman overboard!"

Chapter Twenty-one

I was head over heels into the water, and when I righted myself and came to the surface, I spat salt water and seagrass from my mouth. Out of habit, I touched the top of my head looking for my prayer cap. It was soaking wet, but still in place.

Blane, Lois, and the rest of the kayakers were staring at me as I floated in the water.

"It's only four and half feet deep here, you should be able to stand up," Blane said.

I floated in place and tried to put my feet under me, but the bottoms of my shoes slipped on the seagrass.

I closed my eyes for the briefest of moments and took a breath. When I opened them again, I was face-to-face with the mother manatee.

Fear gripped me, but it soon dissipated. The calf floated near her right shoulder and stared at me as if I were the wildlife to be marveled at.

Behind me, I could hear the other kayaks oohing and ahhing.

"Hold still, Millie," Lois called. "I'm taking a photo."

I turned my face away from Lois so it wouldn't be caught in the picture. It went against my Amish beliefs to have my picture taken, but at the same time, I was very happy that Lois was able to catch this moment. It was something that I would remember the rest of my life.

The calf floated within six inches of me. I wanted to reach out and touch him, but I remembered that Blane said not to do that. Instead, we floated in place and stared at each other.

The mother made bubbles with her nose and the calf swam back to her, and then the pair went under and disappeared into the seagrass.

"Whoa," Blane said. "You just got one of the closest encounters with a manatee and her calf that I have ever seen. That was rad."

"Totally rad," Lois agreed.

The others on the kayak tour chimed in.

Blane on his kayak paddled over to me. "Are you all right, ma'am? You weren't hurt when you fell in, were you?"

"I'm fine," I said. "Exhilarated really. I feel so blessed to be so close to those beautiful creatures."

"Man, I would too," he said. "You've gotten closer than I ever have." He hopped off his kayak into the water with the lightest of splashes. "I will hold your kayak and help you back in."

I nodded and wondered how I would be able to climb back in the kayak and preserve my dignity at the same time. It was impossible. I lay on my torso and with Blane's help lifted my legs over as well. With some rolling back and forth like a beached whale, I managed to roll over and sit down. When I accomplished it, everyone clapped. I blushed.

Lois floated over to me. "I got photos of you climbing in too."

I scowled at her.

"Not to worry. It's just for us to remember the trip. I won't show them to anyone, but when I am ninety, I will look back on them and laugh."

"I surely don't need pictures of that to remember my awkward climb into the kayak," I said.

"Maybe not now, but in ten years when I remind you of it, I might need the evidence." She grinned. "I have to say, Millie, I was shocked that it was you who tipped yourself out of the kayak instead of me. You seemed to be the real pro at kayaking."

"I didn't tip myself over. Something bumped my kayak," I said under my breath just loud enough for her to hear.

Lois's eyes went wide and I knew she was dying to ask me what I meant.

"I'm sure glad you fell into the water where there were manatees and not alligators," Blane said.

"Aren't alligators freshwater creatures?" Lois asked, looking around the estuary as if she was afraid that an alligator was going to jump out of the mangrove at any moment.

The guided nodded. "Usually, yes, they are, but we are in brackish water where the salt water and fresh water meet. Depending on the season, the salt in the water is lessened enough by the rains and fresh water coming from inland that the alligators can survive in it."

"I'm just glad that you didn't become a gator's lunch," Lois said. "I would have a lot of explaining to do when I went back home."

"I'm glad too," I said.

Blane hopped back into his kayak like he was skipping over a crack in the sidewalk and landed in his seat. "Well, I would say that this has been a successful start to our trip! Are you all ready to paddle to the next site?"

The consensus was yes for certain. One of the other guides took the lead, and Blane floated to the back of the pack where Lois and I were. "I just wanted to make sure you're okay. I know you landed in water, but there could be some sharp stones and shells down there. Did you hit anything?"

I shook my head. "*Nee*, but thank you for your concern. I know this might be an odd thing to say, but I am grateful that it happened. Had I not fallen in, I wouldn't have had that encounter with the manatee and her calf."

"For sure. I've been doing this for ten years, and I have never been that close in the water to them. I have to say I'm a bit jealous. It's been my life's work to protect them. They are gentle animals, but any mama creature can be fierce. Clearly, she let you see her calf because she sensed that you were a friend."

I smiled.

Blane cleared his throat. "What I can't understand is how you lost your balance. From what I could tell, you were a pro with a paddle," Blane said. "It wasn't like we were going through rapids or anything."

I shrugged and squeezed the water out of my skirt the best that I could. What I didn't say was I hadn't lost my balance at all. I had been tipped over. Maybe one of the manatees swam under my kayak and bumped it. Maybe not.

Chapter Twenty-two

I insisted that we finish the rest of the tour despite how wet I was. A kind woman in the group handed me a towel from her backpack. I dried myself off the best that I could.

As we continued the trip and paddled through coves and above seagrasses that swayed in the tidal waters, we didn't see any more manatees. However, I was satisfied. Despite feeling like a wet dog slowly being steamed by the relentless sun, I had come face-to-face with a mother manatee and her calf. It was a memory that I would cherish the rest of my life.

Blane guided us into another cove and used a net to pick up creatures from the floor of the estuary. "This is an anemone."

The animal's tentacles wiggled this way and that in a slow rhythm like they were fingertips drumming on a tabletop.

"Does anyone want to hold it?" Blane asked.

Lois paddled over to me. "Not me. Keep that monster away from me."

"They are essential for the health of the estuary."

"Good," Lois said. "They can do that in the water."

"I guess you wouldn't be interested in the sea slug either, then."

Lois turned a bit green at his comment.

Blane went on to hand the anemone to someone else.

When he floated away, Lois shivered. "Did you see the suction cups on that thing's legs? There is no way that I am going to help one of those leech the life out me."

"I don't think they do that," I said.

Lois cocked her head. "How do you know? When was the last time you saw one?"

"I have never seen one before," I said looking around the kayaks. Other than Blane, the only person I knew was Scott Lawrence, Pastor Ross's right hand-man.

As far as I knew in this group of people, he was the only one who might know that Lois and I were working on the murder. Had he flipped my kayak to warn me? Was he trying to protect Pastor Ross from our investigation?

He had been close by, and everyone had been so densely packed to see the mother manatee and her calf. As a group, we were too mesmerized to notice if anyone was causing trouble.

I shook my head. It just seemed to be far-fetched. I was letting my imagination run away with me. First of all, why would Scott do that? He knew next to nothing about me. Second of all, even in the commotion of watching the manatees, I would have noticed if someone stuck an oar or hand under my kayak to tip me over. At the same time, I knew the tumble had not been my fault. I had been canoeing many times before on both rivers and lakes. I knew how to steer a canoe. A kayak wasn't that much different from a canoe. I had not caused myself to fall into the water. That much I knew.

"What's wrong?" Lois asked.

I blinked and looked at my friend. "What's that?"

"I asked you what was wrong. Your forehead is wrinkled and your frown lines are showing. I always know that you are mulling something over when that happens." She paused. "By the way, I have a great cream that could practically erase the frown lines overnight. I swear by it."

"I'm seventy years old. My frown lines are always showing, and I consider them a gift that I have earned."

Lois frowned. "Not me." Then she smiled. "I would like to thank the cream and fillers for that. I offered the cream because I know you would never consider fillers."

She was right about that. I paddled closer to her until our kayaks were touching. "I think it's possible someone flipped my kayak."

Her eyes went so wide that her false eyelashes reached her hairline. "What? How? We were packed in like sardines all trying to see the manatees."

I frowned. "I don't know exactly, but I felt a thump under my kayak and the next thing I knew, I was in the water." I shook my head. "Maybe I just imagined it all and lost my balance."

"Could it have been the manatee? Blane said sometimes they float under boats unnoticed. Maybe one was under your kayak. Maybe another one was swimming by and no one noticed it. It could have been that huge male that was in the water . . ."

"It would be pretty hard for it go unnoticed. He was enormous, and everyone was staring into the water."

Lois glanced around the group of kayakers who were listening to Blane's lecture about how the sea life in the estuary was all interconnected. I would have found what he had to say interesting too if I had not been so preoccupied with being tipped into the water.

"Who was near you when you went over?" Lois asked.

"The only person I knew was Scott."

Lois narrowed her eyes.

"He's someone that we will have to keep an eye on. He might know more about Caroline than anyone else at the conference. He admitted that they worked together before Caroline left to join the Amish."

Lois narrowed her eyes. "I have my eye on him for sure."

I knew that Scott couldn't have capsized my kayak without being seen, but even so, I had my eye on him too.

"This has been a great trip, but it's time to head back," Blane said. "We will go back through the mangrove and be at the docking area in no time at all."

"Back through the mangrove," Lois moaned.

Blane laughed. "It won't be that bad this time. The water will be a little deeper, and the aisle is wide enough to let two kayaks pass. People won't get as easily stuck."

"It might not be as easy to get stuck, but I'm sure that I will manage it," Lois said.

Like before, Lois and I were the last ones, and I followed my friend to make sure she didn't get caught in any of the mangroves' many roots and branches.

Blane had been right. The mangrove trees grew much farther apart from each other in this section of the estuary, so Lois and I could paddle side by side. It was much easier to keep her kayak on course this way.

Having been soaking wet most of the trip, I looked forward to getting back to the bungalow and changing my dress. This trip to Florida had certainly been hard on my garments, from my prayer caps to my shoes. I would have to make a whole new wardrobe when I returned home to Harvest.

The kayak ahead of us stopped, forcing Lois and me to stop as well.

Lois leaned forward and said to the kayaker just ahead of us, "What's the holdup?"

"They saw an ibis up ahead."

"A whatbus?" Lois asked.

"Ibis. It's a large white marsh bird with a hooked beak. There are thousands of them down here."

That must have been what I saw during the first time through the mangrove.

"I want to see him," Lois said.

"I think you will," the man said. "Blane is letting everyone slowly float by him one by one. He doesn't want to spook the bird."

"Yes," Lois said. "Spooking the bird would be the last thing that we want."

When it was the turn of the kayakers ahead of us to see the bird, Lois and I waited in the mangrove. We could see Blane and one of the other kayakers up ahead. He had a giant camera and was taking one picture after another of the bird.

"He must be a birdwatcher," I said. Birdwatching was a popular pastime for the Amish as well. Some were surprised when they saw Amish walking around Holmes County with large cameras like the one the man in front of us had.

After the man finished his pictures, Blane waved Lois forward into the mangrove for a look at the bird.

I floated by the mouth of the mangrove waiting for my turn when I heard a shout behind me.

Had someone else fallen into the water?

I paddled backward out of the mangrove to see if someone needed help in the inlet. If they had fallen out of their kayak, I would be able to tell them how to get on from my own experience.

Behind me, a voice snapped, "It's your fault that she died."

I froze with my oar in mid-backward stroke.

"Stop saying that," someone said back. "It's not true."

The voices were barely above a whisper, and because of that, I couldn't tell if they were women or men. I had to see who they were.

"Someone is coming," one said.

I heard a splash just before I was able to turn my kayak and face the estuary just beyond the entrance to the mangrove.

No one was around. I didn't even see a single bird,

but I watched the tail end of a kayak disappearing into the mangrove.

"Millie," Lois called. "Blane and the others are leaving. We don't want to be lost out here without them."

She was right.

As carefully as I could, I turned my kayak around and paddled back to the mangrove.

Chapter Twenty-three

Safely back on land, I removed my life jacket and shook the water from it.

"Millie, I hardly ever say this to you, but you look a mess," Lois said as she poked at her perfectly dry hair.

I smiled. "Falling out of a kayak will do that to you."

"Or being tipped over will," Lois said in a low voice. "Do you really think that's what happened?"

I set my life jacket on top of the bin for life jackets. As mine was the only one that was wet, I didn't want it to dampen the others. I stepped out of the way as other guests from our kayak excursion placed their life jackets in the bin.

I shuffled over to Lois. My tennis shoes squished. It seemed that wet feet were going to be my permanent state while in Florida. How I longed for warm, dry toes again.

"I can't know for sure. All I know is I felt a bump on the bottom of my kayak before I went over." I shook my head and decided to put it out of my mind. "Maybe I got snagged on a log or something."

"I don't remember seeing any logs floating around the estuary." Lois adjusted her purse strap on her shoulder. "News like this makes me hungry. We should talk about this more over ice cream."

"Let me guess, the ice cream place where Caroline's friend worked."

She grinned. "It's high time that we talk to someone else who knew Caroline, don't you think?"

I did. If Kimber was really Caroline's best friend and roommate for a short while, she might know more than anyone else why Caroline went to Ohio. I knew her trip to Ohio had to be the thread to unravel this murder.

Scott Lawrence waved at us as he stuck his life jacket in the bin with the others. "Did I hear someone say ice cream?"

Lois eyed him. "Millie and I are headed to Double Dutch Ice Cream. We hear they have the best ice cream in Pinecraft. I think with all the paddling, we burned enough calories to earn it."

Scott's face grayed slightly with the mention of the ice cream shop, but it quickly cleared. "They are very good. My favorite is the double chocolate."

"We will keep that in mind. Would you like to come along and have ice cream with us?"

If Lois was three inches closer to me, I would have tapped her on the back of the head for saying that. How could we have an honest conversation with Caroline's friend Kimber with him around?

Scott's eyes went wide. "I would love to, but I need to get back to the conference."

"I'm sure you have much work to do," I said.

He nodded. "The conference is so time consuming that I consider myself lucky that I was able to get away for this excursion."

"I'm sure," Lois said. "And more of the responsibility must be falling on your shoulders because of what happened to Caroline."

"I'm happy to help Pastor Ross any way that I can. When I came to Florida, he welcomed me into his church and offered me a position even though I had no experience to speak of. He really saved me. I had nothing and he gave me all he could."

Lois arched her brow. "Where did you live before you moved to Florida?"

"Here and there," he said vaguely. "I did a lot of traveling across the country when I left home as a young man. When I landed here in Pinecraft, it felt like home." He looked over his shoulder.

Conference-goers still milled around the vans. No one seemed to be in a hurry to return to the resort. I imagined that after a morning in nature, returning to a meeting room to argue about church doctrine and procedure felt quite tedious.

Scott rubbed the back of his neck. "When we spoke before, you mentioned Amish Marple."

Lois perked up. "Yes, I did. That's what we call Millie back in Harvest."

I snorted. It was what *Lois* called me. No one else in Harvest or anywhere else has ever used that name.

"I looked it up on my phone and some articles came up. You've solved murders back in Ohio?" he asked.

"I wouldn't take complete credit for solving the murders. However, from time to time, Lois and I have helped the police. It's a team effort."

"I don't agree with that at all," Lois chimed in. "We are definitely the crime solvers in Harvest . . . or one of them. Bailey King isn't that bad either."

Scott's brow knit together. "Is that what you're trying to do in Caroline's case?"

"We want to help Pastor Ross, of course," I said vaguely.

"I—I don't think you are equipped for solving a murder in Florida. Things are much different here."

Lois cocked her head, and I knew she was thinking the same thing I was. Was his statement advice or a warning? His tone was neutral, but I had a bad feeling about the words coming out of his mouth.

"Detective Marcs has asked us to stay out of the investigation," I said.

His shoulders sagged as if in relief. "Good. That's exactly what you should do."

"Why?" Lois asked.

"Scott!" someone outside the van called. "Come on. The van is leaving."

He waved at his friend before saying to Lois and me, "You should do what the detective says. It's the smart choice. Trust me." He walked over to the van and climbed in.

As Lois and I watched the van drive away, Lois wrinkled her brow. "Smart choice? Because he doesn't want us to find out what he or Pastor Ross did?"

"I don't know." I walked to the bike rack where our dilapidated scooters waited for us.

Lois pulled her scooter out of the rack. "Being vaguely threatened really builds up a sweet tooth. I'm going to get a giant cone."

I removed my scooter with a little bit more care. I was starting to get the hang of riding the scooter, but I still didn't fully trust it or trust myself on it.

Lois, on the other hand, was bursting with confidence.

"Follow me. My phone will tell us how to go." She kicked off from the gravel parking lot, and I had no choice but to follow behind her and pray that she didn't hit anything.

After a harrowing journey in which Lois pulled out in front of two pickup trucks and one buggy, we finally made it to the ice cream shop parking lot.

She parked her scooter next to a white picket fence. "See? These e-scooters couldn't be simpler to drive."

I set my scooter beside hers. "Simple is not the word I would use to describe that trip."

The ice cream stand was a small building no bigger than a shed back in Ohio. There were three young Amish women inside the stand running this way and that, filling ice cream orders. The line was long even though it was a cool afternoon by Florida standards.

Back home all the local ice cream stands like this shuttered their doors from October until May. It was far too cold to make folks stand outside for a cone. It seemed all the northern visitors were missing this warm weather treat.

Lois rubbed her hands together. "I don't know how

I'm going to decide what to get. Every flavor looks like my favorite." Her eyes boggled as she scanned over the list.

"The line is long enough that it should give you more than enough time to decide."

She gave me a look. "Do you know me at all?"

She was right. Lois was often torn when ordering food unless fried chicken was on the menu—then she always had fried chicken. She said there were too many things that she liked. I kept it simple. Any time I ordered dessert and blueberry was an option, I took it.

When we finally walked up to the window, a rosy-cheeked girl with glasses smiled at us. "What can I get you?"

"I will have a small blueberry cone," I said.

"Sure!" She looked to Lois. "And for you?"

"Can I taste the moose tracks?"

The girl nodded and took a tiny plastic spoon from its dispenser. She returned with a miniature scoop of ice cream on it.

"Yum," Lois said. "Can I try butter pecan?"

The girl's smile wavered, but again, she grabbed a little spoon and went to retrieve the ice cream. She handed the second sample to Lois.

"The moose tracks. I'll take a large in a waffle cone."

The girl nodded and went to retrieve our ice cream.

"You are never going to be able to eat that much ice cream," I said.

"Sure, I can," Lois replied.

The girl returned with our ice cream. Lois's was even larger than expected. I guessed there was at least a pint of moose tracks ice cream in her waffle cone.

I accepted my much smaller blueberry cone and paid for the ice cream. "Is Kimber working today?" I asked.

The girl blinked. "Not yet. She should be arriving any time. She works the late shift."

"*Danki*," I said and carried my blueberry cone over to one of the picnic tables in front of the shop.

Lois followed me. "So, what's the plan? We lie in wait for Kimber like a couple of sharks?"

I licked my cone. "*Nee*, but we do wait for her to arrive like a couple of polite elderly ladies."

"Watch who you call elderly," Lois said. "I'm seventy years young and proud of it."

I chuckled.

Twenty minutes later, we were still sitting at the picnic table with our ice cream, and Lois was doing her best to finish hers.

"It's okay to admit that you can't eat it all. No one will judge you."

"I just hate to waste food. It's left over from my Great Depression–era parents."

"Then I will make that choice for you." I took the cone from her hand and threw it away.

As I did, a young *Englisch* woman on an electric bicycle turned into the gravel lot. Her dark hair was pulled back in a tight bun on the very top of her head, and she wore shorts and an oversized sweatshirt with "Double Dutch Ice Cream" embroidered across her chest.

"Kimber?" Lois whispered.

I nodded.

Lucky for us, the bicycle rack was right next to the picnic tables.

She parked the bike and secured the chain around the bike rack. Of all the bikes and scooters there, including our less-than-attractive scooters, I noted that she was the only one who chained up her bike. The rest must have been trusting Amish.

She smiled at Lois and me as she made her way to the ice cream stand.

"Are you Kimber?" I asked.

She froze and looked at me. "Do I know you?"

"*Nee*, but we both know Caroline Zook," I said.

Her mouth fell open and then she burst into tears.

Chapter Twenty-four

Lois walked over to her and started rubbing her back. "There, there." Lois guided her to the picnic table. "Have a seat."

Kimber wiped her eyes on the sleeve of her sweatshirt and left a streak of her makeup behind. "I can't. I have to go to work."

"You can't go looking like that. Your eye shadow is in your hairline, and you smeared your foundation."

Kimber touched her face. "I didn't bring anything with me."

"Oh, honey, you have nothing to worry about. I always have eye shadow and emergency concealer with me just for a moment like this. You never know when you will run into a woman in need." Lois reached into her purse and came up with a cosmetics bag. She opened the bag, and inside was a slew of unopened makeup. She also removed a wet wipe. "I'll get you all squared away."

Kimber stared at her in disbelief. *I might have too if*

I didn't expect these items to appear from the depths of Lois's beloved purse.

Lois dabbed at the sleeve of Kimber's sweatshirt, deftly removing the stain. "These are a dream. I tend to be a messy eater, and I always have a packet of these with me wherever I go."

"This is so nice of you." She glanced at the ice cream shop. "My boss isn't here today. I guess I can take a few minutes to talk to you. You've been so nice." She smoothed the concealer that Lois gave her under her eyes. When she was done, she started to hand it back to Lois.

"No, no, you keep it. You need it more than I do," Lois said.

Kimber nodded and tucked it in her backpack. "How do you know Caroline?"

"We met her on the bus coming here from Harvest, Ohio," I said.

"I told her not to go to Ohio. I knew from the start that it would be a mistake, and now she's dead." Tears came to her eyes, but this time she managed to hold them back.

I sat next to her at the picnic table. "Why was it a mistake?"

Her face turned red. "Be-because she just got married. Now wasn't the time to be running off to Ohio on a whim. I knew that Cainan wouldn't like it. She thought that she knew him, but he is an Amish man. Amish men like to control the women in their lives. It's how they were raised. From birth, they are taught the men are the head of the household and make all the decisions. Even though Cainan is more progressive than many of the people in his district, he is still an Amish man and didn't want his new bride leaving him so soon after they married. If she really wanted to be Amish, she was starting off the wrong way." She plucked at the sleeve of her sweatshirt. "I told her that, but I wish I had been more forceful about it. If I had, she might never have gone and would still be here." Kimber dropped her hand from her sweatshirt. "I know you're Amish, and I don't want to come off judgmental. I live in Sarasota. I have a lot of Amish friends. My boss and his family, who own this ice cream shop, are Amish. They have always been lovely to me. I don't mean to offend."

"You're not offending me," I said. "I know very well how Amish view marriage and family."

She nodded and some of the color dissipated from her flushed cheeks. "I don't want my Amish friends to think badly of me because I don't agree with everything they do."

Lois patted her arm. "Oh, honey, you can disagree with a person on some things and be the very best of friends. See Millie and me sitting right here? We are as thick as thieves, and I think it's crazy that she gets up before the crack of dawn every morning, and she doesn't understand my need to express myself through fashion. It doesn't mean we love each other any less. We respect what the other person is and does, but we don't have to do it ourselves." Lois whipped a packet of tissues out of her purse and handed one to Kimber. "There, there, you were a good friend to Caroline."

Kimber dapped at her eyes. "I hope that's true. I really wanted to be. I've known her since I was a baby. My family goes to her church, or what was her church." She paused. "The church where her father is pastor."

"Do you still go there?" I asked.

She shook her head. "My family moved to Fort Lauderdale a couple of years ago. I stayed back because I didn't want to change high schools. Then I stayed longer because I got into a college close by. I grew up here. I didn't want to lose all my friends. I went to Caroline's church through the end of high school, but even if I wanted to, I couldn't stay any longer after she left. I knew Pastor Ross would grill me every Sunday asking where Caroline was. What was I going to say, that she was hiding out in my apartment?"

"She *was* staying with you," Lois said.

Kimber's eyes were wide. "How did you know that?"

Lois pointed at the two mangled e-scooters in the bicycle rack. "We rented from Zook's Scooters. They look a mess but run great. Cainan told us."

Kimber's jaw fell open. "That's Caroline's scooter."

"What?" Lois yelped.

"The scooter with the bent handlebars. That is Caroline's. I would recognize it anywhere."

I shivered. It was the scooter that Lois had been riding all around town. This also explained to me why Cainan's brother-in-law, Malachi Grabill, found it odd that Cainan rented the scooters to us.

"Are you sure?" I asked.

Kimber got up from the table and walked over to the bike rack. She leaned over and looked at the scooter. "See? Right here. On the post. Their initials are etched into the metal. 'CZ + CH.'" She returned to the picnic table and sat down. "Isn't it weird that he would rent out his dead wife's scooter?"

It was odd, I did admit to myself, but Cainan had been in such a state. Perhaps he wasn't thinking straight.

"Caroline Hanniford," I said. "She had the scooter before they married."

Kimber nodded. "Cainan gave it to her a couple of years ago when we were still in high school. Her father wanted to buy her a car, but she said the scooter was enough for her to get around Pinecraft. And it is. I get around town by e-bike. It's just easier to maneuver in Sarasota traffic, and there are so many bike lanes nowadays, you can actually go place to place a lot faster too."

"What happened to the scooter?" Lois asked.

"Oh, that's easy. The e-scooter is so messed up because she was in an accident. Someone ran her off the road. Someone tried to kill her before she was killed." Her words were so bare and factual, it took a moment for their meaning to seep into Lois's and my minds.

When it did, we were shocked.

"Someone tried to kill her before?" Lois gasped.

Kimber nodded. "At the time everyone thought it was just a freak accident, but now I'm not so sure."

"When was this?" I asked.

"It was before she left home," Kimber said. "She had a concussion and a broken rib. The doctors said it was a miracle that she wasn't injured more. The car that made her drive off the road made her collide with a parking meter. The parking meter was fine. Not even a scratch."

I folded my hands in my lap. "Where was this?"

"The main road that runs parallel to the beach."

That was the road that Lois and I were staying on, and the road that held the Dutchman Resort and Zook's Scooters. I couldn't say if that tied anything together, but it was interesting.

"Were there any witnesses?" Lois asked.

Kimber shook her head. "No witnesses, but Caroline told me everything that happened."

"Can you tell us?"

Kimber stopped and looked at us each in turn. "Why? I don't even know you. I don't know why I have been talking to you for so long as it is. My shift leader is going to ding me for being late, and I already have two black marks on my performance."

I nodded. "That's a very *gut* question to ask. Like we told you before, we met Caroline on the bus coming from Ohio. We both liked her very much. She was a sweet, earnest girl who I could tell was going to make a lovely wife and mother one day." My voice caught as I said the words. It was startling to me in the short time that I had known her how much Caroline's kind spirit had touched me.

Across from me, tears gathered in Kimber's eyes. "She was the best friend that I've ever had." She licked her lips. "I wasn't thrilled that she was going to be Amish, but I wasn't afraid that I would lose her as a friend because of it. Caroline was the most loyal person you could ever meet. I knew that we would still be friends and see each other all the time."

"We want to find out what happened to her," I said.

Again, she looked from Lois to me and back again. "How? You're . . ."

"Old," Lois supplied. "It's okay. Don't sugarcoat it. We're well aware that we have a nineteen at the beginning of the year that we were born."

Kimber blushed.

"We have some experience solving murders back home," I said.

Kimber's brow wrinkled. "I don't know what it can hurt at this time. What do you want to know?"

"Tell us about her scooter accident."

She took a deep breath. "It was a few months ago. She used to work here at the ice cream shop but had recently left because her father asked her to work for him at the church. He was planning this huge pastors' conference, and he needed more help. Caroline was so smart and really organized. She was just the person you would want to plan something for you."

"Did she work with Scott Lawrence?" I asked.

Kimber wrinkled her nose. "Yeah."

"I take it you're not a fan," Lois said.

Kimber shuddered. "No, not even a little bit. One of the reasons that I didn't mind stopping attending Caroline's church was to avoid Scott. He has a crush on me, and it's so awkward."

Lois and I shared a look.

"Isn't he quite a bit older than you?" I asked.

"He's old. Like over thirty."

"Definitely ancient," Lois agreed.

"He not from Pinecraft," I said. "He told us that."

She shook her head. "No, he just started coming to

the church five or six years ago. I can't remember exactly."

"To work for Pastor Ross?" I asked.

She wrinkled her brow. "Not at first. I think he started working at the church after about a year."

I frowned. None of this proved that Scott had done anything wrong but still it was interesting information about the pastor's assistant to tuck under my prayer cap and save for later.

"Did Caroline like working with Scott?" Lois asked.

Kimber shrugged. "I guess. The only thing she ever said about him was he was nervous and wasn't thrilled that Pastor Ross brought her on. I guess he thought he could handle everything himself."

"So, he was offended that Pastor Ross brought his daughter in."

Kimber shrugged again.

"How long after that did she leave home and move in with you?" I asked.

"It was about a month."

"So, she was only working for her dad for a month."

Kimber nodded. "We had so much fun while she was there. I was upset when she said she was going to marry Cainan. I wanted her to wait a couple of years. I mean, we are eighteen. What is the rush? She had been in love with him since we were in middle school, but I guess I really didn't think that she would marry him and become Amish. She was always the good pastor's daughter who did everything that her father told her to do. Except in this one big thing."

"Do you think that got her killed?" I asked.

"Are you asking me if I think her father killed her for marrying an Amish guy?"

I nodded.

"I sure hope not." She shivered. "I think she was killed because of her trip to Ohio. I'm positive it was that. She was so anxious about it. I told her a million times not to go. Who wants to go to Ohio in February?"

It was a great question, and the state was my home.

"Why did she go?" Lois asked.

Kimber looked left and right as if she was afraid that someone was listening to our conversation from behind the palmettos along the edge of the gravel lot. "I don't know." She looked around again, and I knew with all my heart that she was lying.

Kimber stood up. "I really have to get to work. My boss is going to be upset if I'm too late."

"Understood," Lois said, and she stood up too.

Kimber looked from Lois to me. "I'm glad I got to speak to someone about Caroline. She deserves to be remembered. She really was a great friend to me."

"Kimber, one more question," I said.

She turned and looked at me.

"I know the Amish and *Englisch* in Pinecraft are around each other all the time, but there is some natural division. How did Caroline get so close to Cainan?"

"Volleyball," she said.

"Volleyball?" Lois asked.

She nodded. "Caroline loved volleyball. She played since she was little, and for the high school team too. All the Amish kids play volleyball in the evenings on the beach. Caroline started going and asked to play.

That's how she met Cainan. She went to that beach any chance she could get to play."

Lois cocked her head. "She wasn't very tall to be a volleyball player."

"Yeah," Kimber said. "She was always upset with the fact that she wasn't likely to play for a Division One university because she was just too short. I think that's when she started thinking college wasn't for her. I also think that's why it was so important to her to play with the Amish kids. It wasn't as competitive. It was just fun. If you want to find out more about the volleyball thing, you should go to one of their games."

"When are they?"

"Tonight at eight thirty just beyond the pier."

Lois and I shared a look.

"I really have to get to work." With that, she walked away.

Lois and I watched her go.

"She knows exactly why Caroline Zook went to Ohio," Lois said.

"She does." I brushed ice cream cone crumbs from my skirt. "And she is too afraid to say it."

Chapter Twenty-five

Lois and I rode our scooters back to our bungalow without incident. All the while, I wondered about what we learned from Kimber. It seemed to me that the reason for Caroline's murder was connected back to Harvest, and ironically Lois and I were nowhere close to home to find that answer.

Lois propped her e-scooter against the bungalow, and I did the same.

I unlocked the door and went inside. Lois was more reluctant to enter. "Is the coast clear?"

"Are you worried about Jethro or Ruth being here?" I asked over my shoulder.

"What do you think?"

"You're in luck on both counts. No one is here."

She let out a sigh of relief and came into the room.

"I'm going to change out of my wet clothes," I said.

When I came back into the main room feeling much more like myself, I found Lois at the small dining table. Her phone was in the middle of the table and she stared at it. "Finally. I thought you would never come out of there."

"Is there a problem?"

"Other than murder and the fact that Ruth and I are sleeping under the same roof, no, I don't think so." She patted the seat of the chair next to hers. "Come sit."

I twisted my mouth and wondered what my friend was up to. However, rather than argue, I perched on the chair next to her and waited.

"What we need is boots on the ground," Lois said.

I arched my eyebrows at her. "What?"

"We need someone in Ohio to look into that side of the investigation, and I know just the person to do it." She reached for her phone and tapped the screen. While it was ringing, she propped the phone up against the vase in the middle of the table.

Bailey's name was on the screen.

"I thought Bailey was in New York?"

"Phones work in New York, Millie," Lois said.

The call was picked up, and Bailey King's pretty face filled the screen. Her dark hair was back in a ponytail as it always was when she was working at the candy factory, and she wore a Swissmen Candyworks sweatshirt.

"Lois? And Millie?" she said with a smile. "How is your trip? I hope you're having a great time." Her face fell. "Aiden told me about your gruesome discovery on the beach."

"It was unpleasant," Lois said.

"Jethro is here in Florida," I said. "Juliet said that you couldn't take care of him since you were in New York."

"I got back last night, so what she told you is true. I will admit that I miss my little bacon bundle. However, I'm getting a lot more work done without his mischief," she said. "It was straight to work at the candy factory. Easter is in March this year, so we don't have much time to ramp up production between Valentine's Day and Easter. The number of chocolate bunnies we have to churn out is daunting." She smiled. "But I'm happy for all the orders. I knew the factory was a good idea, but I never thought that it would do as well as it has."

"That's all to your credit," I said.

"How's the wedding planning?" Lois asked.

She wrinkled her nose. "It's coming along. To be honest, the summer wedding is the best choice. I don't have any big holidays that I will have to juggle with the candy." She shook her head as if she didn't want to think about it at the moment.

I couldn't blame her for wanting to put the wedding out of her head. If you asked Juliet, the wedding of her son Sheriff Aiden Brody and Bailey King was going to be the biggest event that Harvest had ever seen. I suspected that Aiden and Bailey would want to have a much smaller wedding if they could get away with it without upsetting their parents and the whole village in the process.

"I hope Jethro is behaving himself," Bailey said. "Aiden told me that he was the one who found the body. By the way Aiden told it, the detective down there was very put off. I guess they aren't used to a crime-solving pig."

"Detective Marcs doesn't know what to make of the likes of Jethro, or Millie and me, for that matter," Lois said.

Bailey laughed and then her face became sober. "My guess is you're calling about the murder."

"We are," I said.

"And we need your help," Lois added.

Bailey listened intently as Lois told her about Caroline Zook leaving home to marry an Amish man and shortly after the wedding going to Harvest for some reason.

"That's pretty unusual for an English person to convert to the Amish way to marry an Amish man," Bailey said.

"Very," I agreed. "And we're convinced the reason she was in Harvest was the reason she was killed."

"I'm sure that someone here in Harvest spoke to her. I'm sad to say that I don't remember ever seeing her." She made a note on a piece of paper in front of her. "I'll ask around."

"Bailey!" someone called behind her.

Bailey looked over her shoulder. "I have to go. That's Charlotte calling me. We have a factory tour starting in a few minutes." She turned back to the screen. "Don't worry, I will find out what I can about Caroline." She said good-bye and ended the call.

Lois set her phone on the tabletop. "If anyone can get to the bottom of it, it's Bailey."

"I hate to put another thing on her when she is already dealing with the candy factory and the wedding."

"Pish," Lois said. "We have her future mother-in-law, Jethro, and Ruth Yoder down here and out of her hair. She is working with far fewer complications than she usually would be."

Lois had a good point.

The door to the bungalow flew open and slammed against the wall.

Lois and I gaped as Ruth Yoder stormed into the bungalow. "I have never been so insulted in all of my life!"

"She's a big complication," Lois whispered under her breath.

That she was.

I stood up from the table. "Ruth, what's wrong?"

"What's wrong? What's wrong? I will tell you what's wrong!"

"We asked you to," Lois quipped.

"I will have none of your lip, Lois Henry. I have had the most horrible of horrible days. I can't stand an ounce more." Her voice wavered.

Lois and I shared a look. Was Ruth Yoder about to cry? In all the time I had known Ruth, which was the entirety of my life, I had never seen her cry.

I hurried over to her and guided her to the table. "Ruth, have a seat and tell us what happened. Lois, can you get her some water?"

Lois, with her mouth still agape, retrieved a cold bottle of water from the refrigerator and set it on the table in front of Ruth.

Ruth stared at it. "I need it in a glass. I'm not a man working in the fields."

Lois rolled her eyes. "She's fine." Then Lois went to the cupboard to retrieve a glass.

"I'll need ice too," Ruth said.

I could almost hear Lois grinding her teeth.

I sat across from Ruth. "What has happened? Why are you so upset?"

Lois set the water glass in front of Ruth next to the bottle without a word. I was impressed with her restraint.

Ruth looked at the bottle as if she was contemplating asking Lois to pour her water for her. In the end, she opened the bottle herself. I guessed that even Ruth knew that was taking it too far.

She filled her water glass and took the smallest sip I had ever seen before setting it back on the table.

"So?" Lois said. Her patience was coming to an end.

"That horrible young man at the conference said I wasn't allowed to listen to this afternoon's session on church and district management." She stared at us. "Can you imagine? I have been the bishop's wife for over fifty years. I know more about managing a church district in my pinkie finger than he ever will."

"What did you say when he turned you away?" I asked.

"I said that the bishop and I were both leaving, but Bishop Yoder stayed. He told me to go lie down and take a nap. I'm caring for a large Amish district. Do I look like a person who naps? I haven't had a nap in decades."

"Might explain a lot," Lois muttered.

I kicked her lightly under the table.

"Ouch," Lois grumbled.

"My own husband said this in front of the entire assembly. I was humiliated. Why shouldn't I be in the sessions? What am I to do here? Go to the beach while my husband listens to these speakers? I had no intention of speaking up as a wife, that is not my place, but I can quietly listen. Should I not have all the information too?"

"That's not very Amish of you," Lois said.

Ruth's head snapped in her direction. "Lois Henry, don't you dare tell me what is Amish and not Amish."

I held up my hands. "Please, the two of you, let's not fight. Ruth, I'm sorry that you weren't able to stay at the session. I would find that upsetting too, but I'm sure Bishop Yoder will tell you everything that happened."

She narrowed her eyes. "He had better. I have spent most of my life with my husband, and I have never felt so betrayed. He never treated me so poorly back home. He would know there that I deserved respect. I believe this *Englisch* conference is a bad influence on him. It's filling his head with ideas."

"Yeah, we don't need any of those," Lois said.

I kicked her a second time.

"Millie, I'm seventy years old and can bruise easily," Lois complained.

I'd barely grazed her leg.

I reached across the table and patted Ruth's hand. "I am very sorry this happened. Just because we as women do not run the church does not mean we should not know what is happening."

Lois sat back in her chair. "I've been around Amish my whole life, and from what I have seen, women are the backbone of the church. You all are the real leaders and keep everything going. The men just don't know it."

Ruth glanced at Lois. "I do appreciate the support. There are times . . ."

"There are times, what?" Lois asked.

Ruth sighed. "I believe that *Englischers* think that Amish women are just pushovers because we allow men to lead the church. That is not the case."

"I would never call you a pushover, Ruth," Lois said sincerely.

For a moment, however brief, the adversaries were at peace. I wished that women had more decision-making power in the district. I knew how lucky I was that Uriah treated me as his equal, not as just his wife. I wished that for all women, not just the Amish ones.

"Did Scott say why he didn't want you at the meeting?" I asked.

"He claimed it was a *closed* meeting. Whatever that might mean." Ruth gripped her water glass, although she didn't drink from it again. "I never liked that boy not even when he was in Harvest."

Lois and I stared at her. "What?" we cried at the same time.

"Scott," she said. "I never liked him."

Before I could fully comprehend what she was saying, Ruth added, "Oh, and I forgot. The pig is outside."

Chapter Twenty-six

"What?" I jumped from my chair. "Jethro is outside?"

"Yes, in the stroller. Juliet insisted that I bring him back here to you in that contraption. That was also very insulting. Back home, no one would dare ask me to do such a task. If I had my horse and buggy with me, I would leave in the morning for home."

"That would only take you a hundred years to get back to Ohio by horse and buggy," Lois said.

Ruth glared at her, and peace time was over.

They continued to argue as I threw open the front door and found a stroller sitting outside under the awning. At least Ruth had the good sense to put Jethro in the shade. Pigs could sunburn, and the sun was high in the sky and beating down on Pinecraft and the surrounding area.

Jethro sat up in the carriage that I believed was meant for a dog. There was a mesh cage around the seat. I had seen *Englisch* women in Harvest pushing their dogs around the shops in Harvest in such contraptions. I had always thought it was utterly ridiculous. An Amish person would never walk a dog in such a way, but it just went to show the unlimited differences between the *Englisch* and the Amish.

I unzipped the top, and Jethro stuck his head out.

I leaned forward. "Are you all right?"

He licked my face up one side and down the other.

I pulled a handkerchief from my pocket. It was the very first time that a pig had kissed me. I was grateful that no one had been there to see it.

I opened the door to the bungalow and rolled Jethro and the stroller inside.

Lois and Ruth were still arguing when I walked into the room. While they bickered back and forth, I removed a bowl from the cabinet and filled it with water. I picked up the pig and placed him on the tile floor next to the bowl. He started to drink right away. Poor little oinker. Even in the shade, he must have been hot outside. He wasn't used to hot weather this time of year.

While Jethro drank, I sat back at the table and flattened my hands on the top of it. "Ruth, you can't leave Jethro alone like that."

She looked at me. "It was only for a few minutes."

"Do you have any idea how much trouble he could get into in that time? That's why he needs constant supervision."

Ruth sniffed. "I did not come all the way to Florida to be a pig's babysitter."

"Neither did we," Lois said. "But here we are."

I pinched the bridge of my nose. "*Danki* for telling us Jethro was outside, but please go back and tell us how you know Scott Lawrence."

"I never forget a face," Ruth said. "As soon as I saw him, I knew I recognized him from somewhere. It had to be back in Ohio. I have only left the state three or four times in my lifetime."

"Why didn't you say that you knew Scott before?" Lois asked.

"I didn't know I knew him. It took me some time to place him."

"I thought you never forgot a face," Lois said.

Ruth glared at her. "I haven't seen him in over a decade, and he was just a teenager at the time. I believe you should be impressed that I remember him at all."

Lois held up her hands. "I am. I can't even remember what flavor ice cream I had today."

"It was moose tracks," I said.

"Oh, that's right. It was so good. We have to go back there for more before we leave Pinecraft. It's a long time before the ice cream stands are going to open back home. I can't wait until April for my next ice cream cone."

"Why are we sitting here talking about ice cream?" Ruth folded her arms across her chest. "I thought the two of you wanted to hear about Scott."

"We do!" I shot Lois a look.

She held up her hands as if she was surrendering.

"Please tell us how you know him," I said.

Ruth cleared her throat. "As I said just a moment ago, I never forget a face." She narrowed her eyes at Lois as if daring Lois to contradict her. "I knew the moment that I met Scott that I had seen him before. At first, I thought maybe he was just a tourist that I had seen once or twice in Harvest. You know that we have repeat visitors every year. The faces are familiar over time. We even learn the names and lives of some of the tourists."

This was true. I knew that there were annual visitors in Harvest at Darcy's café on the square. I might not know all of their names, but I knew them when I saw them. That being said, I would never say that I would be able to recognize them out of state and out of context like Ruth had. If that was true, she really never forgot a face.

"They aren't usually young men in their thirties, though," Lois said.

She scowled. "I told you that I was trying to place him, and being a tourist was my first thought. However, the more I thought of it, I guessed that wasn't right because young men his age don't usually come to Amish Country alone. Scott said he wasn't married. If he was married, I would have thought that he came with his family."

"Okay," Lois said. "So how do you know him?"

"He's Amish. He's Ohio Amish."

We stared at her.

"I see that I surprised you."

We both nodded.

"Are you sure?" Lois asked with doubt creeping into her voice.

Ruth scowled at her. "You are no better than any of them at the conference."

"How's that?" I asked.

"After he treated me so poorly, I said to him that he should know how to treat a bishop's wife since he had grown up Amish himself." She slid her glass of water away from her on the table as if it had offended her in some way. "Pastor Ross was dumbfounded at my revelation, and Scott denied it. Even my own husband told me not to make a scene." She sniffed. "I wasn't making a scene. I was stating a fact that as a former Amish young man, he should have known how to treat a bishop's wife."

I wrinkled my nose.

"He wasn't from our district," she said as if I should have known this from the start. "I know members of many districts since my husband is a bishop. The bishops visit other churches from time to time within the order. Even though each district is run separately, it is still *gut* to know what is expected of each congregation."

"Which district is he from?" I asked.

"A much smaller one in Harvest. I have half a mind to write a letter to the bishop's wife of that district and tell her that Scott Lawrence is here."

"Lawrence isn't an Amish last name," Lois said.

"He changed his name when he left the Amish way. Many young Amish do."

"What was his name before?"

"Isaac Zukes," she said.

I thought over the name Zukes, but it didn't mean anything to me. I couldn't think of a single family that had that name, either Amish or *Englisch*.

Lois's phone started to buzz, indicating that she had a video call.

I leaned over the table to see who was calling.

Bailey's smiling face appeared on the small screen.

Lois tapped the screen and propped the phone against the vase. "Bailey, we didn't expect to hear from you so soon."

"As it turned out, I didn't even have to leave my candy factory to find out some news about Caroline Zook." She blinked as she looked at us from the tiny screen. "Ruth, I didn't know that you were there too," she squeaked.

Ruth sniffed. "It is not by my own choice."

"Ruth and Bishop Yoder are attending a church conference here in Pinecraft, and they just so happened to need a place to stay while we were here. Out of the kindness of our hearts we offered them a place," Lois said.

"Oh," Bailey said. "That was very kind of you."

I picked Jethro up from the floor. "He's here too."

Bailey's face broke into a bright smile. "It seems like all the usual suspects are in the same place. It makes me wonder why I'm not down in Florida. Instead, I'm freezing to death in Holmes County and making candy."

"We haven't had the nicest time," Ruth said. "I would much rather be back home in the cold than here where there is no one I can trust."

"Who do you trust in Harvest?" Lois asked.

Ruth glared at her.

I groaned. "Bailey, I'm sure that you are very busy, as you always are. You don't need to listen to us bicker on the phone, you can get enough of that in person when we get home."

Bailey laughed because we all knew it was true. If Lois and Ruth were in the same room, there would be plenty of back and forth. The two of them thrived on it.

"I happened to mention to Charlotte that all you were in Pinecraft this week. When I say all of you, I mean Lois and Millie. I didn't know that you were there, Ruth."

Ruth folded her arms. "Go on."

"She was surprised because she had spoken to an Amish girl who was visiting Ohio from Pinecraft just a few days ago."

"Caroline," I said.

Bailey nodded.

"She said that Caroline stopped by the candy factory and stayed for hours just floating around the gift shop. She didn't want to ask her to leave because it was so terribly cold, and the girl wasn't dressed for the weather. She just had a hooded sweatshirt over her dress and no hat or gloves."

I nodded. It was the same clothing that Caroline had been wearing on the bus.

"Finally, Charlotte asked her if she was all right. She said her name was Caroline and she was waiting for someone, but the person was late and she was afraid they weren't going to come at all. Charlotte invited her to stay a while longer, at least until the factory closed at four. She gave Caroline cookies, a mug of hot chocolate, and a scarf from the gift shop."

I remembered the scarf. At the time, I didn't think much about it, but I realized that perhaps I should have. It was not very Amish. It was bright blue and green. It wasn't the dull colors that were more common among the Amish. Now it made sense to me that it would be from the Candyworks gift shop, which would cater more often to *Englisch* customers, not Amish.

It made me wonder what happened to the scarf. I had not seen it on the beach the morning that Caroline was found. Perhaps Cainan had it at home. He did say they went home before she walked out of the house during their argument. She would not need a thick wool scarf like that in Florida.

"Did the person come?" I asked.

"Not as far as Charlotte knew. At four, as much as she didn't want to, she asked Caroline to leave the factory so she could lock up. She offered her a ride to wherever she might need to go, but Caroline said that she was fine and left. That was the last that she saw her."

"You didn't intervene?" Ruth asked.

Bailey winced. "I would have tried to help her if I knew about it, but I was in New York. I didn't hear about it until today. I wish I had been there. I feel like I would have been able to get the full story out of Caroline."

This was true. Bailey had a knack for convincing people to talk.

Ruth sniffed as if she didn't approve of how Bailey conducted her business. This was likely true. Ruth didn't like how anyone but herself conducted business.

"Does the name Isaac Zukes mean anything to you?" I asked.

Bailey shook her head. "No, should it?"

"*Nee,*" I said.

Bailey looked over her shoulder. "I have to go. We have another tour going in a few minutes. The tours have become very popular at the factory. I'll see what else I can dig up."

Lois ended the call.

The three of us sat back in our chairs.

"Who do you think Caroline was meeting at the candy factory?" Lois asked.

I drummed my fingers on the tabletop. "I don't know, but that meeting could very well be the reason why she was killed."

Chapter Twenty-seven

"We need to make another call," Lois said.

Ruth leaned back in her chair. "To whom?"

"My granddaughter Darcy. If there is any gossip floating around Harvest about Caroline being in the village, Darcy will have heard it at the Sunbeam Café."

Ruth pursed her lips together. "You think the Sunbeam Café is the center of Harvest?"

Lois widened her eyes in mock horror. "It's not?" She tapped on her phone screen.

A moment later, Darcy Woodin's pretty face appeared on the screen. Darcy was Lois's daughter's daughter. Lois's daughter no longer spoke to Lois, and from what I knew, barely spoke to Darcy. It was a touchy subject for Lois, so I rarely brought it up.

However, between grandmother and granddaughter, there was a strong resemblance. Lois and Darcy had the same small nose and gray eyes. Darcy had curly blond hair that looked just like her grandmother's had forty years ago. Sometimes looking at Darcy was like looking back in a time machine to Lois. However, that's where their similarity came to an end.

Darcy was in her late twenties and had never been married. She was a career-minded young woman and had always wanted her own café. She opened the café when she was just twenty-four years old, and now it was one of the most popular places to eat in Holmes County. It was a nice break for tourists and locals alike, away from the heavy Amish fare that could be found in the majority of the area's restaurants, and as Lois said, it was the place for gossip. Both Amish and non-Amish went there to share the latest news about their friends and neighbors in the village.

Darcy looked harried, and I realized that we were calling her at the start of the lunch rush.

"Grams, is everything okay? You're not in jail, are you?" Darcy wanted to know.

"I think it should be noted that asking about jail was one the first questions that came out of Darcy's mouth. That's telling," Ruth said.

Lois rolled her eyes. "I was taken in for questioning, both Millie and I were, but they did not keep us."

"Grams!" Darcy shouted, and then she said to a customer, "I'll be right back with a refill for you." She turned back to the screen. "If you're not in jail, what's wrong? I'm in the middle of the lunch rush."

I could see the collection of teapots in the hutch by the front door. Darcy loved teapots, and Lois took it upon herself to buy every one she could for her granddaughter when she did her weekly loop through all the flea markets in the county looking for vintage furniture and jewelry. That added up to a lot of teapots.

There was a lot of chatter happening on Darcy's end of the call. She ran the Sunbeam Café practically on her own with some part-time help, like that from her grandmother. However, the bulk of the work landed on her shoulders. I believed that was how she liked it too.

"I won't keep you, my girl, but Millie and I found a dead girl."

"Grams!"

"Hush now. We all knew it was going to happen."

"Oh-kay."

"Yes, well, she was the young woman who arrived late to the bus stop. Do you remember her?"

"Oh, yeah, Caroline."

Lois almost dropped her phone. "Wait. You knew who she was?"

"I didn't know her, not really, but she was at the café a few times in the last few weeks."

"Where was I?" Lois asked.

"I think it was always on Tuesdays, and those are your flea market days."

Everyone knew how seriously Lois took flea market shopping.

"Yes, that's right, because she was always there at a slow time. Tuesday is our slowest day for tourists."

All the while Darcy was speaking to her grandmother, she was waiting on her customers. She buzzed from one end of the café to the other, not missing a beat. I supposed to own a busy café, a person needed to be able to multitask, and Darcy was especially good at it.

"She was a sweet girl. I chatted with her a bit. Every time she came in, she just ordered coffee and toast. I don't think she had much money. One time, I was able

to convince her to eat a full breakfast on the house."
She shook her head. "She finally agreed if I let her
wash the dishes."

"Where was she staying?" I asked.

Darcy shook her head. "I don't know. She said she
just moved out on her own."

"Didn't that strike you odd for an Amish girl to say
she moved out?" Lois asked.

Darcy face clouded over. "I didn't want to pry. I know
what it's like to not get along with your parents."

I glanced at Lois, and a blank look crossed her face.
It was the same look that she always got when Darcy's
parents came up.

"Did she say anything else or where she was from?"

Darcy shook her head. "No." She sighed. "It's awful
to hear something happened to her. If she was planning
to stay in Harvest, I would have hired her. She was a
hard worker. She washed all the café's pots and pans in
half the time that it takes me to do it, and they were
sparkling when she was done." She shook her head.
"All I remember was she said she was in Harvest for a
few weeks because she was looking into something for
her father."

Lois and I shared a look. If she was looking into
something for Pastor Ross, he must have known why
she was in Harvest.

"Miss? Miss?" one of the tables called in the back-
ground.

"Sorry, Grams, I have to go. The place is getting
slammed. I'm so sorry about Caroline. Love you." With
that, she ended the call.

Ruth got up from the table. "I'm going to my room

to lie down. I don't know the last time I had such a trying day." She walked to her bedroom and closed the door behind her.

We could hear the lock click.

Lois tapped her colorful nails on the table. "What is she locking her door from us for?"

I ignored her comment because I was grateful that Ruth decided to take a nap. I didn't know how much more I could stand with Lois and Ruth in the same room together.

And I wasn't the only one. Jethro sat on my lap and visibly relaxed when Ruth left the room. It was like all his bones were made of jelly and his little self slumped into me.

"We have to go to the Dutchman Resort and talk to Scott, Isaac Zukes, or whatever his name is," Lois said.

I agreed. I didn't know how this revelation fit into Caroline's death. In truth, it might not be related at all, but I felt in my gut that it was.

Since Jethro was coming with us because we weren't going to leave him with Ruth, I tucked him back in the stroller. At first he kicked at me. He did not want to go into the stroller, and I couldn't say that I blamed him. It must have felt like being in a rolling jail cell. However, I had no choice. The little pig could be unreliable on a leash, and this vacation had already been too eventful with murders and secret identities as it was. I didn't know what Juliet had been thinking when she left the little pig with Ruth.

I pushed the pig's stroller onto the sidewalk as soon as we were out of the bungalows.

"This might be the most memorable scene I have

ever witnessed in my life. An Amish woman walking down a palm tree–lined street pushing a pig in a stroller. Now I have seen everything."

I adjusted my grip on the handlebars of Jethro's stroller.

"That pig travels in style," Lois said. "Oh!"

I looked around. The sidewalk was busy with afternoon walkers, Rollerbladers, and the occasional e-scooter that should have been on the road, but I couldn't blame the rider for wanting to be on the sidewalk as the traffic to the beach picked up with the rise in temperatures that afternoon.

"Hey, isn't that Cainan's sister Tabitha?" Lois asked.

I looked down the sidewalk and saw that she was right. Just like Cainan, Tabitha had striking white-blond hair. The prayer cap did nothing to mask it, and I didn't believe that she would want to hide it. She had gorgeous hair. By the way she patted it here and there, it was clear to me that it was a feature of pride for her.

"It is," I said.

Tabitha marched with purpose down one of the many side trails between the hotels and gift shops that led to the beach. She had her head bent down as if she was concentrating on every step.

"She looks angry," Lois said. "Then again, she might always be in a foul mood. She has that air about her, just like Ruth Yoder. I bet she and Ruth would get along great."

When we reached the trailhead where Tabitha had disappeared from the sidewalk, Lois took a sharp left down the path.

"Where are you going?" I asked.

"Where does it look like I'm going? After Tabitha."

"I thought you wanted to go to the resort and speak to Scott," I said.

"I do, but we can't pass up this golden opportunity to talk to her. She is on our suspect list. I mean, she didn't want Caroline marrying her brother, right? And the scooter shop where she works is just a short walk down the beach from where Caroline's body washed up. Motive, opportunity." Lois ticked the two points off on her fingertips.

This was true.

The gravel path gave way to sand, and Jethro and his carriage got stuck.

"The stroller is never going to work on the beach," I said.

Lois sighed. "Listen, you stay here and I will just walk to the end of the path to see if I can spot her. Maybe she just went for a walk."

While Lois walked down the path in search of Tabitha, I tried to pull Jethro's stroller out of the sand. With the pig inside the carriage, the wheels would not budge. I tried to pick up the stroller instead of rolling it, but it was too awkward and I nearly fell.

There really was only one answer. It was to remove Jethro from the stroller and then move it back onto the gravel.

I sighed and unzipped Jethro's carriage. The little pig looked up at me with his round brown eyes and bopped me in the nose with his snout.

"I'm going to take you out while I move the stroller," I told the little pig like he could understand me. "While I am moving the stroller, you stay put. Do you hear me?"

He just looked at me with those doe-like eyes. I had no confidence that he understood a word that I had said.

I pulled him from the stroller and set him in the sand. "Stay."

He sat on his behind, and I thought for a moment that might actually have gotten through to the little pig. I think other than Bailey King, no one else had before.

I pulled back on the stroller's handlebar and now, free of the pig, it moved easily onto the gravel. I turned to pick up Jethro to put him back into the stroller, but he was gone.

Chapter Twenty-eight

I rubbed my forehead. That little pig was going to be the death of me. When I returned home I promised myself that I would never complain about the antics of my goats, Phillip and Peter, ever again. The two of them combined were easier to take care of than one toaster-sized pig.

"Jethro!" I looked up and down the path.

It was empty. There was no sign of life, much less a pig anywhere around me.

I wasn't cut out for pig sitting. I would gladly turn those duties back over to Bailey. Juliet would be very hard-pressed indeed to convince me to care for Jethro again after this trip.

"Jethro?" There was just a hint of panic setting in when I called him the second time. I suspected that the urgency was in my voice because there was a faint whimper coming from the shrubbery to the right that lined my path.

I walked over to the bush's edge. "Jethro?"

The whimper came again.

The bush wasn't really a bush at all but a large cluster of sea grapes, a native plant along the beaches of Florida. When I wasn't speaking to Caroline on the bus on the way here, I had been reading all about Pinecraft from a tour book that Lois had brought with her. It had proven to be a wealth of information.

I pushed the leaves away for a better look and saw Jethro in the middle of the tangled roots of the massive plant. He lay on his belly under the sea grapes. His hooves were stretched out around him windmill style. It took my breath away seeing him like that until I heard him snoring.

It seemed that Ruth wasn't the only one who needed a nap that afternoon.

I put my hands on my hips. "Jethro, this is no time for a nap. Don't you know we are investigating a murder?"

He looked over his shoulder at me and then laid his head back down again in the sand.

"Come out of there."

I looked up the path that Lois had taken, but there was no sign of her. I didn't know how long she would be gone, and I didn't want Jethro to be spooked by a bird or lizard and run off.

"Please come out," I told the pig.

He didn't move.

He was too far in the middle of the shrub for me to reach, so I had no choice but to climb in to get him.

I pushed the stroller to the side of the path and

moved the sea grapes for a better look at Jethro. Muttering a prayer, I bent in half and shuffled into the shrub.

When I was a young Amish girl growing up in Holmes County, this was not something I would have imagined that I would be doing in my twilight years.

Something creepy-crawly fell onto the top of my head, and I batted it away. I gave a full body shiver. Typically, I wasn't so squeamish when it came to nature, but that was back home where I knew every kind of plant and creature I might find. Here, I didn't know much more than what I read in that travel book Lois brought.

Jethro jumped up with a squeal and bolted out the other side of the sea grapes. This was exactly what I didn't want to happen.

As quickly as I could, I made my way through the dense shrub, but I was a seventy-year-old woman, not a terrified small pig. When I came out the other side, I was covered in twigs and leaves, and who-knew-what-else. I didn't see Jethro anywhere.

I was beside a large shed that stood with its doors wide open. Behind the shed was a dune covered with tall grass. Just on the other side of the dune was the beach. I imagined Lois was on the other side of that dune, doing one of her "sting" operations while she stalked Tabitha.

Jethro was nowhere to be seen, and I grew worried. My best guess was he went into the shed to hide.

If I didn't find him soon, I would have to look for help. If anything happened to that little pig, I would never forgive myself.

Outside the shed, there were a number of bicycles and scooters in different states of disrepair.

I stepped into the shed. To my left, ten or twelve e-scooters were plugged into the generator, all being charged up before they could be rented out again. Clearly, this was Cainan's work area for the shop.

"Hello? Is anyone in here?" I called.

No one spoke back.

I stepped forward again, and my foot slipped. I braced myself on a nearby stool. There was a thin coating of sand on the concrete. I supposed sand was something a person couldn't escape if their business was this close to the beach.

When I found my footing, I took everything in. A bicycle lay on its side. It was just the frame. The wheels had been removed. Bits of wire and metal were strewn all over the table. It was as if the bicycle was in the middle of surgery.

As Amish we didn't embrace most *Englisch* technology, but many *Englischers* were surprised at how many Amish were skilled at mechanics and engine work. We had to be just to survive.

"Jethro? Are you in here?" I asked in a hoarse whisper.

Nothing.

"Jethro, you are clearly causing me to trespass, so if you could make yourself known, I would appreciate it."

A snuffling sound came from the back of the shop.

I found Jethro in the very back corner of the shop with his face buried in a cat food bowl. It seemed in times of stress, like many people, myself included, the little pig turned to food. A large brown tabby glowered down from a shelf as he saw his dinner disappear under Jethro's nose.

Before Jethro could take off again, I leaned down and picked him up. "This will be the last time that you run away from me on this trip."

He looked up at me and licked my nose. His breath smelled like cat food.

I turned and apologized to the cat for Jethro's poor behavior. She hissed in reply.

"This is not the way to make friends," I told the pig.

I stepped around the shelves when I saw movement at the other end of the shed. A tall Amish man with broad shoulders and a dark brown beard stepped into the shed. It most certainly wasn't Cainan Zook but his brother-in-law Malachi Grabill. Malachi walked over to the worktable and began clearing away the bits of wire and metal. He dropped them into a five-gallon bucket.

I looked around with the hopes of finding a back door or other means of escape, but there was nothing. I didn't feel like I could march through the shed and say I was just here for the pig.

Tabitha came into the room. "One of those nutty old ladies from Ohio followed me all over the beach. I couldn't make it to the spot without being seen."

"Well, you are going to have to find some way to get there," Malachi said gruffly. He picked up a wrench and began loosening one of the bolts on the bike frame.

"Malachi, I have done all that I can for this mess that you have put us in. I wash my hands of it."

Malachi turned around. "You can't be done with it. You're my wife, and you have to do what I say."

Tabitha scowled at her husband.

"Or do you think of yourself as Amish like Caroline claimed to be Amish," he scoffed.

"How can you say such a thing? I am nothing like that *Englischer*. She just wanted to marry my *bruder* to run away from her problems. She didn't care if she was going to ruin his life in the process."

"She can't ruin anyone's life now," Malachi said.

The words hung in the air between them.

Finally, Tabitha spoke. "I didn't want this for her or for my brother."

"You put it in motion."

Tabitha paled. "I didn't. You did. It was your idea."

"Because I was doing what you wanted. You were furious over Cainan running off and getting married to that *Englisch* girl. I found a way to make her leave."

"She is gone. She's dead," Tabitha said. "It's not what I wanted at all. I would never want that."

I jerked back. Was I listening to Tabitha and her husband Malachi confess to murdering Caroline Zook? With the beach just a few hundred feet away, they had the opportunity. Did they kill her because she married Cainan? But why? She converted to being Amish for Cainan, something that was rarely done by an *Englischer*.

I bumped into the shelf, and the jars of nuts and bolts above my head rattled. The cat jumped off the shelf onto the floor. Jethro and I froze.

"What was that?" Malachi shouted. "Is someone else in here?"

"Who else would be in here?" his wife asked. "Cainan is at the resort."

The large brown tabby looked up at me and gave the slightest of nods before sauntering out into the open.

"It's just Macy the cat," Tabitha said.

"That cat is a menace," Malachi grumbled.

"Don't say anything like that about Macy. She's a very *gut* cat."

Malachi snorted as if he didn't fully agree with his wife.

"I don't want to discuss this anymore," Tabitha said. "I have made up my mind. I'm not going to be involved in this any longer. If you wish to continue, that is your choice. Now come inside, I have lunch ready for you." She walked out of the shed. Macy, the brown tabby, followed behind her.

Malachi remained at the worktable and swore. He then threw his wrench on the table. It hit the bicycle frame and went careening onto the floor. He swore a second time and then stomped out of the shed.

Jethro and I didn't move for several minutes. I don't think either of us dared to take a breath.

Finally, the little pig in my arms whimpered.

"You're right," I whispered. "It's time to get out of here." I stepped out from behind the shelves and looked this way and that.

There was no one there. I hoped Malachi and Tabitha were safely inside the shop enjoying their lunch.

I squinted at the bright sunshine when I stepped outside the shed. When I could see again, I tried to decide which way I could get away from Zook's Scooters without being seen. If I climbed over the dune to the beach,

I would be making a target of myself, and if I walked back the shop, I would surely be seen in one of its many windows.

I had one and only choice. Back through the sea grapes I went.

Chapter Twenty-nine

When I came out on the other side of the shrub, I found Lois sitting in the middle of the path next to the stroller with the entire contents of her massive patchwork purse strewn all around her. It was an amazing number of things. She had brushes, hairpins, lipstick, and packets of tissues, which were all things that you would expect in a woman's purse. But she also had a full-sized stapler, lockpicks, a bag of gummy worms, and a brick. The brick was a staple in Lois's purse.

She was chomping on a gummy worm when I came out of the sea grapes. Her mouth hung open and half of the gummy worm that had been in her mouth fell to the sand. "Millie, where have you been? I thought you were abducted by aliens."

"Aliens?" I asked as I removed one of the flat, palm-sized leaves of the shrub from the top of my head.

"Sure," she said. "The stroller was just sitting here alone on the path like you had been snatched away."

"And why did you empty your purse?"

"I thought I would organize it while the aliens had you. From what I read, when they reject someone, they drop them back in the same spot where they found them. I guessed that after fifteen minutes with Jethro on their spaceship, they would send you back."

I squinted at my best friend as if to see if she was making this all up.

She gathered up her things and tossed them back into the purse. If she was hoping to be more organized, I didn't think that was the way to do it. When everything was back in the bag, she stood up.

"Did you find Tabitha?" I put Jethro into the carriage and zipped it shut. He wasn't getting away from me again.

Lois shook her head. "She lost me. I think she knew she was being tailed. It's never good when the mark knows."

"The mark?" I asked.

"Spy talk. You wouldn't understand."

No, I wouldn't.

"Well, while you were getting organized, I was chasing after Jethro." I picked up the tissue and lipstick and handed them to her.

Lois shook her head. "I should have known it was the pig that ran off. That makes a lot more sense than an alien abduction."

I decided not to comment on that.

"Jethro ran into a shed behind the scooter shop, and Tabitha and her husband Malachi were there."

"Oh?" Lois brushed sand from her backside.

"I was inside the shed looking for Jethro, and they didn't know I was there when they came in."

"And you hid, right?"

"Of course."

Lois nodded her approval. "That's my girl. They don't call you Amish Marple for nothing."

"They were talking about Caroline and some kind of spot, at least that is what Tabitha called it 'the spot.'" I paused. "They were talking about Caroline, and I think they just might have admitted to killing her."

Lois stared at me with her mouth hanging open. "How? Tell me everything word for word."

I promised Lois that I would, but we still needed to speak to Scott Lawrence/Isaac Zukes.

"Let's walk and I will tell you on the way," I said.

I pushed the stroller off the path and back onto the palm tree-lined sidewalk. The stroller moved much more easily on the sidewalk even though it was making some kind of grinding sound as the sand worked itself out of the wheels.

While we walked, I filled Lois in on what I had overhead in the shed.

"There you go," Lois said, holding up her hands. "We have our killers. Let's tell the police and let this be the end of it."

"We don't know for sure that either Tabitha or her husband killed Caroline. I don't want to make accusations like that if we could be wrong. The family tension between Tabitha and her husband and Cainan is already very high."

"We can't sit on this information," Lois said.

"We won't," I said. "Let's talk to Scott first."

"And give Jethro back to Juliet."

I looked down at the little pig, who had fallen asleep

in the stroller. He had had a very big day. I had too. A nap sounded like a perfect solution, but I knew I never would be able to fully rest until Caroline's killer was caught.

We walked up to the resort and were surprised to find dozens of people standing out on the sidewalk. There were people in resort uniform, Amish people, *Englischers* in all manners of dress from shorts and tank tops to summer dresses and professional attire.

I walked up to one of the Amish ladies standing on the grass. "What has happened?"

She looked at me. "There was a fire somewhere in the resort. We have no choice but to leave. The fire marshal said that the whole building could go up."

I placed a hand to my chest. "How horrible."

She nodded. "It was, and we were in the middle of a really interesting session about children in the church. I hope they will continue it when we go back inside."

"You're here for the conference?" I asked.

She nodded. "My husband is a bishop here in Pinecraft and was asked to come. He was hesitant at first."

"Why?" I asked.

Before she answered the question, she asked one of her own. "Where is your district?"

"Holmes County, Ohio," I said.

She nodded. "You looked to be Ohio Amish to me."

I nodded, understanding what she meant. Perhaps to the *Englisch,* Amish and even conservative Mennonites all looked the same, but there were subtle differences that we, as Amish, could see. I could easily note the differences between an Old Order Amish person and New Order Amish person.

"I'm Millie Fisher Schrock," I said.

She smiled. "Aggie Troyer. My husband is Bishop Troy Troyer. Why his parents named him Troy with their last name I will never know. To make matters worse, our son is named Troy too because my husband wanted a junior. I'm certain that legacy will go on and on through the family line. I don't think my husband's parents thought all that out when they named their son."

"Troy Troyer is a strong name and not one you will soon forget."

"*Danki.*"

"Why was your husband hesitant in attending?" I asked.

"Because the Amish and *Englisch* here in Pinecraft are already so close and intertwined. You will find that it's different than what you are used to back in Ohio."

"I have noticed some differences," I said.

"Part of the reason that it's challenging to separate ourselves here is because of space. We are surrounded by *Englischers* or the ocean. There isn't anywhere to spread out. We don't have the large farms and wide expanses that you have in Ohio. Children are more easily exposed to the *Englisch* way here. We cannot keep it from them."

It was becoming more and more difficult to keep Amish children in Ohio away from *Englisch* influence as well, but I knew it had to be that much more difficult in Pinecraft.

"My friend Lois and I rented e-scooters from an Amish business close to here. I just wondered if you know it."

"You must mean Zook's Scooters. *Ya*, we know it

well. The Zook family have been longtime members of our district. Cainan and his sister Tabitha grew up in the district. We were so proud of Cainan when he opened his shop when he was still a teenager. He's been so successful, and he has shared that success with his family and the district. From the start, Tabitha and her husband have been part of the business. I know it is the Amish way to work with family, but it's not always enjoyable." She said this as if she was speaking from experience. "But from what I know, Tabitha and Cainan truly enjoyed working together until lately."

"Until Caroline joined them?" I asked.

She made a pained expression. "*Ya.* I believe Tabitha didn't believe that anyone would ever be *gut* enough for her *bruder*, but an *Englischer* would be her very last choice. She is very protective of Cainan. She is quite a bit older than him and mostly raised him herself. Their parents passed when Cainan was small."

I nodded. Now it was making more sense to me why Tabitha was so protective of Cainan. She didn't see him as a brother; she saw him as a son. That was a major distinction.

"I was so sorry to hear what happened to Caroline."

Her shoulders relaxed. "You know? That is *gut*. It's always difficult to know how much I should and could say."

"You can say whatever you like about it to me," I said, and I hoped that she would. If I knew more about the marriage, then maybe I would be able to find out what really happened to Caroline.

"They were married a few weeks back," I said hoping to encourage her to share more.

"They were legally married, *ya*, in the eyes of the *Englisch*," Aggie said. "But they were not married in the Amish faith. My husband was advising Cainan what to do. The bishop suggested that Caroline live like an Amish woman for a year before they wed. If she did that, she could make a better decision as to if this was the life she wanted. I didn't doubt that she loved Cainan. However, love seems hardly enough to give up your whole life."

"So, it would be like a reverse *rumspringa*."

"*Ya*." She nodded. "It would be very much like that. Just like Amish young people need to see the *Englisch* ways to decide about joining the church, so do *Englischers*."

"She didn't take that time," I said.

Aggie shook her head. "They were young and impulsive. Truly, I did not know why they were so set to rush into marriage, especially since Caroline grew up *Englisch*. I read that the *Englisch* are waiting longer and longer to marry now."

"I think she needed a place to live," I said.

Aggie nodded. "That might be the practical reason, but no reason to rush into a marriage. We also would have set her in an Amish home so she could learn the Amish way before her wedding. It's terrible what happened to the poor girl—and her father. My husband has been close friends with Pastor Ross for a very long time. Our hearts break for him. However, I believe that Cainan and Caroline would certainly butt heads if they'd had the chance. There were already cracks in the foundation of the marriage. They were only married a few days when she left for Ohio. The bishop spoke to Cainan after she left. He told him that this was not a *gut* way to start life with another person, and even so early on, he worried that the two of them would end up divorced." She paused. "And he wasn't the only one. Everyone in the district was concerned, and it seemed that we had *gut* reasons to be. However, we never thought that it would end like this. Tabitha did not approve of the marriage, but few members of the community did."

"How far do you think she would have gone to stop it?" I shifted my stance.

Aggie looked me in the eye. "To any length."

I shivered.

"False alarm!" a young man in a firefighter's uniform called. "There is no fire. It was just a prank. You can all go back into the building."

"A prank?" someone yelled in the crowd. "What do you mean by prank?"

"Someone pulled the fire alarm. I reset the system. You can all go back inside. It's safe. There was never a fire to begin with."

Slowly the crowd of employees made their way back inside. Lois walked up next to me while pushing Jethro in his stroller. "You spoke with that Amish woman for a long time, and you were speaking your language. I could only understand a handful of words." She shook her head. "Who is she?"

"She's the wife of Cainan's bishop."

"Oh? Did you learn anything?" She rolled Jethro's stroller back and forth.

I watched the line of people going back into the resort. "Just how much Tabitha hated Caroline."

Chapter Thirty

Lois and I finally made our way into the resort. Pastor Ross stood in the entryway directing people who were attending his conference where they should go next.

Lois push Jethro's stroller up to him. "Don't you have someone else who can direct traffic for you?"

Pastor Ross pressed his lips together. "Typically, it would be Scott who would do this, or he would ask one of the volunteers, but I haven't seen him since last night." He shook his head. "It's not like him at all to just leave and not tell me."

"That's strange," Lois said. "He was on the kayak trip the conference organized this morning."

"He was?" Pastor Ross asked. "I didn't know he was attending that. I know he was upset by something that one of our attendees said, but he can't just abandon the conference when we still have two days left."

"Bishop and Ruth Yoder are staying with us. We know that Ruth claimed that Scott was Amish and she knew him from Ohio. She said that he was very upset when she made the announcement."

"He was upset and insulted, I would say," Pastor Ross said. "She must have him mixed up with someone else. Scott swore to me up and down that he wasn't Amish and had never been to Ohio."

Why would he deny he grew up Amish? Why would it matter? And why was it such a tightly guarded secret?

Over the years, I have met many people who grew up Amish. They all wanted to share about it in varying degrees. Some were happy to speak about it and others wanted nothing to do with it. However, I had never had anyone deny it before.

"Why, though?" Lois asked as if she had been able to hear my thoughts. "Would it make any difference to you as his boss?"

Pastor Ross shook his head. "No, not at all." His face grew pinched. "I just do not understand why he would leave me in a lurch at a time like this. He, more than anyone, knows what I have gone through with my daughter and how much pain I am in over losing her."

"Is there anything that we can do to help?" I asked. "We can direct traffic for you."

"No." He shook his head but stopped mid-shake. "Is the pig in there?"

Lois rocked the stroller back and forth as if she was putting Jethro down for a nap, but she didn't need to do that as the pig was already out cold. "He's had a very eventful day. I am sure that he would be very happy to be reunited with Juliet."

Pastor Ross shook his head. "I changed my mind.

There is something that you can do for me. You can take that pig out of this resort and never bring him back. He's just one more complication I cannot handle."

When Pastor Ross walked away, Lois said, "That was rude. I'm glad Jethro is sleeping so he didn't hear what the mean pastor said."

"After the day he's had, I'm sure Jethro would rather be with his mistress than us," I said.

Lois called Juliet to see if she would come down and get her pig. She held the phone to her ear. "It's going straight to voicemail." She tapped on the screen. "Let me call Reverend Brook." She paused and listened. "His call went right to voicemail too."

Jethro woke up in his stroller and sat up.

"Looks like he will be going back to the bungalow with us," I said.

Lois sighed. "Another night with the Yoders and a pig. It sounds like an old country song, but a really pathetic one."

"Before that, we have one more stop," I said.

"The volleyball game. Don't think I forgot. I have been working on my serve."

I narrowed my eyes. "I haven't seen you doing that."

"In my head, Millie," she said with a sigh. "It's all about visualization."

Before going to the Amish youth volleyball game, Lois and I pushed Jethro's stroller back to our bungalow. The little pig hopped out of the stroller as soon as we opened it in the bungalow's kitchen.

He pressed his snout to the floor in search of food. When he didn't find any, he looked up at Lois with his big brown eyes as if he was asking her for mercy or for some spaghetti. According to Juliet, he really loves Italian food.

I didn't have any pig food on hand but went to the kitchen and found him a snack of crackers and apple slices.

Lois went into our bedroom door. "What does one wear to Amish volleyball?"

I looked down at my dress. "Probably what I'm wearing."

"Millie, I love you, but no. I'm not going that deep undercover. Let me change and we can head out."

"What about Jethro?" I asked as he happily munched away.

"What about him?"

"Should we leave him here or take him with us?"

Lois put her hands on her hips and looked down at the little pig. "Hmm. I vote for taking him. He might break the ice for us. I mean, he is a conversation piece." She wagged her finger at the little pig. "But if you try to run off, your bacon is fried."

He covered his eyes with his hoof.

Ten minutes later, Lois reappeared from the bedroom. She was wearing bright orange capri pants, a flowy pink blouse, and a baseball cap covered in rhinestones. She cracked her knuckles. "I'm ready to serve!"

I shook my head and snapped Jethro's leash on him. "Please be a *gut* pig."

He looked up at me as if to question why I would think he would be anything else.

"It's going to be dark out on the beach," I said.

Lois put her hand in her purse and came out with a

large flashlight. "We could see Mexico with this thing."
She turned it on and hit me in the eyes.

"Ahh! Lower the light."

"Sorry. Just a little trigger happy."

As we left the bungalow, I was still blinking black
dots from my eyes.

Lois pointed the flashlight at the ground, but she
was right, it was powerful. We could see fifty feet in
front of us at least.

When we walked over the path on the dune to the
beach, we quickly learned that the flashlight wasn't
needed. To our right was the outline of the pier, and beyond that was a volleyball court that was lit up like an
Englisch Christmas tree.

"Are those electric lights?" Lois asked.

I nodded.

Jethro lifted his snout in the air and sniffed.

The Amish youth also had a fire going where they
were roasting marshmallows. Jethro loved marshmallows. He had infamously attacked Juliet's marshmallow frosted wedding cake. It was a bit of Harvest
lore at this point.

He tugged on his leash.

"All right, Jethro, we are going that way, but I don't
know that Juliet wants you to have any sugar this time
of night."

He pulled on the leash hard. I began walking with
him because I didn't want him to pull so hard that he
ripped the leash out of my hand, even though I had the
end of it wrapped around my hand. Twice.

As we crossed under the pier, Lois turned off her

flashlight and tucked it back into her purse. There was plenty of light to see. The volleyball court was bright, as if it was high noon. Four lights rose ten feet in the air, all on wheels. It was quite the setup. It seemed that the Pinecraft Amish took volleyball very seriously.

A generator hummed nearby with a snake's nest of electrical cords running out from it to the various lights. For someone not used to the Amish, this must have all looked very strange. Here they were using electric lights for recreation. Not all Amish would do that, this is true. However, the Pinecraft Amish tended, by reputation, to be a bit looser on their rules, and most of the youth at this volleyball game were still in *rumspringa*. When they are in *rumspringa*, they can experiment with the *Englisch* life.

This not only applied to the lights but to the clothing too. The dress varied quite a bit, so Lois really wasn't that out of place in her outfit even if it was much brighter than anything the Amish young people were wearing.

Some of the girls were even wearing jeans and capris. If I didn't know that this was an Amish youth gathering, I might have mistaken many of them for *Englisch* teenagers.

A volleyball game was in progress when Lois and I came upon the group. A tall Amish man served the ball, and the two teams volleyed back and forth for a little while until the same Amish man spiked the ball into the other team's court.

"Game!" one of the people on the sidelines called.

The winning team cheered, and the losing team was good-natured enough to congratulate them.

The players, both men and women, walked off the court.

The young man who spiked the ball dusted sand off his shoulder and stood just a few feet from Lois, Jethro, and me.

"Is that a pig?" he asked.

I looked down at Jethro. One very *gut* thing that I had to say about the pig was he was an excellent conversation starter. People always want to talk to someone who is walking a pig. I could vouch for that.

I picked Jethro up and walked over to him. "It is. We are pigsitting for a friend of ours."

"An *Englisch* friend, I would guess," he said with a laugh.

"To be sure," I agreed. "Nice work making that final point."

"*Danki*. All our games are for fun, but I would be lying if I didn't say that I wanted to win. Volleyball is my favorite sport."

"I remember playing it when I was your age. Now I don't think that my knees could take it."

He looked from Lois to me and back. "I'm Edgar. Are you looking for someone?"

"We are Millie and Lois," Lois said. She pointed at me and then herself. "We were out for a walk looking for crabs. I'm very interested in crabs," Lois said. "I heard they came out at night. I was looking for any sign of them."

He gave her a strange look as if he didn't quite believe what she was saying. He had *gut* reason not to, since she made it up on the spot.

"Well," Edgar said. "You will want to turn around

here. You can't go any farther up the beach with a flashlight. Up ahead lights at night aren't allowed because sea turtles might be nesting."

Lois clapped her hands. "I would love to see that, but we won't go any farther. We don't want to upset the sea turtles. I will also have you know that I never use disposable straws because of them."

Edgar wrinkled his forehead.

"I did have one question," I said. "Is this where Cainan Zook played volleyball?"

The young man's eyes went wide. "Why are you asking about Cainan?" His tone turned from friendly to guarded in a moment.

Lois had a ready answer. "We rented scooters from him and heard about his wife. It's so tragic."

Edgar relaxed a bit. "*Ya*, it is horrible. I'm sorry if I snapped at you. Cainan is a *gut* friend of mine, and I know that he's hurting. You won't find him here. Cainan doesn't come to the volleyball games anymore. He hasn't since he got married."

"I didn't expect to find him here," I said. "We are friends of his wife Caroline and just wanted to see a place that she talked about all the time."

He looked at Lois and me and back again with suspicion. "The person you want to talk to is Becka. She knows Cainan and Caroline the best."

"Where is she?" Lois asked.

Edgar pointed at a tall blond Amish girl. She wore a long plain skirt, but on top she wore a Mickey Mouse sweatshirt. The crossover of Amish and non-Amish made my head spin.

"You can talk to Becka if you want to talk about this. I don't want anything to do with it." Edgar backed away.

"Why's that?" Lois asked.

He didn't answer and walked away.

"Well, that was rude," Lois said.

"I think we should be happy that we got out of him what we did."

Lois and I walked across the sand to Becka. She was standing with another Amish girl by the fire roasting marshmallows. Jethro's tail wiggled with anticipation at the closeness to the marshmallows. He licked his lips.

"Becka?" I greeted.

The blond girl turned and looked at us. "*Ya.*"

"We would like to talk to you about Caroline and Cainan."

The other Amish girl who was with her suddenly walked away.

Becka watched her friend leave with narrowed eyes. She wasn't going to forget this abandonment.

"We were told you know Cainan well."

"*Ya,* as we were promised to each other."

"What?" Lois asked. "He married Caroline."

"I know that," Becka said. "But he was promised to me. His parents and mine are close friends, and they always encouraged us to marry one day. I thought that Cainan was planning to do that too. He gave me the impression that he was until Caroline showed up."

"Did he say he'd marry you?" Lois asked.

"*Nee,* but that is not how it works in our community. You court. I was being courted, or at least I was until that *Englischer* showed her face here. When that happened, it was like I had never existed."

I pursed my lips together and could not help but wonder if Becka misread the signals from Cainan. In Amish courting, intentions were made clear from the beginning. So it was also possible that he simply left Becka for Caroline too.

"It was too late when I realized what was happening. I would see them talking and laughing at the volleyball games, but I wasn't worried. She was *Englisch*. Nothing would come of it. Little did I know all that time they were plotting and planning behind my back." She poked her marshmallow deeper in the flames. I wondered if she was imagining it was Caroline or maybe even Cainan.

She pulled the marshmallow out of the blaze. It was still aflame. She blew on the blackened husk of a marshmallow. "It wasn't until Tabitha came to one of the volleyball games and got into a fight in front of all our friends with Cainan over courting Caroline that I learned what was happening. By that time, it was too late. He made up his mind it was Caroline he wanted. There was nothing I could do or say to change his mind. But I knew she wasn't right for him. He ruined his relationship with his sister and all his friends for her."

"But you were right for him?" Lois guessed.

"I would have been, but I'm not taking him back now," she snapped.

"Now that Caroline is dead," I said.

She narrowed her eyes at me. "I didn't wish her dead, if that's what you are implying. I just wanted her gone. *Nee*, I wanted her never to have shown her face on this beach." She smashed her charcoal marshmallow between chocolate and graham crackers. "That's all I have to say about that." With that she stomped away.

Lois watched her go. "I can respect a girl who will wait until she constructed the perfect s'more before storming off."

My shoulders sagged. "I just can't see that young girl killing anyone."

"Jealousy is a major motive for crime."

An old Amish proverb came to my mind: "Every time you turn green with envy, you are ripe for trouble."

"I know that, but to drown someone and hold them under the water. That's just too cruel. You really believe a girl like that could do it?"

"I've know my share of mean girls in my life. I wouldn't put it past them."

I heard a snuffling sound at my feet, I looked down to find Jethro had knocked the marshmallow bag from where it was sitting on the log and had his face buried in it.

"Get him out of there," I said. "He could suffocate."

"What a way to go, though," Lois said as she pulled the pig's face from the bag. "With a mouth full of delicious marshmallows."

Jethro was free from the bag and gulped down the four marshmallows in his mouth before I could take them away from him.

"He's going to sugar crash hard," Lois said.

"I think we are all going to crash hard. Let's head back to the bungalow."

Jethro seemed to agree with this idea as he pulled on his lead in the direction of the bungalow. The little pig was smart and ready to go to bed. I can't say that I blamed him. I felt much the same from the kayaking in the morning to the volleyball game at night.

"Let's walk up to the road," Lois said. "I feel a little bad about having a flashlight on the beach with sea turtles around." I agreed and we walked away from the water. Over the dune, a building came into view.

"Is that the scooter shop?" Lois asked.

"*Ya*, and the shed where Jethro and I hid from Tabitha and Malachi earlier today."

Lois looked over her shoulder. "Do you think it means anything that it is so close to where the Amish youth play volleyball?"

"I don't know, but it could."

Lois and I finished our climb over the dune. It wasn't so easy for a couple of more mature ladies. It didn't help that Jethro ran this way and that on his leash as the sugar hit his system. The little pig should never have marshmallows. I reminded myself to tell Bailey that when we got home since Jethro spent so much time in the candy shop or candy factory.

The back of the scooter shop's property was quiet. There was a security light, but other than that it was dark.

"If we can climb over that dune," Lois said, "it is easy to believe that any spry young person from the scooter shop would be able to as well."

I nodded.

I knew that Cainan lived over the shop. I looked up at the windows. Just as I did, one of the curtains in those windows moved. Someone had been standing there, waiting and watching. Was it Cainan? Did he wish that he made different choices in his life? Did he wish he never met Caroline and just married an Amish girl like Becka?

My eyes traveled below the window just in time for me to see a figure disappear into the sea grapes on the edge of the property.

"There's someone over there," I whispered. "By the sea grapes."

"What are we waiting for? Let's go get them."

Before I could stop her, Lois took off for the sea grapes at a trot.

"Lois," I hissed, but it was too late. She disappeared into the bushes.

Chapter Thirty-one

I had no desire to climb back into the sea grapes in the dark. My skin crawled at the thought of what bugs, snakes, and other critters might be hiding in there for the night. As usual, Lois didn't have the same problem.

Since I had been inside the sea grapes before, I knew where Lois would come out on the other side. I picked up Jethro and walked as fast as I dared in the dark through the scooter shop's property to the sidewalk. I then came down the path on the other side of the sea grapes just in time to see Tabitha glaring at Lois.

"How dare you follow me like that," Tabitha shouted. "I thought someone was trying to kill me."

"Kill you? Kill you? Do I look like a killer?" Lois wanted to know.

"I don't know. I don't know what they look like. I've never seen one."

I caught my breath and set Jethro on the sandy path.

He had grown heavy in my arms. "Tabitha, we are so sorry that we frightened you. Lois and I were on a walk on the beach and decided to come up to the sidewalk because it was so dark."

"Why are you walking on the beach in the middle of the night?" Tabitha asked. "It's too cold out for such foolishness."

"You should visit Ohio if you want to see cold," Lois said.

"When you saw it was us, why did you run away?" I asked.

"I couldn't see who it was. As you said yourself, it's very dark out. I wanted to get out of the way in case it was someone dangerous. An Amish woman alone can never be too careful."

"I would say any woman alone can never be too careful," Lois corrected.

Tabitha sniffed. "I believe that the two of you have caused enough uproar for the night. I need to head home. My husband will be wondering where I am."

"Do you live with your brother over the shop?" I asked.

"Of course not," Tabitha snapped. "But I was working late and was on my way home. I handle all the books and paperwork for the business. My job doesn't end at closing time. I thought I heard something outside. I knew that the youth were having a volleyball game tonight. I wanted to make sure they weren't up to any funny business on our property. Sometimes they can get rowdy. People don't believe that about Amish teenagers and young people, but it's true. Not all of them are well behaved."

I was very aware this was true, and so was Lois. She had lived in Amish country long enough to know it.

"Since you are working late alone," I said, "I'm surprised that your husband isn't here with you."

She glared at me. "Why would he be? He's a very busy man."

"But doesn't he work here?"

"*Nee.* I mean he does, but not full-time. He helps out with fixing the scooters and bikes, but he has many business ventures. He's very successful," she said with a note of pride.

Lois cocked her head. "Is that what the Amish want to be? Successful?"

"We want to be able to provide for our family and give back to our community, so *ya,* that is true."

I agreed with Tabitha on this point. There was an aspect of entrepreneurship in the Amish community. As a people, we wanted to have work that we were proud of, but I didn't understand why she was so offended by Lois's question.

Tabitha touched her neck. "I left my scarf in the shop." She shook her head. "It's not that cold tonight. I will get it tomorrow. Now, I really must be going. My husband will be worried." She walked quickly to the sidewalk and disappeared around the corners of the sea grapes.

"Something is up with her," Lois said.

I agreed.

Jethro snuffled. I looked down and saw him sleeping on his side with his mouth open on the sandy path. Apparently, Jethro's sugar crash came earlier than expected.

I sighed. "One of us will have to carry him back to the bungalow."

Lois held up her hands. "Don't look at me. I'm already carrying my purse, and it has a brick in it."

I sighed again.

When we got back to the bungalow, it was clear that Ruth and Bishop Yoder were back from the conference and already in bed. I could not blame them. It had been a terribly long day.

I shuffled into our room, got Jethro settled, went through my nighttime routine, and lay down.

I woke in the middle of the night unsure of the time. Ambient moonlight poured in through the window. It was just enough for me to see Jethro sprawled at the foot of my bed like a Labrador.

Lois snored softly in the next bed. Her noise machine hummed away. Her eye mask and earplugs were in place.

According to the clock on the nightstand, it was three in the morning. I sighed and lay back on my pillow. It was too early to get up, even for me. I would have to wait at least one more hour for it to be a reasonable time to wake.

I turned onto my side and faced the large window. It was cracked open, and even with Lois's noise machine humming away I could hear the Gulf lap against the beach. The waves sounded more animated at night. There were weather reports that a storm was headed toward Pinecraft. It wasn't hurricane season, so locals didn't view the oncoming storm with much concern. However, I would be lying if I didn't admit that I was nervous about being so close to the water during a thunderstorm. As beautiful as it was, I found the ocean to be unpredictable, and now when I thought of it, I imagined Caroline Zook's body in the waves.

My eyes were slowly closing again, much to my surprise. I was sure that I would not be able to fall back asleep. However, the busyness of the last few days and the kayak adventure made me sleep more than I ever would have at home.

Just as my eyes were about to shut, I saw movement in the window. My eyes popped open again and a pale face appeared. Fear gripped at my heart and froze. I squinted my eyes to look like they were closed, all the while watching the face in the window.

Scott Lawrence. It was Scott Lawrence. What was he doing looking into our room?

Just as quickly as his face appeared, it was gone again. I waited a few minutes more and quietly slipped out of bed. I walked over to Lois's bed and tapped her on the shoulder.

"What?" she mumbled into her pillow.

"Lois, wake up," I whispered. I gently shook her shoulders.

She pushed the face mask up into her hairline. "Millie?"

I put a finger to my lips to tell her to be quiet.

As soon as I did that, she was immediately awake. "What is it?" she whispered. She pulled her earplugs from her ears.

"Someone was looking into our room through the window."

She jolted up in bed and nearly knocked me to the

floor in the process. She grabbed my hand so that I wouldn't fall down.

"Who was it?"

"It looked like Scott Lawrence or Isaac Zukes. I don't know what to call him anymore."

"What is he doing here?" Her voice was hoarse.

"That's what I want to know. I'm going outside to see if I can find out."

"Not without me, you're not," Lois said.

"Why do you think I woke you up?" I asked. "I don't want to go out there by myself."

"Right." Lois jumped out of bed, threw a caftan on over her pajamas, and slipped her feet into flip-flops.

I twisted my braid into a knot on the back of my head and put a robe on over my nightdress, and then I stepped into my one dry pair of tennis shoes. I was ready too.

"We look like a couple of loony old bats," Lois said.

"That's just what we are if we are going out in the middle of the night to look for a suspect."

"Well said," Lois declared. She then set her purse on her shoulder.

"You don't have to take your purse," I said.

"I always need my purse." She reached into the bag and came up with the ever-trusty brick. Lois set the brick in my hand. "If there was ever a time to use this, it is now."

She took the stapler for herself.

I really didn't know what Lois thought I was going to do with the brick. I was a pacifist. And I didn't want to know what she intended to do with a stapler, but it couldn't be *gut*.

I opened the bedroom door, and Jethro stood up on the bed. "Go back to sleep."

"Right," Lois said. "Pigs aren't meant to be detectives." She shut the door, leaving Jethro in the room.

I might be chasing a killer, but at least I wouldn't be chasing a pig as well.

Before I opened the bungalow door, I turned to Lois, "You have your phone in case we have to call the police?"

She held up her hands, the stapler in one and her cell phone in the other. We could not be more prepared.

I opened the door and yelped. A man sat on the picnic table outside our door. The porch light illuminated his face. It was Scott Lawrence. I didn't expect that he would be that easy to find.

Lois held her stapler high as if she was ready to strike.

Scott looked at me. "I need your help."

Chapter Thirty-two

Scott held his head in his hands. "I'm sorry to be coming to you in the middle of the night, but I didn't know what else to do. I am in real trouble."

Lois lowered her arms. "Is that because you killed Caroline Zook?"

I winced. If Lois was really going say things like that, she should be the one holding her purse brick just in case the suspect lunged off the picnic table at her. I didn't think the stapler was going to be the kind of protection that she needed. She did look as menacing as a seventy-year-old woman holding a stapler could, but Scott was less than half of our age. He was nimbler and stronger than Lois and I combined.

I stood on the balls of my feet just in case I had to grab Lois and run back into the bungalow because Scott was in a rage.

Instead of lunging at Lois, Scott seemed to melt into the table. "It is my fault that she's dead."

Lois and I shared a look, and I wrapped my robe more tightly around my shoulders.

"Did you kill her?" I asked.

He looked up. "No. I would never do that, but it is my fault she's dead. I've tried so hard for so long to keep something like this from happening, but I have to accept my fate. I can't run from it forever."

Lois folded her arms. "You had better cut to the chase, young man, or we are calling the police." She waved her phone around as if to put a fine point onto her threat.

"Please don't. I came to you for help."

"Why?" I asked. "If you're in trouble, why don't you go to Pastor Ross?"

"I can't. Pastor Ross can't know what I did. He would be so disappointed."

Lois ground the toe of her shoes into the sandy gravel. Her patience was short, and I couldn't blame her. We were in the wee hours in the morning, and the breeze coming off the Gulf was chilly, even if it was a Florida chilly and not an Ohio chilly. Those are two very different kinds of cold.

"What did you do?" I asked.

He looked down at his hands.

"If you're not going to talk to us, we have no choice but to call the police. We have very *gut* reasons to suspect you for the murder of Caroline Zook. I suspect that she found out that you were Amish, and your connection to the Amish in Harvest was the reason that she was in Ohio." I paused. "And her trip to Ohio is the reason she was killed."

"I don't know why she was killed," he said. "I mean, I'm not certain why she was killed."

"But you have suspicions," Lois said.

He looked up at us. His eyes traveled to Lois, who was still holding the stapler ready to strike. "I came to you because Reverend Brook and Juliet spoke so highly of you. They said that you solved murders in the Amish community, and that is just what I need help with."

"How did you know where to find us?" Lois asked.

"Juliet told me where you were staying," he said.

Lois rolled her eyes. "Of course she did."

"I can understand needing help," I said. "But why now? It's the middle of the night. Why didn't you wait until later in the day? Why are you here peeking into our window?"

His face flushed red. "I am sorry about that. I shouldn't have done that."

"You shouldn't have," I agreed.

"Yeah," Lois added. "It's super creepy and something a killer would have done."

He licked his lips. "I'm not a killer. I promise you, I'm not."

"Promises at this time of night don't mean much," Lois said. "That's how I ended up married to my third husband, and I can assure you that one didn't end well."

"You mentioned when we met that you were an early riser and liked to go out and see the sunrise. I thought I would wait for you here until you did. It's not like I can sleep anyway. I haven't slept in days."

As if to prove his point, the electric light from the lamppost highlighted the dark circles under his eyes.

"Why should we help you when you tipped over Millie's kayak? She could have drowned."

Scott opened and closed his mouth. "That was an accident. I bumped the back of her kayak with my oar."

"You bumped it twice," Lois said.

"I guess I did. I was trying to turn the kayak around."

"Why didn't you say anything after I went into the water?" I asked.

He looked like he was on the verge of tears. "I knew that you were already suspicious of my because of Caroline's death and didn't want to make it worse."

He appeared to be so frightened and shocked by the idea that I tended to believe him. I glanced at Lois and knew she wasn't convinced.

"When we were paddling back to the loading area, I heard you whispering in the mangrove with another man," I said.

He eyes went wide. "You did?"

"Who were you talking to?" I asked.

Rather than deny it was him, Scott said, "It was one of the pastors at the conference. He said since Caroline didn't want to work with me at the conference office she ran to her Amish boyfriend. If I had been better to work with she would have stayed and not have been killed."

For the sake of getting the information that we needed, I chose to believe him.

"How are we supposed to trust a Peeping Tom?" Lois asked.

His face flushed red. "I peeked into your window to

make sure I had the right bungalow. Juliet was a little vague on the details about which bungalow was yours. It was a stupid thing to do."

"You bet it was," Lois agreed. She lowered her stapler, but I didn't doubt for a second that she would bring it out again if she had a need. "You had better start at the beginning."

He nodded.

The sky was starting to lighten in the east. "Let's go talk on the beach. There will be fewer prying eyes there."

"She means Ruth can't spy on us if she wakes up," Lois said.

I nodded.

Lois waved her stapler at Scott. "Don't think for a second that I won't clock you with this if you try any funny business."

Scott, Lois, and I walked to the beach in silence.

That morning was so much like the morning that Jethro found Caroline Zook's body. A handful of beachcombers were walking up and down the sand looking for interesting shells and lost trinkets. A man jogged barefoot along the water's edge.

I shivered. Maybe coming to the beach had not been the best idea for this heart-to-heart with Scott.

Lois dropped her purse in the sand and reached inside. She came up with three beach towels.

Scott stared at her purse in awe. "What else do you have in there?"

"You know, that's a question I get asked just about every day." She smoothed the towels on the sand.

Lois plopped down on one, and I waited to see where

Scott would sit before I picked my spot. I wanted to see his face while he was speaking. I was a good judge of character, and I would know if he was lying to me.

He kneeled on the edge of the towel and then sat looking away from the ocean but back at Lois.

I slowly sat down by Lois.

"Now, you better sit there and tell us your story," Lois said. "Because if you run off, there is no chance of us catching you. You have to take into account our age and how long it takes us to stand up again."

"I'm not going to run," Scott said. "I told you that I came to you for help, and I meant it. I am in a terrible spot. It's gone on too long and too far."

"What does this have to do with Caroline's death?"

He looked down at his hands folded in his lap. "I pray it's nothing. I pray every day that it is nothing, but I'm afraid it might not be."

"Start at the beginning like Lois asked."

He nodded. "I grew up Amish in Ohio."

"And your name was Isaac Zukes when you were Amish," Lois said.

Even in the dim light, I could see his cheeks darken. "Ruth Yoder told you this, I take it."

"We don't reveal our sources," Lois said.

He blinked at her. "What Reverend Brook and Juliet said about the two of you is true. You are good at this."

Lois buffed her brightly painted nails on her shirt. "We like to think so."

"What happened when you lived in Ohio?" I asked.

He looked at me. "I was in *rumspringa*. I knew from an early age that I didn't want to be baptized into the district. For me, being Amish was too restrictive. I thought that one could be a Christian and serve God without following so many rules. It felt like the Amish faith, to me, was more about earing points to get into heaven than about doing good for others just because it was the right thing to do."

"Why didn't you just leave at the beginning of your *rumspringa*?" Lois asked.

It was a fair question, but I had a feeling that I knew that answer.

As Scott spoke, I knew I was right.

"If you grow up Amish and know you're going to leave even as child, it's still hard to leave. You have to walk away from everything you have ever known. You have no support from family or friends to start a new life. You're effectively alone because you picked yourself over your family and your community. You're punished for that. I'm not talking about shunning. Since I was never baptized, I wasn't shunned."

What he said was true, I knew. It was also the experience that I had heard from many other people I knew who left the Amish faith. Even if the people who left the community weren't shunned, there would always be a distance between them and their family.

"Because I knew I would have to strike out on my own, I wanted to stay in the district for a few years after I reached the age of fourteen so I could save up enough money to leave and be able to take care of myself. At the same time, I quietly got my GED without my parents knowing about it. It wasn't easy to do that. The job I was working was in construction, which meant that I left for the jobsite before first light and came home after dark every day but Sunday. Sunday was full of church activities that I participated half-heartedly in to keep up appearances. The only time I had to study or work on my schoolwork was late at night with a pen flashlight after my brothers, who I shared a room with, went to sleep."

"This is all very interesting," Lois said. "But I don't know how this leads to Caroline. She was younger than you and born to an English family in Pinecraft."

He nodded. "I'm getting to that. I hated work like that. I felt like such a failure. I was an Amish man who hated working with his hands. I wanted to be studious. I would much prefer a day at the library than a day on the jobsite. I also knew that I wasn't any good at it. I continually made mistakes. The only reason that the contractor, Zeke Klemp, gave me a job was because he was my father's best friend. If they hadn't been such good friends, I would have been fired a long while before."

"Why didn't you quit and find another job like in a store or restaurant in Harvest, if you were so bad at construction?" I asked.

"In hindsight, that is exactly what I should have done, but I stayed in the job because it paid much better than any of that work would have, and like I said before, I was saving money as quickly as I could to escape from Holmes County. As hard as it was to leave, I didn't want to stay there one day longer than I absolutely needed to."

Out over the water, I could just see the horizon lighten, but it would still be a long while before the sun fully showed itself.

Scott swallowed hard and his Adam's apple bobbed up and down. "Despite my little mistakes, I was getting by. I was able to fix or cover up the mishaps I had here and there, and up to that point no one was ever hurt."

"Up to that point?" Lois asked.

He nodded. "Until my last day on a jobsite. We were working on a house to turn it from an English home to an Amish home. It was very old and the plumbing and wiring were outdated. Almost everything needed to be replaced. Zeke was working on the plumbing. Somehow an electric wire was too close to the lead pipe plumbing. To remove the pipe, he told me to turn off the breaker to that room."

I shivered because I had an idea I knew where this was going. "If it was going to be an Amish home," I said, "why didn't you just turn off all the power to the house?"

He sighed. "Zeke didn't see the need for it. Since the house had power, we could use it to work and power our tools. He wouldn't have to bring a generator in or spend money on fuel for the generator."

"What happened?" Lois asked.

"I turned off the wrong circuit breaker. They weren't labeled well, and I thought I knew which one was which. I told my boss that I had done it. A few minutes later I heard this terrible cry." He shivered as if he was hearing the sound again in real time. "I ran into the room, but he was already dead. I just froze. I didn't know what to do. I had killed him."

Chapter Thirty-three

A female jogger ran along the beach as the first glimpses of sunrise shone on the sand. She had a large black and white dog running beside her. If I squinted hard enough, the dog looked a lot like my black and white goat Phillip. Seeing them run made me homesick for my goats, cat, husband, and farm. I was also homesick for my routine and knowing where I was going and what I was doing every day. Lois and I were leaving Florida in two days, but that seemed like such a long way away when I was face-to-face with a young man who just confessed to murder.

"It wasn't murder," Lois said. "It was an accident."

"I would still be sent to prison even if I didn't mean to hurt my boss."

"I guess it could be manslaughter," Lois mused.

I stopped myself from rolling my eyes. I didn't know how Lois thought that was going to make him feel any better.

"Scott, it was an accident. You can't torture yourself

for the rest of your life for it. Have you made amends with the family?"

He looked away from me. "In a way."

What did that mean?

"Was anyone else there? Did anyone see what happened?" Lois asked.

"Zeke and I were the only ones working at the house that day. Usually, we had a much bigger crew, but until the plumbing issue was handled, no one else was coming in on the job."

"Why were you there?" Lois asked. "Did you work in plumbing?"

He shook his head. "No, I was awful at it, like I was on most things on the jobsite. I was just the general gopher for my boss. I would run and grab the things he needed and clean up the site at the end of the day. He didn't trust me with any important work."

"He trusted you to turn off the breaker," Lois said.

Scott hung his head. "Yes, and he shouldn't have in that case either. You don't know how many times over the years I have thought about that day or how much I want to take it back. I wish that I could make it right. My father's friend died in the accident. He left behind a wife and seven kids and three grandchildren. They all depended on him and his business. I took that all away from them in one second. All it took was one second of a mistake, so many times I wanted to tell them I was sorry."

"Then why did you run?" I asked.

"I thought it was my only chance. If I stayed, I would be thrown in jail, and prison is unkind to the Amish." He dug his right hand into the sand. "I was a dumb, afraid kid." Tears came to his eyes. "I know now that I should have stayed and faced whatever there was to face. To run away was a cowardly choice. If I could go back and fix it, I would." He shook his head. "But too much time has passed now, and too much more has happened."

"How much time has passed?" I asked.

"I was fifteen at the time. It's nearly twenty years."

"How does this relate to Caroline?" I asked because as sad as his story was, Caroline was still at the top of my mind.

"She found out," he whispered. "And when she found out, she wouldn't let it go. It left me again with few choices."

Lois narrowed her eyes. "Did you think she was going to report you to the Holmes County sheriff's department?"

He shook his head.

Lois yanked her stapler out of her purse and held it in the air. "Are you telling us that you killed Caroline?"

He held up his hands to protect his face as if he were afraid that Lois was going to throw the stapler at him. There was a good chance that she would, so it was a very good idea to protect himself. "No, no, no, I would never do that. Caroline is the daughter of Pastor Ross. Pastor Ross is my mentor. I would never do anything to hurt him. Caroline was the most important person to him."

"How did she find out?" I asked.

He swallowed. "We worked in the charity office together and she found some questionable checks."

"You were stealing from the conference?"

"No, I mean, yes, but not for myself. I was trying to make up for what happened in Ohio all those years ago. I wanted to help Zeke's family. I personally don't have anything to give. I'm in church work. I barely make a living wage. It's little better than volunteering. I have free housing in the parsonage, but without that I wouldn't be able to house and feed myself on what I make. I don't have a dime to spare for Zeke's and his family." He licked his lips.

"But the church has money," I said.

"Yes, a lot of money through gifts and donations and through money earned through the conferences. Conferences are not cheap to put on, but Pastor Ross is well liked and respected in the community, so many of aspects of the conferences are comped, so he has more money to give to his charities." He looked out at the Gulf. "I didn't think he would notice if a few hundred here or there went missing."

"Why did Pastor Ross trust you so much?" I asked.

"Because I had proven myself to him over the last few years. I knew that I wanted to do church work, but I didn't have the education to do most of it. Then I saw an advertisement about an internship here in Pinecraft. It was at Pastor Ross's church. It was unpaid, but room and board would be provided. It seemed like the perfect fit for me. Maybe it was dumb of me to move to a place that was full of Amish and one which Amish from Ohio came to visit every year. Ruth Yoder wasn't the first one to recognize me over the years. Others did too, but I was always able to put them off by laughing and joking that I must have a twin somewhere in the world. Ruth wasn't that easily deterred."

"She never is," Lois said from experience.

"Tell us about Caroline," I said. "Why didn't she just go to her father when she found out? I imagine that would have put an end to it."

His face fell. "I still can't believe that she is gone. She and I had a great relationship for so many years. She was like my little sister. There were times that I would tell myself that she and Pastor Ross were my real family and everything back in Ohio was just a dream."

"So, you always got along?" I asked.

He frowned. "Yes, up until she was a teenager and became curious about the Amish. She started working at an ice cream shop, and most of the girls there were Amish. They were her friends. She loved their big families and how close they were in the community. It was the opposite of the way she was brought up by her father. Pastor Ross was a good dad to her," he added quickly. "But he was a pastor of a large church and running a conference as well. He didn't have much time for his daughter. She really didn't have any other family but me, and I was a poor substitute. I would have done anything to impress her father. I cared more about that than her."

"We know all about the ice cream shop," Lois said. "We spoke to Kimber."

His face grew bright red.

"She told us that you had a crush on her. Aren't you a little old for her?" Lois asked.

He grimaced. "Yes, that's why I never pursued her."

"That's not how Kimber felt," Lois said.

He braced his hand on the sand. "I'm sorry Kimber felt that way. She never said anything to me about it."

Lois folded her arms. "What is she going to say? She's a teenager, and you're a grown man."

"You had a problem with Caroline's interest in the Amish," I said.

He nodded. "When Caroline told me that she wanted to learn more about the Amish, I snapped at her and said she could never really understand it. I thought I was helping her. I thought her infatuation with the Amish world was just a passing thing. I know better than anyone what it is really like to be Amish. I know how hard it can be. Even when you're Amish in Holmes County, you're still balancing two worlds. You have to be in the English world to some degree to succeed and care for your family, but you have to be in the Amish world to be respected by your family. It's a hard balance, and one I clearly failed at." He looked down. "It caused a rift between us. I think in many ways I pushed her into wanting to learn even more. I didn't know until later that she started to going to Amish youth gatherings on the beach and picnics with her friends. I knew Cainan was her friend from childhood, but I never thought she would go as far as to marry him."

"She fell in love with Cainan," I said.

He nodded. "Pastor Ross found out about Cainan and forbade her from seeing him. He made her quit her job at the ice cream shop and come work in the conference office with me. He said it was a better fit for her. Caroline was a whiz at math. She could do equations and figures in her head that I wouldn't even know how to write down. Pastor Ross hoped she would go to college and do something with her gift. She didn't have any interest in college. She just wanted to be with Cainan."

"How did Pastor Ross find out about Cainan?" I asked.

He looked me in the eye. "I told him. I told him everything."

"Did she know you told him?" Lois asked.

"Yes, I was very vocal in my support of her father. I even got into an argument with Cainan over it."

Lois folded her arms. "We heard. On the beach in front of all their friends."

His face was red. "I thought I was helping. I thought I knew what was best for her. She was upset with me, which I think spurred her to double-check my work. That's when she found I was skimming money from the church."

"And?" Lois asked. "Did she tell her father?"

He hung his head. "Yes, but he didn't believe her. I denied it, and he believed me. He said that she had already betrayed him by staying with Cainan when he forbade their relationship."

"Then what happened?" I asked.

"Nothing," he said. "She was just gone. Pastor Ross and I knew where she had gone. She ran to the Amish. She went to be with Cainan."

"Why did Pastor Ross file a missing person report if he knew where she had gone?"

"Because he knew the Amish would hide her if she joined them. He wanted to make a point." He shook his head. "In the end, it didn't matter. She was over eighteen and an adult. If she wanted to leave, she could."

Lois stood up. "Now we know why she went to Ohio. It was because of you."

Scott scrambled to his feet. "We don't know that."

"Sure we do. She went to Ohio to find the proof that you were stealing from the church. She wanted to prove to her father that she wasn't lying, and I might add, she wasn't. She needed a witness, and it cost her life."

I thought Lois just might be right about that.

Chapter Thirty-four

I stood as well and picked up my towel. "Scott," I began. "You came all this way early in the morning. You have told us your story, but you said you needed our help. What exactly do you want us to do?"

He swallowed. "That police detective, Detective Marcs, came to the church conference yesterday. He was asking a lot of questions about the church conference. I think that he believes Pastor Ross or I had something to do with the murder."

"Detective Marcs is no dummy," Lois said.

"I promise you Pastor Ross and I are innocent."

"We are looking for the killer," I said. "And we can't rule out that it was you. You have told us a pretty clear motive."

"It's not!"

A group of seagulls took off at his shout.

"Keep your voice down," Lois admonished. "Do you want joggers to think you are trying to kill us? You don't want any more of those sorts of problems."

He paled.

Behind him at the horizon, the sun was starting to peek over the waves. It would be light soon, and our investigation would be back in action. An old proverb came to my mind: "The only time to look down on someone is when you're bending over to help." Scott Lawrence—or his Amish name, Isaac Zukes—needed our help. He was asking for our help. We could not turn away.

"We will get to the truth," I said. "And we will help you if we possibly can."

Relief flooded Scott's face. "Thank you. I don't know where else to turn."

"However, I do think you should tell Pastor Ross the truth about taking money from the church."

"I—I can't."

"You will or we will."

His eyes were wide.

"Honesty is always the best way forward for the Amish and *Englisch*," I said.

"I'll tell him," he said finally, but he would not meet my eyes when he said that. "I need to get back. Breakfast at the conference will be served soon, and there is much to do." He said good-bye and turned and walked down the beach in the direction of the Dutchman Resort.

Lois bent over and picked up the beach towel that Scott had left in the sand. "He could have at least picked up his towel," she grumbled. "And I would bet all my vintage jewelry that he's not going to tell Pastor Ross about that stolen money."

"If I was a gambling woman, I would not take that bet," I said.

When Lois and I went back inside the bungalow, we found Ruth Yoder, fully dressed and ready for her day, sitting at the small dining table across from Jethro. Both of them were eating Cheerios. Ruth daintily ate her breakfast with a spoon while Jethro had his snout buried in his bowl.

"Are you two having a bonding moment?" Lois asked.

"I don't know what you feed pet pigs," Ruth said. "He was trying to steal my breakfast from me. I can't have a pig trying to eat my food. I had to give him something so that he would leave me alone."

"So, you set his food bowl on the table?" Lois asked.

Ruth narrowed her eyes at Lois. "I did what I could."

"How did he get out of the room?"

Ruth pressed her lips together. "I knocked on your bedroom door to see if you were up. When no one answered, I opened the door just a crack to peek inside and he ran out. I have never seen a pig move so fast in all my life."

"That was your first mistake," Lois said.

Ruth scowled at her. "Why didn't you take him with you? I thought it was your job to watch him."

"The last time we were on the beach with Jethro, he found a dead body. We didn't want a repeat of that," Lois said.

Technically, the last time we were on the beach, he ran into a shed and got us tangled up with murder suspects, but I didn't correct Lois.

Ruth sniffed and picked up her bowl and set it in the sink. "Now that you are back, I assume that you will take over the responsibility for him."

"We will," I said. "We thank you for feeding him." I wiped milk from Jethro's chin. "It's clear that he enjoyed his breakfast."

"We were on the beach with a friend of yours," Lois said.

"Who?"

Lois glanced at me. "She is definitely counting us in that number of non-friends."

"Who was it?" Ruth asked.

"Scott Lawrence," I said before Lois could make another joke.

"I have no use for that man." Ruth set her spoon back into her cereal bowl. "Did he lie to you too and tell you that he wasn't Amish?"

I shook my head and grabbed a roll of paper towels from the counter. I cleaned up the mess around Jethro the best I could. In truth, the little pig could probably use a bath, but that was far beyond what I agreed to when I said I would watch Jethro for Juliet.

"He admitted it. He said he grew up in Holmes County and was Isaac Zukes."

"Oh," Ruth said as if she was surprised that he would admit it. "Well, if he was just going to come out and say it to you like that, I don't know why he made such a scene about it at the conference yesterday."

"You might have caught him off guard." I picked Jethro off the dining chair and set him on the floor.

He looked up at me and grunted. Apparently he was offended at being treated like a pet and not a human.

"Why did he want to talk to you?" Ruth asked.

"Juliet told him that we could help him."

Ruth snorted at this. She sounded a lot like Jethro when she did that, but I knew better than to say it.

"He wants us to find who killed Caroline because he felt responsible for what happened to her. He's afraid the police are going to blame him."

"He should," Ruth said.

"Why do you say that?" Lois asked.

Ruth patted her prayer cap. "I just don't feel like he is an upstanding young man. Anyone who will lie about who they really are shouldn't be trusted."

Lois wrinkled her nose as if she didn't like that answer. I can't say I was fond of it either.

"Do you know anyone by the name Zeke Klemp?" I asked. "From back home?"

Ruth sipped her coffee and thought. "The only Zeke Klemp I know of died years ago."

Lois poured herself a coffee. "Millie, would you like any?"

I shook my head and sat at the table across from Ruth.

"Scott was there when Zeke was killed. He just told us that."

Ruth stared at me. "I always heard that Zeke was alone."

"Not according to Scott," I said. I wasn't ready to go so far as to say aloud that Scott's mistake killed Zeke.

Ruth seemed to consider this. "I think Isaac/Scott/ whatever the name he goes by now ran off about the same time. I can't be sure. We were from different districts, but of course, it was talked about in their community. Any time a man is killed, it is talked about."

I nodded. If I had been around at the time, I would have known about it too. When Scott worked for Zeke, I was living in Michigan caring for an ill sister. By the time I moved back to Harvest, over a decade had passed. Zeke Klemp's death was old news by then, and since he was not a member of my district, it made sense that I would hear nothing about it.

"Do you know anything about the Klemp family?" I asked.

"It was a big family. I believe Zeke was the father of seven or eight children. They received help from their district after that, but there is only so much that the district can do. I believe the oldest child at the time was twelve."

"That many kids under twelve?" Lois gasped.

"I believe they had infant triplets at the time of Zeke's death. That does stand out in my mind."

"That poor mother," Lois said.

"At twelve, the oldest boy could go to work and earn for his family," Ruth said. "He became the man of the house at that point."

I pressed my lips together. I had similar stories in my own family. My niece Edith lost her husband when her oldest son was just eight years old. At eight, he was considered the man of the house. It was not easy for my great-nephew and had ramifications for him to this day, and he only had his mother and two younger siblings to think of. I can't imagine what that twelve-year-old boy with eleven people relying on him dealt with.

Ruth got up from her chair and took her dishes to the sink. "Bishop Yoder left an hour ago for the conference. I suppose I should walk over there now."

"I'm surprised that you're going back after the way you were treated," I said.

"My husband asked me to be there. He will be giving a talk this afternoon about Amish and *Englisch* relations in Harvest. I should be there to support him." She sniffed. "It's a topic that I know much about. I also would like a word with Scott Lawrence now that you have told me his connection to Zeke Klemp. I don't trust that young man. There is something off about him. You will see."

"We never claimed to trust him," Lois said. "We just heard him out."

"Not everyone deserves that," Ruth said. "This is the last day of the conference. I can't tell you how happy I am about that. If I had my way I wouldn't go to the closing service tonight, but I know the bishop would like me there for that too."

"What happens at the closing service?" I asked.

"People are invited to get up and speak and share how the conference has changed them and what they plan to take back to their community." Ruth sniffed. "It's a terrible format, if you ask me. It is my belief you shouldn't just let anyone speak up in a church setting. You have to know what they are about to say, or they might confuse people."

"I think people should share their stories. You never know who they might reach," I said.

"Millie, there are times I think Lois has too much influence on you," Ruth said.

"I take that as a compliment," Lois said.

Chapter Thirty-five

Lois tucked Jethro into her massive purse and slung the bag over her shoulder before hopping on her e-scooter.

"I don't think this is safe," I said.

"We will be fine. I really feel like I have this scooter riding down, and we have a lot to do today. We can't take the time to walk from place to place with Jethro's stroller. The scooters are the only way to go."

I stepped on my own scooter. "You are tilting to the side. It looks like the scooter will topple over at any second."

She adjusted her stance to be a little more upright. "Is that better?"

"Not really."

"We don't have time to debate it. We need to be at the closing service tonight."

I agreed with her on that. I too wanted to be at the closing service to speak to Scott again and find out if he kept his promise and told Pastor Ross about taking money from the church. He came to Lois and me for help, but I didn't see how we could help him when he was still withholding information.

Lois revved her e-scooter. "Let's ride."

I was beginning to tire of that expression.

Our first stop was Zook's Scooters, and I was happy that we made it there in one piece. There were a couple of times that Lois almost veered into traffic because the weight of her bag was causing her to list to one side, but she was always able to right herself at the last second.

We parked our scooters outside the door. Jethro poked his head out of Lois's purse, and she firmly pushed it back down. "I doubt pigs are allowed in here."

The bell over the door rang, and Tabitha was at the sales desk. When she looked up and saw us standing there, she frowned. We were not the people that she wanted to see.

"Is there something wrong with your scooters? I believe you have them rented for two more days." She narrowed her eyes as if she were offended that we would dare to turn them in early.

"There is nothing wrong with them," Lois said. "They are great fun. We're having the time of our lives on these things."

"If everything is fine with your scooters, I don't know why you are here," Tabitha said.

"You should really work on your customer service skills," Lois told her.

I stepped forward. "We wanted to talk to you about Caroline."

Tabitha jerked back. "Why? I have nothing to say about her."

"She was your sister-in-law," I said.

"In whose mind? She wasn't married in the district. She and my *bruder* might have been married in the *Englisch* view, but they certainly were not married to me. Marriage is a sacred service that should be performed in front of your church and congregation. Otherwise, it is meaningless."

"You didn't welcome her into the family, I take it," Lois said.

"Why should I? I could see from yards away that she was only going to ruin Cainan's life. He was doing so well in the shop. He didn't need the distraction. Caroline came to him with too many problems. We don't like drama in our community, and I feel like that was all Caroline was bringing." She paused. "I don't have anything else to tell you."

The top of Jethro's head popped out of Lois's purse. She deftly pushed him back down into the bag.

"Is that a pig in your bag?" Tabitha asked.

"It's just a stuffed animal. It is a gift for my granddaughter Darcy back home."

"How old is your granddaughter?"

"Twenty-six, but she's a kid at heart. Loves stuffed animals and has dozens." Lois shrugged.

I groaned inwardly. Lois wasn't fooling anyone, and Darcy would be horrified if she heard her grandmother say she loved stuffed animals at her age. Then again, Darcy Woodin knew her grandmother well and had heard her say even more outlandish things before.

Tabitha wrinkled her nose.

"Why did you dislike Caroline so much?" I asked.

"She is not one of us. It would spoil our family. I warned her to stay away from my *bruder*. He wasn't going to become *Englisch* for her."

"But she became Amish for him," I said.

She snorted. "She thinks she can put on a prayer cap and a dress and be Amish? She would never really be one of us. She proved that when she left my brother just a few days after they married. She made a fool out of him. She didn't embarrass just him but my husband and myself too. Now we are the talk of the district. Not only did she up and leave, but she also had to get herself murdered."

"This woman is awful," Lois whispered into my ear.

I silently agreed.

"I would have done anything to get her out of my life," she said.

"She is out of your life. She's dead," I said.

She glared at me. "I had nothing to do with it. I believe it was just *Gotte's* way of correcting a mistake that Cainan made. Now he can find a decent and respectable Amish wife."

"Caroline wasn't a mistake," Cainan said from the back of the shop. "I loved her, and she loved me. She converted to the Amish way for me. I know what a big change that was for her. Maybe I should have left the Amish life to be with her. If I had been willing to do that, maybe she would still be alive."

"Don't be ridiculous," his sister snapped. "You can't leave the Amish life."

"After this week, I am thinking about it."

"You would have to walk away from everything, including this shop," Tabitha said.

"I don't have to leave my business to be *Englisch*," he said.

Tabitha paled. "Malachi and I would no longer work with you if you were *Englisch*. We couldn't condone it. You have already been baptized. You would be shunned."

"Maybe that's what I deserve after the death of my wife," he snapped.

"She wasn't your wife," she spat. "She left you. She put her family first and died for it."

"What do you mean by that?" Cainan asked.

Tabitha's face grew red as if she realized she had said too much.

The front door to the shop opened and Malachi walked inside carrying a bicycle wheel. He took in the scene in front of him. "What is going on in here?"

"What do you mean by that, Tabitha?" Cainan asked again, walking toward his sister.

"I don't mean anything. I misspoke."

Cainan ran over to the desk and glared at Tabitha. "Don't lie. You know something."

Malachi dropped the wheel, and it clattered to the concrete floor. "Don't threaten my wife like that."

"She knows why *my* wife was killed," Cainan shouted at the top of his voice.

"I really don't want to get in the middle of an Amish family brawl," Lois said.

Neither did I.

"I'll tell you why she died," Malachi said. "She died because she put her father before you. When you marry, you are supposed to leave your old family behind and start a new one. She wasn't able to do that. She went to Ohio to prove to her father that she was right about Isaac Zukes, but you might know him by another name."

Lois and I looked at each other. This was the confirmation we need that Caroline had gone to Ohio to prove Scott stole money from the church. Her father hadn't believed her over Scott. She needed real evidence to prove Scott had been lying.

Scott could very well be the killer and gave us his sob story to make fools of us. He wasn't going to get very far doing that, not with Lois and me on the case.

Chapter Thirty-six

Detective Marcs was not impressed when Lois and I called him a little while later and told him our theory that Scott had killed Caroline.

"Stop! Stop!" the detective shouted into the phone. "I don't want to hear any more about this. Scott Lawrence or whatever his name might be did not kill Caroline Zook."

"How do you know that?" Lois asked.

"Don't you think that we checked the alibi of everyone who was close to her? Her husband, father, Scott, and others all have alibis for the time the coroner said that she was killed."

"What was Scott's alibi?" I asked.

"He and Pastor Ross were onstage in front of all their conference attendees leading an evening prayer service, and the services were live-streamed on the internet. I have seen it."

Lois whistled. "Drat. That is a pretty good alibi."

It was the perfect alibi, I thought, but I wasn't convinced that he was completely innocent.

"That may be true, but he has motive," I said.

The detective sighed. "What is it?"

As briefly as I could I told the detective about Scott's life when he was Amish and the death of Zeke Klemp. "Caroline found out about Zeke's death and Scott's involvement. She wanted to go to Ohio to prove that it was true."

"That was dumb on her part. Make a phone call. Did she really have to go to Ohio?"

"You have to remember that you are dealing with Amish," I said. "She could have sent a letter, she could have called whichever shed phone the Klemp family was attached to, but there was no guarantee that she would be able to contact them. The only way to truly find them and speak to them was in person. That meant she had to go to Ohio."

"What she should have done," Detective Marcs said, "was report to the police that Scott Lawrence stole from her father's church. We would have taken it from there."

"If she did, it would have made the news. It would have embarrassed her father and the church. I believe she only wanted her father to fire Scott and be done with it," I said. "She needed to prove he was stealing on her own to do that."

"I see your point," the detective muttered.

"Detective, tonight is the closing service at the conference. I think you should be there to speak to Scott yourself," I said.

He sighed into the phone. "Do the two of you think this is my only case?"

"We know that it's not, but a young woman in her prime, a newlywed, is dead just days after she was married. She deserves justice."

"Fine. I can't promise you anything, but I will try to be there. I can never make promises in this line of work. I never know what will happen."

We thanked him, and Lois ended the call. It was the best we were going to get.

"I say our first order of business is to get Jethro back to his mistress," Lois said. "It's just not practical to have a pig in tow when you're sleuthing. I'm sure all the great detectives like Sherlock Holmes and Miss Marple would agree with that."

I would have to take her word for it.

"I agree. Let's take him back to the resort. I want to go there anyway because I have a question."

"What's that?"

"Ever since yesterday, I have been mulling it over in my mind about that fire alarm at the resort. Who set it off? Why did they do that?"

Lois nodded. "Those are good questions."

We popped Jethro back into the stroller for the walk to Dutchman Resort. The little pig didn't seem to be upset about being cooped up in the stroller after his marshmallow binge the night before. He was still recovering from that.

Lois had called Juliet to tell her that we were bringing Jethro back, and Juliet met us at the entrance of the resort.

As soon as we walked through the revolving door, Juliet clapped her hands. "Oh, I'm so happy to have my little darling back." She bent over the stroller. "Did you miss Mama? Did you?"

Lois rolled her eyes.

"How was he for you?"

I was certain that marshmallows were at the top of both Lois's and my minds.

"He was a little angel," Lois said.

"I know he was." Juliet peered closer to the pig. "He looks so tired. He always has a ball with the two of you. Thank you for bringing him back. As an extra thank-you, I want to invite you to the closing service this evening. There will be a nice dinner and lovely speeches."

"What's the attire?" Lois asked. That was always the question at the top of her mind.

"Cocktail or Sunday best. There will be a gamut of outfits. Pastors aren't known for being fashionistas." She laughed. "Reverend Brook and I have a table, and we would love for you to sit with us."

Lois wrinkled her nose. Even though I knew she would love the idea of getting dressed up, sitting through speeches was not how she liked to spend her time.

"We will be there," I said.

Juliet clapped her hands. "Lois, I will text you the details with the time and everything just as soon as I get up to my room." She looked down at Jethro again. "It seems to me that this little one needs a nap before tonight's festivities."

"We could all use a nap," Lois said.

I could not agree more.

"Before we let you go, Juliet, have you heard who pulled the fire alarm?"

Juliet looked this way and that as if she wanted to make sure that no one was listening. "It was an Amish man."

"What?" I asked.

Juliet nodded. "Yes. They caught him on security footage."

"Who was he? Someone here at the conference?" Lois asked.

"They don't know that. The camera couldn't see his face, but he was definitely in Amish dress. Pastor Ross is quite upset about it. He's afraid the resort will blame the conference since there are a number of Amish in attendance. However, I told him there are so many Amish in Pinecraft, they can't assume that it's someone from the conference. I don't believe so." She grabbed the handlebars of the stroller. "Now, I must really get my little dear into bed. He's just completely spent." She turned the stroller around and made her way to the elevators.

After Juliet left, I turned to Lois. "Why would an Amish man pull the fire alarm at the resort?" I asked.

"Why would anyone pull a fire alarm?" Lois asked. "It's because they want to empty the building."

"For what?" I asked.

"That's what we need to find out. I think we need to have another chat with Pastor Ross."

I could not agree more.

Chapter Thirty-seven

Finding Pastor Ross in the massive Dutchman Resort was easier said than done. I stopped one of the pastors outside the auditorium. "Do you know where Pastor Ross is?"

He shook his head. "He's been running around all day. I would start looking in his conference room."

"Where's that?" Lois asked.

The pastor pointed down the hallway. "Take a left at the corner."

We thanked him and went on our way. With the pastor's directions we found the conference room easily. The door stood open, and Scott Lawrence was inside sweating and shoving papers into a duffel bag.

"He looks like a bank robber in an old B movie," Lois said.

As usual, I had no idea what she was talking about.

"Scott, are you okay?" Lois asked.

He looked up at us like he was seeing an apparition. "How did the two of you get in here?"

"We are looking for Pastor Ross and were told this was the conference room that he was using for his office."

"It's both of our office during the week," Scott said.

"Oh-kay." Lois looked around the room. "Is he here?"

"No, does it look like he's here?"

Lois cocked her head. "What are you doing? You appear to be a bit," she paused as if looking for the right word, "frantic."

"The conference is ending, and I'm just packing up." He wiped sweat from his forehead.

"Do you need help packing, then? Millie and I are great at packing."

I was great at packing. Lois not so much. She brought three suitcases to Florida for a five-day trip.

"No!" he said a little too quickly and a little too shortly. As if he realized his tone, he said, "I'm sorry to snap. There is so much to do for the ending service, and we have to be out of this room by eleven tomorrow morning. I thought I would take some time to make the process easier tomorrow."

Lois and I looked at all the papers and folders and signs on the tabletop and then on the floor. It didn't look to me as if he was making the process easier at all.

"Do you know anything about the false fire alarm yesterday?" I asked.

He looked up at me. "What?"

"The fire alarm," I said.

"Oh, that was just a prank."

"We were told that the security camera caught an Amish man pulling the alarm. It didn't show his face, but he was in Amish dress."

"The Amish can pull pranks too," he said hotly.

I raised my hand. "I'm not denying that, but it just seems like odd behavior. I assume that most of the Amish here at the resort are here as part of the conference. I can't envision a pastor or bishop setting off a fire alarm just as a prank."

"I can't know why anyone does what they do," Scott said.

"No one can," I said. "Scott, you asked us for help this morning. That's why we are here, to help you. Maybe the fire alarm is related to everything that is happening."

"You're right. I know you're just trying to help, but I promise you the fire alarm is not involved. It can't be." He gathered the last few papers off the table and shoved them into the bag. "Now, I have a lot of work I have to do. I can never thank you enough for your help, but I do have to leave." He walked to the door. "I can't leave you in here."

Lois and I stepped out of the door after him. When we walked through, he locked the door with a key behind us. We weren't going to be able to go back in there and snoop around.

"Truly, thank you for your help," Scott said and then scurried down the hallway.

Lois reached into her purse and pulled out her lockpicks. "It's sure a good thing that I have these." She shook the lockpicks at me.

"Okay," I said. "Just make it quick."

She nodded. "Cover me."

While I watched the hallway, Lois put her lockpicks

to work. She wiggled them into the lock, and in a matter of seconds the door popped open.

She stepped back. "I am getting really good at that!"

"I'm not sure it's a skill to be proud of," I said.

"Sure it is." She dropped the lockpicks back into her purse.

We stepped into the conference room that Pastor Ross and Scott had turned into a makeshift office. The papers that Scott had been in such a rush to pack up had been in a plastic rolling filing cabinet. The drawers to the cabinet stood open.

Lois picked up several sheets that fell to the floor. "These are all financial records for the church and conference," Lois said, picking up one of the papers. "Why would he be in such a rush to take them in such a disorganized way? And why are they here and not at the church?"

"He'd want to hide anything that would prove Caroline's accusations against him," I said as I looked over the papers.

"This isn't a great way of hiding something, and the records must be in other places too. I mean, this must also be on a computer somewhere. No one deals with paper anymore."

I gave her a look.

"Okay, no English person deals with paper anymore. Why would this be printed out?"

I shook my head.

The doorknob started to rattle like there was a key in the lock. Lois and I stared at each other. There were voices on the other side of the door. Lois dropped the paper back on the floor like she had been shot.

I pointed at the door in the corner of the room. Lois and I ran to it and jumped inside just as Pastor Ross and Scott walked into the office.

I stepped back into the tiny utility closet and a broomstick poked me in the back. Lois held her finger to her lips and inched close to the door to hear. However, there was no need—Pastor Ross and Scott were not keeping their voices down.

"I apologize, Pastor Ross," Scott said. "I know the office is a mess. I mistakenly knocked over the filing cabinet."

"He's lying. He didn't knock it over," Lois whispered in my ear.

"Shh," I hissed and listened for any indication that they had heard us.

"That just seems to be the way everything is going," Pastor Ross said in a forlorn voice. "When you get it cleaned up, let me know. I just wanted to look everything over. I have this feeling that the funds aren't right." He took a breath. "I wish that Caroline was here to look at it all. She was such a whiz at math." His voice caught.

"I'm sorry, sir."

"I'm glad that I have you at my side, Scott. I don't know how I would get through the rest of this conference without you. You really are like a son to me."

"Thank you, sir." There was a waver in Scott's voice this time.

"Clean it up and then call me in," Pastor Ross said. "I'm glad that the conference is over tonight. We need to get back to the church, and I need to put my life back together. Lord willing."

We could hear the outer door open and close and then the sound of Scott, who must have remained in the room, picking up papers and opening and closing drawers. Finally after what seemed like an eternity, the outer door opened and closed again. We waited a few minutes for any more sound. There was nothing.

Lois busted out of the closet. "That is not the place to be in when you have claustrophobia." She leaned over and gulped air.

"I didn't know you were claustrophobic."

"Me either until I was trapped in that closet forever."

I looked around the room, and everything was neat, tidy, and put away. "We had better not be in here when Pastor Ross comes back to look over those papers."

"Right," Lois said. "We should go back to the bungalow and get ready for the closing service tonight. If you ask me, something is going to go down."

I thought she just might be right.

Chapter Thirty-eight

My prayer cap was in place, and I pinched my cheeks to put a little bit of color into them. The Amish do not wear finery or makeup, but we aren't completely immune to a bit of vanity. Everyone wants to look their best and make a *gut* impression.

"I'm so glad that I brought this dress," Lois said. "You might believe that I overpacked, but if I hadn't, I never would have brought this." She twirled in her bright floral dress. It was made of tulle and satin. It was as bright as her hair, and considering how bright her hair was . . .

Lois's jewelry was just as loud. She wore huge gemstones on her fingers and a large, bejeweled necklace around her throat. One would have thought she would change her purse for the occasion, but I knew better. Lois never went anywhere without her giant patchwork purse. She never knew when she might need the lockpicks or the brick she carried.

The conference's closing service was our best chance

to talk to Scott and find out what he really knew about Caroline's death. He had told us a lot that morning, but I was beginning to wonder if he had only done that to throw us off.

Thankfully, we got into the conference with Juliet. Goodness, with as many times as we took care of Jethro the last few days, it was a small favor to grant.

We stepped into the large room. There was a stage set up at front with a band and a pulpit. A young man played the guitar while people found their seats.

"This is like a banquet." Lois rubbed her hands together. "I'm starving."

My stomach rumbled telling me that I was hungry too. We had been so caught up in Caroline's murder that there hadn't been much time to eat.

The hostess at the door gave us our table number, and I was relieved to see it was in the back of the large ballroom. In my opinion, it was always a smart idea to know how you could leave a place as soon as it was polite.

I was relieved to see that Ruth and Bishop Yoder were already seated at our table. Ruth shifted in her seat and looked down at the silverware. "Why are there so many spoons?"

"They all have a different purpose," the bishop said. "It's not very practical, but it is very *Englischer*."

"The person who made the decision of how many spoons each person would get isn't the one washing them," Ruth said. "It's wasteful."

Bishop Yoder pulled at his long white beard. He looked as uncomfortable as his wife, but he was far less vocal about it. I understood how he was feeling. Because I was so close with Lois, I had been exposed to more *Englisch* ways of life than other Amish of my generation, but this was fancier than I had ever seen.

"Just enjoy it, Ruth," Lois advised.

Ruth sniffed, and I knew that she wasn't going to take Lois's advice for one second. Even so, I was proud of her when she didn't snap back.

Another couple I didn't know joined our table, but Bishop Yoder greeted them warmly. I assumed that they were another pastor who was attending the conference and his wife. Finally, just before the dinner was set to begin, Juliet and Reverend Brook slipped into the ballroom.

Juliet was stunning in a sequined dress that was surprisingly free of polka dots, but she couldn't get away from her favorite pattern. Her large handbag was covered in black and white gems in a polka-dotted pattern.

"That's quite a large bag," Lois said. "Did you bring snacks if the food is bad?"

Juliet blushed. "You are always carrying a large bag, Lois."

Lois reached under the table and held up her giant purse. "I am, but I never know when I will have to jump into action and help Millie with a case. It's all part of being a sidekick."

I set my water glass on the table. "You are far from a sidekick, Lois, and you know that very well."

"I'm happy to be Amish Marple's sidekick any day." She grinned.

Reverend Brook pulled out his wife's chair, and she

tucked her bag under the table. Before placing her napkin on her lap, she looked down again as if to reassure herself the bag was still there.

"I'm so glad that you could come to the last service," Juliet said. "It should be so moving. I think this conference gave many pastors and their spouses the tools to go back and reach more people in their congregations."

"I can't think of a single lesson Bishop Yoder and I will use," Ruth muttered.

"That's because the only person she listens to is herself," Lois whispered to me.

The music began and the room stood to clap and sing all together. I stood out of respect for the service, but it was much different from how the Amish worshiped. Bishop Yoder stood quietly at the table too, but Ruth remained in her seat.

As the final notes of the song ended, the band moved off the stage, and Pastor Ross walked up to the pulpit. "Good evening, everyone. Praise God that you are here with us this evening to celebrate an amazing few days of leading and learning." He paused. "On a personal note, I want to thank you all for the outpouring of love and understanding you have given me through the week over the loss of my daughter Caroline. I can never thank you enough. She was a brilliant young woman, and I am adrift without her." His voice caught.

Tears came to my eyes as he spoke. His pain was palpable. Even though I knew his relationship with Caroline had been strained over the last few months because she wanted to marry Cainan and join his

Amish community, it was clear to me that Pastor Ross loved his daughter very much.

Pastor Ross noisily cleared his throat. "Our first speaker for the evening will be my right-hand man, Scott Lawrence. I know many of you have met Scott this week as he has helped you with everything from microphones to being the liaison to the resort and registration. Scott has been my behind-the-scenes man for years. He's never wanted to step into the limelight and speak about his faith, so when he came to me earlier this evening and said he wanted to share with the assembly, I knew he had something important to say."

Scott walked up the pulpit, and Pastor Ross gave him a hug before stepping back.

Scott stared out into the room. "I don't like to be the center of attention, but I know there is something I must share." He licked his lips. "I've made mistakes. Mistakes that I have been covering up my whole life. I'm not proud of them even when they were back in the farthest corners of my mind." He looked at Pastor Ross. "I'm sorry. These last few years, you have treated me like a son. I haven't been good to you. I have stolen from you. I have lied to you. I have caused the greatest loss in your life. If I had never walked through the doors to your church, Caroline would still be alive." He looked down. "Because of that, I'm so sorry."

There was a hush in the grand room.

Pastor Ross stared at Scott as if he were seeing him for the very first time.

"I'm just telling you now, you won't have to worry about me any longer. I'm going to make amends for what I did." He stepped away from the pulpit and ran down the steps and out the side door.

Pastor Ross glared after him.

I was on my feet. I didn't like the sound of what Scott said at all. Was he planning to hurt himself?

Lois jumped to her feet and in the process tipped over Juliet's large gem-covered bag. Jethro came shooting out of the bag and ran around the table.

"There is a pig loose!" someone cried.

"Don't worry," Juliet cried. "It's just Jethro. It's my pig."

She and Reverend Brook were on their feet running after the pig.

Lois was about to join them when I grabbed her arm. "Let Juliet deal with Jethro this time," I said. "We have to find Scott. I'm scared for him."

I didn't have tell Lois twice. She went straight out the door with me.

Chapter Thirty-nine

The wind was so strong, Lois and I had to double at the waist to make our way over the dune.

"Millie, are you sure Scott came this way?" Lois asked.

"I'm sure," I said. "When I came outside, he was running over the top of the dune."

"This wind is something. At least it's not raining." Just as she said that, it started to rain. Large drops pelted us.

"Maybe we should go back," Lois said.

"We can't. We don't know what Scott will do. I'm afraid for him."

The wind was too strong for much talk, so Lois grabbed my hand. That's when I knew she was with me.

"Did you find him?" someone shouted behind us.

We turned to find Pastor Ross running out onto the wet beach. His face was etched with worry. "I can't lose another important person to me. I can't." He hurried over to us.

"Take a breath, Pastor Ross. We will find him. He's upset, but all will be fine," I said.

"I'm surprised you ran out here looking for him after he admitted what he did," Lois said.

"He's like a son to me."

I nodded. "Okay, we will find him."

Other than the wind and rain, the beach was empty. No one else was dumb enough to go out into the storm. From what I could see, we didn't have a choice. I was certain that Scott planned to do something terrible to himself. I would never forgive myself if I didn't at least try to stop him.

"There is a light over by the pier," I shouted at Lois.

She gave me a thumbs-up sign to tell me that she heard me.

Doubling over again, we shuffled forward through the wet stand, which clung to our shoes and the hems of our dresses. Lois had been so excited about her dress, but after tonight I knew it would be ruined.

Pastor Ross's suit was no better.

When we were under the slight wind barrier that the pier had to offer, Lois pushed her now-flat purple spikes out of her eyes. "This weather is crazy, and it's not even a hurricane. If we were back home, I would say a tornado was coming for sure."

"Let's hope it's not that," I said.

We stood at the part of the pier that was closest to the dune, but at the far end where the pier met the edge of the water, there was a light flashing back and forth.

Lois and I moved from pylon to pylon making our way toward the light. When we were within ten feet, we could clearly see it was Malachi Grabill holding a battery-powered lantern. Scott was in the sand on his knees in front of him.

"You are the reason that my siblings and I didn't grow up with a father." The shout pierced through the storm. "Do you even know what that did to us? Our mother never recovered. She was just a shell of a person." Malachi shook with every word.

"I'm sorry. You have every right to hate me," Scott said.

"I took the money you stole from the conference, and that's how I made you pay for it. You had to ruin it by telling that girl." Malachi pointed a gun at Scott's head.

"I didn't tell Caroline. She figured it out on her own. She noticed that some of the money from the church was missing. It was a small amount over several years. I thought it wouldn't be missed, but she figured it out. When she asked me about it, I told her she was wrong. She didn't believe me and kept digging. I thought that she would stop when she got into that accident."

"You mean when you tried to run her off the road?" Malachi spat. "You just made her more determined."

Next to me, Pastor Ross covered his mouth. In a muffled voice, he said, "Caroline was telling the truth about Scott. My little girl was telling the truth, and I pushed her away."

I reached over and held his arm because I thought he might crumple into the sand.

"I knew why Caroline went to Ohio to meet with one of my brothers. She wanted proof that you were sending money to my family for killing our father."

I realized that Malachi's brother must have been the person Caroline planned to meet at the candy factory.

"When she came back, she knew I was Zeke Klemp's son," Malachi said. "She wanted to talk to me about it. She wanted me to tell her father that you have been giving me money for years to prove that you have been stealing from the church. Why would I do that? The money would dry up then."

"You killed her?" Scott asked.

"I didn't have a choice. She would ruin everything. I knew I wouldn't be getting anything more from you if she told her father what you did. You should be grateful I removed her. Everything would have been fine if you had just let it be and stopped involving those old crones."

"Are we the old crones?" Lois whispered.

I nodded, still trying to keep Pastor Ross steady. It was no easy feat. He was at least a foot taller than I was.

"I'll show him an old crone," Lois said.

"You're right. You can shoot me," Scott said. "It's what I deserve. If I hadn't come here at all, Caroline would still be alive. I wished I had never met her or Pastor Ross."

"What you should wish is that you hadn't killed my father!" Malachi snapped. "I'm not going to shoot you. You are going to do that to yourself." He flipped the gun around and held the barrel in his hand and the handle out to Scott.

Lois shoved her hand into her purse and came out with the brick. She hurled it at Malachi and hit him on the forehead.

"What a lucky throw," Lois said. "Not many people know this, but I was high school state shot put champion back in my day."

I scooped the gun out of the water just as we heard a commotion down the beach. It was Detective Marcs and his officer. He was going to be furious about getting wet.

"I finally used the brick!" Lois cried in delight.

Epilogue

As Lois and I stood in line on the charter bus waiting our turn to disembark onto the Harvest Market parking lot, Lois said, "Can you believe that we had the same bus driver for the ride home? He wasn't too happy to see me."

"He wasn't happy when he saw your luggage," I said. "Since you slept to and from Florida, I don't believe that he had a problem with you at all."

"I hope you're right, because he's kind of handsome, and I'm in the market for another husband."

I rolled my eyes and was grateful when the line of passengers moved forward and Lois and I could finally get off the bus. It had been a very long trip home and an even longer week. Pinecraft was beautiful, but I didn't think I had a desire to go back any time soon.

I rubbed the scarf that was around my neck. It was blue and green, much brighter than I usually wore. The morning after the conference's closing service, Cainan had found it at Tabitha's desk. He immediately recognized it as Caroline's. When he confronted his sister, she admitted that her husband Malachi gave it to her. I shivered at the thought of Malachi killing Caroline and then stealing the scarf only to give it to his wife as a gift.

I didn't want to take it, but Cainan, as Lois and I were leaving Pinecraft, insisted I accept the scarf as a reminder of Caroline. I could not refuse such a gift from a grieving husband.

I didn't think I would wear it often, but wearing it home on the bus as Caroline wore it on the bus before seemed fitting.

When I stepped off the bus, the smiling faces of Uriah and the goats were waiting for me. And Darcy was waiting for Lois.

Darcy threw her arms around Lois. "I'm not letting you go on trips without me anymore. You get into too much trouble."

"You're going to have to blame this one on Millie," Lois said.

"Hey!' I complained.

Lois laughed.

Phillip and Peter were jumping up and down and pulling Uriah this way and that as he had a death grip on their leads. I looped my arms around each goat's neck and hugged them tight. They licked my face up one side and down the other. They smelled like hay, carrots, and dirt. It was the perfect combination.

I stood up.

Uriah grinned at me. "We are glad you're back."

"I'm glad to be back." Even with so many people around to see, I leaned forward and kissed him on the cheek. I was home, and that's where I planned to stay.

Visit our website at
KensingtonBooks.com
to sign up for our newsletters, read
more from your favorite authors, see
books by series, view reading group
guides, and more!

Become a Part of Our
Between the Chapters Book Club
Community and Join the Conversation

...veenthechapters.net